Secrets & Sake

A Paranormal Yakuza Duet Book 1

CJ Ravenna

Print ISBN: 979-8-9878197-6-0

First edition 2024

Editing by AlternativEdits

Proofreading by Lori Parks

Cover design by Natasha Snow

Content Warnings

Triggers:

Graphic violence, including torture, murder and dismemberment, blood, descriptions of severe burns, and gore

Explicit language

Violence against shifters in their animal forms

On-page abduction of a child through a fully detailed flashback

A character is forced to self-harm on-page

A main character was cheated on, and the cheating is mentioned through dialogue and a non-descriptive flash-back

Discussions of the past sexual abuse of a minor, which occurred off-page

Kinks:

Public sex

Praise kink

Primal play

Knotting

Tropes:

Grumpy x sunshine

Touch him and die

Instalove

Fated mates

High heat (the word cock is mentioned 74 times)

Dedications

I spent two decades trying to write a story like this. There have been many renditions of Raiden and Jinta, so many versions of this story told so many different ways. This duet is by far my favorite. Thank you for being a part of Raiden and Jinta's long journey.

I knew going into this book that it would be one of my most challenging ones to date. This is my first book to feature a non-white main cast and, while I love and respect Japanese culture, I am not Japanese. I knew I would have to ask for help, and I am so glad I did.

Thank you to my amazing beta reader and sensitivity reader who shared their endless knowledge, introduced me to books about Japanese history and the culture, called me in when I messed up, and ultimately made me a better writer.

For more information on Japanese culture, mythology, the yakuza, and more, I highly recommend the following books. They were essential reading material that I resourced frequently.

Etiquette Guide to Japan: Know the Rules that Make the Difference! by Boyé Lafayette De Mente

Tokyo Vice: An American Reporter on the Police Beat in Japan by Jake Adelstein

Strange Tales from Japan: 99 Chilling Stories of Yokai, Ghosts, Demons and the Supernatural by Keisuke Nishimoto

Uncovering Japanese Mythology: Exploring the Ancient Stories, Legends, and Folktales of the Land of the Rising Sun by Lucas Russo

Japanese Mind: Understanding Contemporary Japanese Culture by Rodger J. Davis and Osamu Ikeno

Yakuza: Japan's Criminal Underworld by David E. Kaplan and Alec Dubro

Any mistakes are my own.

The Namikawa-Kai:

Kensuke Namikawa: the leader of the Namikawa-kai yakuza organization. Pronounced Kehn-soo-kay Nah-me-ka-wa.

Raiden Noboru: also known as the Wolf of Asakusa, enforcer and debt collector for the Namikawa-kai. Pronounced Rye-dehn Noh-boh-roo.

Hideyoshi: Kensuke Namikawa's second-in-command, and Raiden's grandfather. Pronounced Khee-Deh-Yo-Shee.

Ren Makoto: Raiden's childhood friend, and owner of the Blue Lotus nightclub. Pronounced Rehn Mah-ko-to.

The Takada-kai:

Saito Takada: leader of the Takada-kai, and Raiden's abusive ex. Pronounced Sah-ee-to.

Hirano Kasamatsu: Saito Takada's second-in-command. Pronounced Khee-rah-no.

The Onodera Family:

Jinta Onodera: a reporter for the Jiji Shimbun. Pronounced Jeen-ta O-no-deh-ra.

Katsuki Onodera: Jinta's big brother, who always stole the spotlight. Heir to the family hospitality business. Pronounced Kahts-kee.

Fumiko Onodera: Jinta and Katsuki's mother. Pronounced Foo-me-ko.

Isshin Onodera: Jinta and Katsuki's father. Pronounced Ee-shin.

Chapter 1

Jinta

A chill runs down my spine as the smiling face of a young woman looks back at me from her own missing-persons' poster. Pity squeezes in my chest. Though I didn't know her, Himiko Nakamura looks like a kind and lovely person from her picture alone.

Tearing my gaze away, I walk until I reach the end of the street. Where was her house again? I check the messages on my phone. Right. On this street, but to the left. I pass more posters of Himiko's smiling face, like she's begging me to help find her.

I will. Definitely.

After I climb the steps of an apartment building, I walk along the balcony until I find the right apartment number.

I double-check the number is correct, then buzz. I lift the edges of my mouth into a polite smile while I wait.

"May I help you?" The woman standing in the door-way regards me with wary confusion through her tired, red-rimmed eyes. The puffy state of her cheeks and nose suggests she was crying before she answered the door.

Chest squeezing with pity, I smile to reassure her. "Excuse me, but are you Aiko Nakamura?"

"Yes," she answers slowly, sniffling.

Giving a bow, I say, "Nice to meet you. I'm Jinta Onodera. I'm with Jiji Shimbun," I hastily say to clarify when she continues to look confused.

She lets out a gasp. "Oh, yes! I'm so sorry. I'd completely forgotten you were coming."

"No problem!" Clearing my throat, I add, "I have some questions about your daughter, Himiko. I'm investigating her disappearance. I'd like to write a story to raise awareness."

"I... I appreciate it. Thank you." Her voice wavers as she steps aside to let me in.

Relief whooshes from my lungs. I was really hoping she wouldn't have changed her mind, though I would've understood why. It can't be easy to talk about this stuff with a stranger. "Thank you so much. And here. For you." I present her with a small box of cookies I bought on the way over. It would have been impolite to show up empty-handed.

She accepts them and lets me in.

"Pardon the intrusion." I step inside after her. In the vestibule, I exchange my outdoor shoes for the pair of hallway slippers she offers me and follow her further into the house.

"Please have a seat," Nakamura says, heading into the kitchen. "Would you like tea? I have matcha."

"Yes, please."

The apartment is small and cozy with pictures hanging on the walls. There are pictures of baby Himiko with chubby cheeks, being embraced by a younger version of Nakamura. In another picture, an older Himiko celebrates her graduation. I don't see any to indicate Nakamura had a partner. Looks like she was a single mom who adored her daughter and did right by her. Envy gnaws at me. I had two parents, and even combined, they aren't even half the parent Nakamura was—is.

Nakamura carries steaming tea to the table, and we sit. Thanking her, I take a cautious sip. The tea warms my stomach as I set out my notepad and pen. "Those are nice pictures. I went to the same university."

"Really?"

I nod. "What did she study?"

Nakamura pulls her trembling lip between her teeth, gaze falling to her teacup. "She wanted to be an engineer. She had started dating this wonderful man. This week, she was supposed to go to an interview."

I make a note. "Sounds like she was really going places."

Until she'd disappeared, like so many others. The victims have nothing in common, not age, not gender, and they aren't even from the same neighborhood. The only commonality is that they were married, engaged, or at least dating someone. Some are foreigners, while others are Japanese citizens. There's seemingly no motive. People go missing all the time, but this isn't right.

"When was the last time you saw Himiko?"

Nakamura exhales shakily. "She was going out with some friends to the Blue Lotus. I told her not to go there. Everyone knows that the club is owned by the Namikawa-kai."

At this, my heart skips. This is it. The connection I was hoping for. The Namikawa-kai is the biggest yakuza organization in Tokyo. They operate primarily in the Taito Ward, where they have a headquarters in Asakusa. Their leader is Kensuke Namikawa, one of Tokyo's richest, most powerful men.

"And? What happened when she got there?" I fight to keep my tone neutral, my heart pounding to escape my ribs.

"Her friends said she caught the eye of this yakuza." Anger tightens her features. "Himiko is non-monogamous, so it wasn't unusual for her to flirt with other men. They danced together, and she left the club with him. That was the last time anyone saw my daughter." With a trembling hand, she wipes away a sudden rush of tears.

Anything could have happened to Himiko. The yakuza have been known to traffic women and children. Wetting my dry lips, I ask, "This yakuza she left with. Who was he? Do you know?"

Could it be? My heart throbs with anticipation.

Sniffling, she nods. "The police did. I gave them the same description Himiko's friends gave me. They knew right away who I was referring to. His name is Raiden Noboru."

This is it! The one thing the victims have in common so far—Raiden Noboru, enforcer for the Namikawa-kai. Noboru has a reputation as big as Tokyo itself. The Wolf of Asakusa sticks to Namikawa's side night and day, except when he's out terrorizing people into paying their protection fees on time. He's my only lead, and so far, he's been seen in the company of two of the missing people.

This can't be a coincidence, can it?

"They didn't even bring Noboru in for interrogation! Claimed there wasn't enough evidence." She huffs, eyes narrowing in anger. "It's well-known Namikawa owns the police. Unless Noboru kills someone and there are witnesses, the police will never hold him accountable for his actions. Not unless they want to risk Namikawa's anger." Sighing, Nakamura says, "The Wolf of Asakusa is untouchable."

A feeling of hopelessness claws at my guts. The yakuza

are so deeply entrenched in this society that it's hard to feel like any fight against their corruption is winnable. They've blackmailed and bribed people in some of the highest positions of government.

"I'm familiar with some folks in the police department," I say. "There are good people, men and women, who are just as frustrated as you are with the corruption. It's not that they believe Noboru is innocent. The opposite, actually. But they'll need serious evidence to charge him with anything. Unless they can prove beyond a reasonable doubt that he's done something to her or the other missing people, they're not going to risk getting on Namikawa's bad side."

Nakamura blinks fast. "He did it. I know he did. He's kidnapped my daughter, and nobody believes me!"

I take her hand before I can stop myself. "I believe you, Nakamura. That's why I'm here. I want to help Himiko and everyone else like her who has gone missing."

She laughs coldly and wipes her eyes. "What can you do?"

I paste a smile on my face. "Well, I can't fix the system, unfortunately. But I'm a reporter. The very least I can do is try to link Noboru to these disappearances."

"And how will you do that?"

"I don't know. Not yet. But I'm going to do whatever it takes to help."

For a while, we sit and talk, and Nakamura tells me more

about Himiko. I take notes for my story and listen. All the while, my mind is running wild. Noboru is involved. I just know it. All I have to do is find a way to prove it.

Raiden Noboru.

The name haunts me as I try to sleep and consumes my every waking thought from the moment I leave my apartment. I overslept, so I have just enough time to grab a packaged onigiri from my local 7-Eleven and run to catch the train. The train is packed but quiet. Once we're in Chiyoda, I book it to the Jiji Shimbun's headquarters on the other side of Hibiya Park.

As I march through the office, waving at my colleagues, a plan takes root. Speak to my editor and convince her to let me chase this lead. There's a story here, I know it, one that could make my career. For years, I've watched my colleagues make the front page with their amazing stories while all my articles got buried in the back. Raiden Noboru and his connections to the missing people like Himiko are going to be my big break.

My editor, Reiko Hasegawa, jumps when I practically barge into her office. Before she can so much as greet me, I blurt out, "Excuse me, Hasegawa, but I've finally got a lead! Raiden Noboru was last seen in the company of Himiko Nakamura and Kohei Asano. They both went missing after leaving establishments owned by the Namikawa-kai. I'm telling you, I think the Namikawa-kai, or at least Noboru, is responsible for these disappearances."

Hasegawa exhales slowly. "Onodera, there's no evidence to back up your claims. None of the other missing people were even involved with the Namikawa-kai."

"I'll find more evidence! Let me chase this lead. There's a connection here. I can feel it!" I'm ready to get down on my knees and beg at this point. "I want to write about Noboru's connection to the disappearances for the morning edition tomorrow."

Hasegawa purses her lips. "Any unflattering press about the Namikawa-kai could get us in trouble. The last person to write a story about them got his face slashed open, and the office received threats. It's too risky."

My shoulders slump in disappointment. "But—"

"I'm sorry," she says, and the finality in her voice shuts me down. "You're a good reporter, Onodera. Keep it up. You'll get your big story one day. Now, here." She hands me an edited copy of a story I sent her last night about a spate of pet thefts around the city. It's covered in red marks. "Make these corrections and send it to me in an hour."

She wants me to write some story about a missing poodle that won't even make the front page. This wouldn't have just been a big story; this would have been the story of my career. If my father could see me now, he'd laugh in my face.

Some reporter I am.

Later that evening, I begin the walk of shame home. The first thing I do once I'm inside is crack open an ice-cold Asahi beer. My apartment is all one room, only a little bigger than my dorm back at university if that dorm room also had a kitchen. I sit on my futon by the window and drink to the soundtrack of honking cars and PSA broadcasts over the speakers.

On the wall above my bed is my growing case map. I've put up photos of Himiko, Kohei, and another of the Blue Lotus, where they both went missing. All in all, there are ninety-five missing people. Hostesses who disappeared walking home at night from their jobs. Drunk salarymen who never made it home to their families. The abductions began in January and have only been piling up. The only positive is that there are no bodies. They're not being killed. So they must be kept somewhere. But why? There haven't even been any ransom demands.

In the center of my little map is a photo of my suspect, taken from a yakuza fan magazine. Raiden Noboru.

If he weren't a yakuza thug, I'd say he was handsome. He's young. Can't be much older than me, if even. He's got high cheekbones, a strong jaw, dark eyes, and midnight-black hair that he sweeps back with a pomade, and the man looks damn good in a suit. Okay. I admit it. He's hot as hell, even if it chafes to admit that about a scumbag like him.

Fuck. Am I going to hell for thinking that if he wasn't a criminal, I'd sit on his dick in a heartbeat? Probably.

My phone rings, making me jump. When I see the I.D., I barely stifle a groan of dismay. I swipe to answer. "Hey, Mom. Is everything all right? It's late."

"I wouldn't have to call so late if you'd just be a good son and call me."

I wince at the cold disapproval in her voice. "Sorry. Things at work have been busy."

"And how is work?"

How do I tell her today was a disaster? "Uh, work's... great!"

Her voice lights up when she says, "Speaking of work, guess what? Katsuki got promoted! He's officially CEO! We're so proud of him."

When was the last time she said that about me? I don't think either of my parents ever have, but they've never been short of praise for Katsuki. My older brother works for my family's hospitality franchise. He's the golden child my parents always wanted, who did what he was told and didn't deviate from the path they expected from him. "That's... great."

A frustrated huff blows in my ear. "Jinta, don't be jealous."

"I'm not." I'm not jealous of my brother's position, just that he's more accomplished than I am.

"Your father and I were ready to offer you a place in the restaurant. You said no." There may be thousands of miles separating us, but there's no escaping the guilt of my mother's disappointment.

"Yes, I did, and I'm fine with that. I'm happy in Tokyo, Mom. I love my job."

"But you haven't even had any front-page stories. You're far away from your family, and we didn't even get to see you for your twenty-second birthday."

Fighting back a groan, I fall backward onto my futon.

"I understand you wanted to be different from your brother, but this is not the way to do things. You were always such a good cook. The customers loved you."

She isn't wrong. I was a good cook, and I loved cooking, but just not with my family. Not when it became clear nothing I did could ever make them happy. So I moved on and found other passions. Why can't my family just be happy for me and support me? Well, they could, but only if I give up my life in Tokyo and become the perfect son they always wanted, like Katsuki.

"Anyway, I just wanted to let you know that your father

and I are coming to Tokyo for Katsuki's birthday." Ugh. I'd rather throw myself in the Sumida River than see my brother, even though we live in the same city while my parents are in Osaka. "We'd love to see you."

"You'd love to see me," I correct before I can stop myself. I haven't spoken to my father in five years. The last time I saw him, he'd screamed at me for deciding to study journalism rather than train under him to inherit the business.

She sighs. "You hurt your father. I know he's always been hard on you, especially, but it's only because he cares about you."

Yelling at me whenever I got lower grades than Katsuki, slapping me when I cried, and constantly comparing me to my brother sure was a funny way to show he cared. I take a swallow of beer so I don't say something nasty.

"Jinta, are you really happy?"

I squeeze my phone until the case digs into my fingers. Maybe I'm not. I've been in Tokyo for five years, and what do I have to show for it? No front-page articles, an angry, disappointed family, and an empty apartment to come home to.

"Things... aren't easy," I admit, and a lump rises in my throat.

"Then come home," she pleads with me in that voice that could always get me to do whatever she wanted. "Forget about this journalism stuff. There's always going to be a place for you here."

I look up into Noboru's dark eyes and find my resolve. No. I can't give up. I know Noboru is behind these disappearances. I've got a huge story on my hands. If I give up now, then what was it all for? Moving to Tokyo, earning my degree in investigative reporting, working my ass off to pass my entrance exam, all those interviews after university.

"I'm staying, Mom. Love you. I'll see you in a few weeks." Before she can guilt me some more, I hang up. I can't give up now. This could be the story that makes everything I sacrificed worthwhile.

Nobody is untouchable.

Not even the Wolf of Asakusa.

Chapter 2

The sun goes down, and the lights of Senso-ji Temple come on, glowing golden over the streets of Asakusa. When Senso-ji closes and the dozens of vendors lining the path to the temple pull down the shutters for the night, it might seem like Asakusa has gone to sleep, but you'd be wrong. As long as you know where to look, Asakusa never sleeps, and I know these streets better than I know myself.

West of the temple grounds is Hoppy Street, a small stretch of street packed full of bars and eateries. The streets light up like a damn Christmas tree, and the crowds gather outside the tiny bars and restaurants, spilling out into the streets with food and drinks.

Through the flashing lights, I spot my destination and beeline for it. The arcade is packed with families playing games. The machines make all sorts of racket that cause me to grind my teeth, and some damn brats nearly trip me as they chase each other around like pups.

I sidestep them, growling low in my throat before I can stop myself. When I look up, I lock eyes with the very man I've come to see. Jiro Suzuki, manager of the arcade, laughs as he plays a zombie shooter with two of his kids. The kids turn their fake guns on him and pretend to shoot him, squealing with delight as he cries, "Oh, ouch! You've got me!"

Looks like he forgot all about our little meeting tonight. "Hey," I bark, my voice making Suzuki jump.

At the sight of me, Suzuki's round face blanches, and his smile falls right off. "Kids, go find Aunty. Daddy's going to take a break." The kids run off, and Suzuki swallows hard as I approach.

"It's Wednesday, Suzuki."

He chokes out a laugh. "O-oh. Is it? I'd completely lost track!"

This asshole really thinks I'm stupid. "You were late last week, and I let it go. Didn't I? It's time to pay up."

"Y-yes, of course." The stink of his sweat makes my lip curl. "Right this way, Noboru."

Smelling like fear and cigarettes, Suzuki leads the way toward the employee's only door where I know his office is.

His shaking hands fumble with his ring of keys and sweat beads on his temple. "Just a moment…"

With an impatient click of my tongue, I lean back against an arcade machine by the door. If this asshole still doesn't have the money, my boss is going to give me shit. After several painful seconds that grind on my nerves, Suzuki gets the door open. "All right. J-just let me get your payment…"

I push off from the machine and approach the door as Suzuki steps inside—then he whips around and slams the door in my face. "Hey!" I bark, shock turning to fury as the lock clicks.

"Go away!" Suzuki hollers through the door. "I'll call the police!"

Idiot. The cops in Taito Ward get paid extra by Namikawa to turn the other way and ignore our dealings. Growling, I slam my foot into the door. One more kick, and the door gives, flying open and crashing against the wall. I smirk at the sight of Suzuki's petrified face, but my satisfaction plummets as Suzuki grabs a framed picture and hurls it at me.

With lightning-quick reflexes, I smack the picture out of the air before it hits my face. But that distraction gave Suzuki the seconds he needed to throw open the window behind his desk.

"Don't run!" I warn him.

"Stay the hell away from me," he hollers, and jumps over

the windowsill. As he runs, the drive to chase, to hunt, possesses me. It's a pull no wolf alive can resist.

"Told you not to run," I snarl as my fingernails sprout claws and my canine teeth sharpen into fangs. The chase is on! I leap out the window and pelt after him. Suzuki tears through the crowd ahead, throwing a fearful look over his shoulder. Tourists shriek as I plow through anyone not quick enough to get out of my way.

Suzuki shoves past people and hurtles toward the street where the light is about to turn red. The bastard runs fast, making it across the street just before the cars start to move. In my half-shifted state, my reflexes are faster than a normal human's.

As the cars rush by, time seems to slow. I bunch my muscles and leap. A woman screams in her car as I come down hard on the hood. Before she can brake, I jump onto a taxi, then onto some rusty truck. Cars honk, tires screech, and people shout in alarm as I hit the pavement on the other side of the street. Not exactly subtle, but I've seen stranger things, and that's coming from a yakuza werewolf.

I catch Suzuki's scent and pursue it. His scent gets stronger as I near a narrow alleyway. There he is, cursing as he's halted by a dead end. Suzuki spins around and gasps. Slowly, he raises both hands. "Please. Let's talk about this, okay?"

I flash him my claws. "Sure. Let's talk." I scrape them along the wall, and he winces at the sound. "Let's talk about how you told me you'd have the money by this week, after I let you off the hook the week before. This is the second time this month you've tried to play me like a fool. If I don't come back with your payment tonight, Namikawa's going to have my balls in a vise. And if you don't pay up, someone's going to visit that arcade of yours and smash it to pieces."

I corner him against the wall. Lifting my claws, I tap them over his plump cheek. I should bloody him up a bit. That usually works.

"Please, I... the boys' mother ran off on us."

My fingers are still against his cheek.

Suzuki hangs his head and laughs bitterly, shame coloring his cheeks. "Just packed her bags last night and bailed. Didn't leave anything to cover her portion of the rent, so.... that's where your fee went. B-but I can have your money by this weekend! I swear!"

I think about those two little kids in the shop. They were even younger than I was when I last saw my mother.

The breath gets stuck in my throat. Before I can stop myself, I reach down and touch my chest. Beneath my shirt, the five-yen coin rests cold against my skin, the same coin my own mother dropped into my hand on a cold winter's morning. Right before she left. I still don't know why. My mother was many things. Kind and warm, at first. Angry and drunk. Miserable. Sentimental? Not really, so I don't know why she decided I needed some parting gift.

Did she want me to have a fortunate life? Was this her way of trying to make amends for betraying me like she did?

Well, joke's on you, Mom.

I'm a damn yakuza thug, and it's all I'll ever be.

Growling low in my chest, I step back. "Fine. I'll be back Sunday evening, same time. Have the money ready. This is your last chance, Suzuki."

I'm such a sucker, but I haven't got it in me to demand anything of him. Namikawa is going to give me a hard time.

A relieved laugh escapes Suzuki, and he smiles. "Th-thank you so much!" He bows in gratitude. "I... I'd heard some people say the Wolf of Asakusa isn't such a bad guy. Looks like they were right."

Flicking open my wallet, I count out some bills and shove them at him. "For your kids. The less money you have to spend on the little gremlins, the faster you can pay Namikawa back."

Tears well up in Suzuki's eyes. "I couldn't—"

Grabbing his collar, I yank him in close and growl, "Take it and shut up. If you aren't paid up by next week, I'm smashing the shit out of your store. Got it?"

He nods frantically. "Yes! Thank you so much, Noboru. I—"

Clicking my tongue in annoyance, I turn away. "Make sure you're paid up."

Namikawa is going to be pissed at me for this. Hopefully, my next collection will go smoother.

Some ten minutes later, I've arrived at one of the many host clubs in our protection racket. Inside the club, the lighting is dim. A singer with a bald head croons some old-timey love song up on the stage. Good-looking hosts serve women glasses of expensive liquor and fuss over them.

"Is Aida in?" I ask the bartender. Aida is the manager of the bar, and the one who owes me money.

The bartender jerks a shoulder to the back door behind him. "Smoke break in the alley."

"Thanks." I walk around behind the bar and through the door. Steam from a vent clouds the alley. I follow the scent of cigarettes through the vapor, waving my hand in front of my face. "Aida! Where are you?"

Someone screams ahead of me.

"Aida?" I run through the steam cloud, and just as my vision clears, a body crashes into me. Aida falls on top of me, pinning me beneath his weight. He's completely limp, neck twisted at an unnatural angle. Someone snapped his damn neck.

Panic spurs me to my feet. I throw Aida off me and scramble to stand, claws and fangs at the ready.

"Oh, dear. Namikawa won't be pleased one of his top payers got killed on your watch, will he?"

That smug, mocking voice makes the hairs on my neck

stand up. At the sight of Saito Takada, leader of the Takada-kai, a snarl rises from my throat. He's shorter than me, with long greasy hair slicked back into a ponytail and eyes like a viper's that x-ray me. Just the sight of him has me fighting bad memories as they pour into my mind, oily slick and black. His degrading remarks. The pain he was more than happy to inflict, even when I snarled at him to stop. I tolerated all of his shit, his insults, the bite of his claws, because I was convinced it was what I deserved, that what we had was as good as it would get.

Things would have carried on like that forever, the hate-fucks, the barbed remarks. I wouldn't have stopped it. Why should I? That's all relationships ever really amount to, isn't it? Pain. Hurt. Anger. Regret. The only reason things ended was because Saito split the gang apart. After he left, I felt different. Saito had dragged me into a black pit, and I hadn't realized how far I'd fallen until he left, and I... I could breathe again. I don't want to go back there. If he tries to touch me again, I'll rip his arm off and beat him to death with it.

"You've got some fucking nerve coming into Namikawa-kai turf and killing one of our debtors!" What's gotten into him? Does he have a death wish? Gang wars have been started for less than this. His gang has always been at our throats, but never like this.

Takada smiles, making his goatee quirk as he bares sharp fangs at me. "And yet you're the one who let me get away with it. The Namikawa-kai must be truly losing its edge if they allow rival gangs to infiltrate their territory. Why, you're all as soft as puppies!"

Fur sprouts over my skin, pressing against my clothes. "Shut your fucking mouth!" Raising a claw, I charge at him.

Takada laughs. "You should have joined my organization when I offered, Noboru! I could have made a real wolf out of you. Instead, Namikawa's turned you into a dog!"

I'm only a few feet away when Takada jumps, scaling the chain-link fence. His boots hit the ground just as I start climbing over. He runs, booking it toward a large black *Cadillac*, and leaping inside. The driver slams on the gas just as I hit the ground running, tires squealing as the car drives off into the sea of blinking neon lights.

"Fuck!" I snarl, helpless to do anything but watch our enemy escape.

Namikawa is going to have my hide for this.

I want to say tonight can't get shittier, but I can't. As shitty as my day has been, it can only get worse. There's a stone in my gut as I arrive on the top floor of the Namikawa-kai headquarters. A guard answers when I knock on the office door. "Come in," he says.

I nod my thanks and head in, dread mounting with every step. He will punish me as he's always done when I fail him. I'll just have to take it like a man and endure, like I always do.

Kensuke Namikawa sits behind his desk. Shadows fill the lines and wrinkles in his face. His hair is shaved short to his head and so silver that it's almost white. There's virtually no fat on his body, leaving him looking frail and too thin. I've never asked how old he is. His age is the subject of many rumors within the clan.

I lower myself into a bow. "Boss." I place the envelope of cash on his desk and push it down toward him. "Here are the payments."

Namikawa accepts the envelope, opens it, and counts, quivering fingers slipping over the notes.

I wet my suddenly dry lips. "Suzuki was unable to pay, but he assured me he'd have the money by this weekend."

Namikawa halts his counting, lips thinning. "You already let him off the hook once before. You were to collect the payment in full today. Did you punish him for his failure?"

"No," I say through clenched teeth.

Namikawa rises, and as anger darkens his eyes, he seems taller. "Do you realize what this will mean for us if word gets out you let him get away without paying not once, but twice?" His weathered voice shakes with barely restrained fury. "People will stop paying their protection fees. They will believe we are soft, weak!"

I fight the urge to flinch at his ice-cold rage. "It's worse," I say, voice quieter than I meant it. When he uses that cold, disappointed tone, it's like I'm still the eight-year-old brat indentured to him. "Saito Takada was in Asakusa. He killed Aida before I could collect from him. Then, he escaped."

Drawing in a breath that makes his nostrils flare, Namikawa walks around his desk. His back is hunched, and his hands are clasped behind his back. My instincts tell me to avert my gaze and tilt back my throat in submission to my boss and alpha.

Before I can offer an apology for my failings, Namikawa strikes. Razor claws gouge open my cheek, tearing flesh down to muscle and bone. In seconds, my healing kicks in and the wound slowly closes, but the pain makes my eyes water, and I gnash my teeth so I don't shout.

"Fool!" Namikawa bellows. The lights in the room flicker. The shadows get darker. "Your failure tonight has brought shame upon this clan. I took you in and raised you as my own, and you humiliate me in this way?"

"My deepest apologies."

When I look up, Namikawa is back behind his desk. He opens a drawer and produces a dagger. He unsheathes it, and the blade gleams in the lamplight. My stomach churns, and the hairs on my body stand on end. Fuck. This is going to suck.

Namikawa locks eyes with me. I can't look away, even if I want to. Deep within my soul, my wolf rolls over in submission, incapable of fighting back.

"Would you kindly pick up the knife?"

"Yes, boss." I try to pull my hands back as they reach out against my will, unbuttoning my shirt. I can't move my own fucking body. No matter how many times this happens, it's never any less terrifying.

Stop. Stop it! I scream at myself, but my lips won't move. I clasp the dagger. Someone. Anyone. Please. I press the dagger into my own skin. The blade is made of silver, and it burns like fire as I carve a bloody line across my chest. I thought I was stronger than this, but I guess not. A hoarse snarl of pain escapes me.

The wound won't heal thanks to the silver, and blood weeps down my body.

Namikawa leans back in his chair and smiles. "Keep going. I will tell you when to stop."

Gnashing my teeth, I cut. And cut. And cut. I can't stop it. Nobody can hear my screams. I never look away from Namikawa's dark eyes, and I hope he feels every ounce of resentment eating away at my insides.

Ever since Namikawa adopted me into the gang, I've lived in a world of endless night. The moon never waxes or wanes. The sun has ceased to shine. All I know is darkness, a darkness that festers within me.

I'll never be free. I will live and die a caged wolf.

Chapter 3

Jinta

My heart is in my throat as I stand outside The Blue Lotus in Asakusa.

This is it. After three weeks of planning, it's finally time to begin my undercover investigation into the Namikawa-kai. I'm going to keep compiling evidence until I've got enough to put out a story that exposes Raiden Noboru in the abductions plaguing Tokyo.

For weeks now, I've been coming to the Lotus every night, getting acquainted with Ren Makoto, the bartender. She's also a good friend of Raiden's, and they've known each other since practically infancy. She's nice, and we connected over stories of bad exes together. Ren told me that the photographer for the Namikawa-kai's fan magazine had died. I let slip that I'm a photographer and that I'd love to photograph such a famous organization, really laid on the fanboy enthusiasm and won her over.

And now, here I am. Or, here's Hiro Watanabe. My alias. Tonight's the night I finally meet Raiden face to face, and I'm *nervous*. I can't stop sweating. We'll sit at the bar, have drinks, and he'll look over my photos and decide if I'm good enough for the job. I can't say I ever imagined using my photography skills to take pictures of yakuza for their fan magazines, but I guess there's a time and place for everything.

I'll get close to Raiden and find out everything he knows. But I have to be careful. If I'm caught... well, it's probably best I don't think about that so I don't throw up all over my nice suspenders.

Heart thumping, I push open the doors to the Lotus.

Here goes nothing.

Blue LED lights illuminate the ceiling, and the walls are backlit in pink. Sofas wrap around tables where guests eat and drink. A DJ plays music on a stage before a throng of writhing, dancing bodies. The music is so loud, it's deafening. How are we supposed to do an interview here? Over at the bar, Ren Makoto bounces a shaker up and down with the confidence of a skilled dancer. She's tall, and her sleeves are rolled up to expose her muscular, tattooed arms. Her sleek black hair is tied back in a ponytail that swings up onto her left shoulder when she looks my way and waves.

"Hey, Hiro! You're early!"

I am, but I've always preferred to be too early than too late. I sit at the bar. "Is Noboru here yet?"

Ren looks up toward a room on the second-floor balcony. "He's in VIP, but he should be down in a few minutes. The usual?"

My heart thumps. I'll be face to face with the Wolf of Asakusa. I wonder why he's called that. Maybe he'll tell me. "Actually, just sparkling water with some cranberry for me." I want to be clear-headed.

Ren grins, eyes twinkling with mischief. "Nervous? Don't be. Raiden isn't as bad as the rumors say."

How can she say that when the guy is behind at least two of the kidnappings? Unless maybe she doesn't know. I paste on what I hope is an excited smile. "I can't believe the Wolf himself actually agreed to interview me! The guy is a legend in this city." I'll admit, I've heard some pretty crazy stories about him from Ren alone. His life couldn't be more different from mine, packed with danger and excitement. Not that I'm glamorizing what he does. The yakuza are scummy people. But I understand the intrigue around their organizations.

Ren looks behind me, and her smile widens. "Be sure to tell him that." She tips her chin over my shoulder.

I turn, and there he is. The blue lights from above stain his dark hair as he strides toward me. A dark, tailored suit hugs his broad shoulders and accentuates his slender waist. His white fitted shirt, ironed to perfection, outlines a muscular chest, and a red paisley tie provides a pop of color where it fits snugly against the base of his pale throat. Damn it. I hate how hot he is. Someone like him has no business looking so good.

As our gazes collide, Noboru freezes as if he's as stuck dumb as I am. Electricity zings down my spine and pools hot in my balls. My dick *jumps* against my trousers.

The last thing I can afford is a conflict of interest, and Raiden Noboru is a walking, talking, tattooed temptation.

Before I can catch my breath and compose myself, he's in front of me. He's even taller up close, making me crane my neck to meet his dark gaze. "I-it's nice to meet you." My neck burns as I stutter. Damn it, Jinta. Get a grip! I bow low. "I'm Hiro Watanabe. Thank you for meeting with me."

"Raiden Noboru," he says, with a long nod of his head. I expected a deep, gruff voice, but the timbre of his voice is low and unexpectedly gentle, almost musical. He motions to the bar. "Ren, another Hibiki. And for you?"

My throat clicks dryly when I swallow, and I have to struggle to hold his gaze as butterflies dance through my stomach. "I'm good with this." I hold up my sparkling water with cranberry.

Raiden shrugs and leans on the bar. His face is hard to read, carefully devoid of expression. I wouldn't say he's friendly, but he's not snappish and rude like I worried he'd be. While Ren grabs a bottle off the shelf, I catch Raiden glancing my way. What's he looking at? Is something on my face?

Ren sets his drink on the bar. "Here you go. Play nice with him."

Raiden makes a noncommittal grunting noise, which isn't very reassuring, then motions toward the VIP section on the balcony above. "It's noisy. Let's talk upstairs."

Nodding, I rise from my seat. "Sure—whoa!" My foot slips in a puddle of someone's spilled drink and slides out from under me. The floor hurtles toward me. I screw my eyes shut—and slam into a hard, warm body as two arms wrap tight around me. My heart jumps up into my throat. For a few long seconds, Raiden inhales deep against my hair. Is he... sniffing me? Arousal heats my skin.

"You okay?" Raiden's breath warms my ear and ruffles my hair.

Face burning, I look up at him. "Yeah. Thank you."

Raiden's dark eyes drop to my mouth so swiftly that I would have missed it if I were capable of looking away from him. This close, I can catch the shadow of barely-there scruff on his chiseled jaw. He doesn't wear cologne, but he smells like clean, ironed linen and aftershave. My mouth damn near waters.

Clearing his throat, Raiden lets me go and grabs his drink off the bar. "You sure? You don't need me to carry you upstairs?"

I'm so surprised, I laugh. "No, no! I'm really fine! Lead the way."

I follow Raiden through the crowd and up the stairs past a burly, bald bouncer guarding the way into the VIP section. There are more guards upstairs stationed around a soundproof booth. Once we're inside, the noise of the club is muffled. The space is dimly lit with dark leather sofas and a white fur rug on the floor. We're the only two people in here, and my stomach flips. I thought I'd gotten over much of my social anxiety, but here I am, feeling sick at the prospect of being one-on-one with a handsome yakuza.

My heart races, and sweat slicks my palms. I don't think he'd try to hurt me. He's got no reason to. But then again, did he have any reason to kidnap poor Himiko, Kohei, and who knows how many others? I can't afford to let this ridiculous attraction distract me from the truth. This guy is dangerous, and he's surely killed and hurt people who didn't deserve it.

The leather squeaks when Raiden sits down and crosses his ankle over his knee, setting his drink on a marble table. He cocks a dark brow. "Nervous?"

"No," I assure him, voice cracking unconvincingly. "Okay. Maybe a little. It's just... wow. I've heard so much about you. I've always been so curious about the yakuza way of life, and you're... you're a living legend in the yakuza world."

Unless I'm mistaken, I think I see a hint of a smile at the corner of his mouth. Or maybe not. It's not bright enough in here to tell.

"Is it true you once fought five guys hyped up on meth?"

Raiden's eyes narrow, and he shifts forward in his seat. Unease turns my skin ice cold. *Shit.* Was that the wrong thing to say? Ren told me that story. She wouldn't have if it was off-limits, right?

"I'd tell you the truth"—Raiden's voice is dangerously low—"but then, I'd have to kill you."

A chunk of ice falls into my stomach. "O-oh." I squeeze my glass so hard I worry it will crack. "I-I'm sorry. We can talk about something else. I didn't mean to—"

And then a big, bright grin springs across Raiden's face, and he throws back his head and laughs. The breath is punched out of me at the unexpectedly sweet, musical sound of his voice. *Fuck.* He's the most gorgeous man I've ever seen, and I made him laugh.

A laugh escapes me, and all tension flees my body.

Mirth dying to chuckles, Raiden slaps the spot beside him. "Sorry, sorry. You're a blast to tease. Come on and sit down. Let's get this interview over with. I'm starving."

He'd seemed so stoic and brooding downstairs. This playfulness is throwing me for a total loop.

Raiden takes a drink. "So. You're a photographer."

"Yeah, I... hold on." *Fuck I am a mess!* I throw open my bag and pull out my photo book. "Here are some examples of my work. And here's my card." I pluck a card from my wallet and hand it to him. Raiden accepts the card and inspects it, front and back, then tucks it away in his wallet. He then hands me his own card, which I accept with both hands. The front has the Namikawa-kai logo of a wolf howling over a mountain. The back has his name and number. Thanking him, I carefully put the card away.

"Are you from Osaka?" Raiden asks me after a sip of whiskey.

He must have noticed my dialect. "Yes. I moved to Tokyo about five years ago."

As I speak, Raiden nods and hums, his eyes never leaving my face. It's… different. I feel seen, heard. I realize I haven't felt this way in a long time. "What school did you go to?"

"Tokyo University of the Arts. Where'd you study?"

Raiden downs the last of his whiskey like water and snorts. "Does someone like me look like he went to university and got a good education?"

"Hey, you look—" I almost swallow my tongue. Best I don't tell him what he looks like.

Raiden arches a brow, and a curious smile hooks the corner of his supple lips.

I clear my throat as I remember the way he glanced at my mouth downstairs. If he's into me, for whatever reason, I should use that to my advantage. "Th-that shirt is very nice," I say.

An amused huff escapes him, then he drags those dark

eyes down my body and back up to my face. "So is yours."

Heat tingles down my spine.

"I wish I had gone to school," Raiden adds, thoughtfully swirling the ice around in his glass. "Maybe things could have turned out differently."

There's a note of regret and bitterness in his voice. My journalistic curiosity perks right up. "What would you have studied if you did?"

"Maybe—" Raiden furrows his brow, then shakes his head. "Doesn't matter. You're lucky you had the chance to go. Ren told you we needed a photographer for our magazines, right? Why are you interested in working for us?"

I guess asking about university ticked him off because he's suddenly all business.

"I know this is probably going to sound strange, but... I want to put together a photo book about the Namikawa-kai. The yakuza way of life is still a mystery to me. I've always been curious about the quieter, more business-like element of the yakuza. The media only ever shows one side of your organization, and I'd love the opportunity to capture another side, to show the world there's more to the Namikawa-kai than the violent aspects we hear about on TV."

Raiden is silent while he churns over my request. "The photos for the magazine aren't a problem. But my boss will get the final say in anything else."

"That's reasonable." Suddenly, my stomach growls. Loudly. My cheeks heat. "Sorry. I haven't eaten since this morning."

"Want to grab dinner?"

Oh, shit. Is he asking me out? Is he just being friendly? Is he really just hungry and I'm completely overthinking this?

"Sure."

"There's a great izakaya nearby."

"Okay. Let's go there."

He grins like I've just gifted him something precious instead of my measly company. "Let's go."

We leave the club together. It rained while we were inside, leaving the ground wet and the air thick with the clean scent of moisture. At the curb, a sleek black beast of a *Mercedes* awaits us. I'm no gearhead, but I know a luxury vehicle when I see it. With the click of a remote, the gull-wing doors soar open, beckoning me into an interior that screams comfort, class, and money. I'm almost worried I'll dirty his seats.

"After you." Raiden motions me into the front seat.

The leather seat is butter-soft and is easily adjustable.

Raiden slides into the driver's seat. "What music do you like?"

"I'm good with anything." I'm curious about what kind of music he likes. "Play me something you like."

"Eighties rock okay?"

I nod, and he puts on a playlist. It's a song in English, and Raiden sings along to every word in a pleasant voice. I can't fight the grin that breaks across my face. "Your English is good! What band is this?"

"Queen. They were really popular in my grandad's day." With a spin of the wheel, Raiden drives us through evening traffic. "My grandad went to see them in concert. He didn't even really know any English, but he was blown away. He loved them, still does. He raised me, made sure I grew up knowing their greatest hits. You know a song is good when it speaks to you, right here." He pats his chest.

"Your grandad raised you?"

Fondness softens his face. "Yeah. Since I was eight."

"Were your parents busy?" Maybe I'm playing with fire, but the journalist in me has an insatiable curiosity for every bite of knowledge this man can give me. His life is worlds apart from my own safe, orderly existence.

He shrugs those big shoulders. "Busy being absent, yeah."

Ouch. I wince.

"So you had a troubled childhood and joined the yakuza."

He smiles ruefully. "Could I be any more textbook?" Neon lights blur outside the windows, streaking over the glass in shades of red, green, and pink. I'm even more curious than before about his past.

Before I can ask, he says, "What about your family?"

"Why? Looking for something to use against me?"

"Yeah. Need to know who I'm going to kidnap in case you betray us." He says it so seriously that my blood turns to ice. Then he gives me a wink. "I'm kidding."

"Are you really?"

"How about this? I promise to only kidnap someone you don't like."

I bark a laugh. "That sort of defeats the purpose of kidnapping, doesn't it? Maybe I'd just let you keep them. Besides, you'd have to kidnap my entire family, and that would be a lot of work. You'd be doing me a favor."

His eyes get comically wide.

I realize I've probably revealed more than I wanted to.

"Guess I'm not the only one with family issues."

"My mom and dad live in Osaka," I say. "They weren't exactly jumping for joy when I announced I was moving."

"But you still did it?" There's no judgment in his voice. We've stopped for the light, and he's taken his eyes off the road, his gaze full of curiosity.

Having his undivided attention makes me squirm in my seat. "It was either move here and get away from them or force myself to do what they wanted of me and be miserable for the rest of my life." I learned not to talk about my family with anyone. When I've opened up about my family in the past, most people call me ungrateful for disobeying them. How could I turn my back on the people who raised me? I get the disapproval, I do. Blood is thicker than water, that's what my father always told me. It's how I was raised, to respect my family and the sacrifices they made for me. I wrestled with my decision for years. It wasn't a choice I made lightly.

I'm a private person, and I value my secrets, so I'm not sure why I'm spilling them in a car with a yakuza. There's something reassuring in knowing he's probably heard way worse than some guy's family woes.

Ever since I was a little kid, I thought I would manage one of the many luxury hotels my family owns all through-out the world, but I discovered a passion for writing and journalism in my last year of high school.

My parents were so disappointed when I told them I wanted to study journalism. My mother cried. Father ranted about how ungrateful I was for throwing every-thing they'd sacrificed in the trash. I'm sure glad I never told my parents I was gay. My father would probably drop dead from shock. My mom would just cry.

With nothing for me back in Osaka, I moved to Tokyo to go to university. I spent years studying journalism and worked long nights in a busy ramen bar to pay for my tuition. All that hard work was supposed to finally pay off when I passed my entrance test. I applied to dozens of newspapers around the city and landed a job at Jiji Shimbun.

Instead, here I am with nothing but a few crummy sto-ries about dull, petty crimes to show for all my hard work. I don't even have a boyfriend to come home to because I've been so busy that I've neglected any kind of social life.

Maybe I should have just done what was expected of me. At least then I wouldn't be alone.

People cross the street in front of us while we're frozen in a quiet little bubble.

Finally Raiden says, "That's brave, defying your family like that."

My face warms. He thinks *I'm* brave. Me. What a joke.

"I'm not. I mean, it took me so long to work up the nerve to tell them I wasn't going to do what they wanted me to do. I wasted years trying to be someone I wasn't." I'd spent so much of my formative years just wasting time when I could have been following my own path.

Raiden turns us left, hands sure and steady upon the leather-clad wheel. "My grandfather has always encouraged me to strike out on my own, but it's easier said than done. Defying your family, forging your own path no matter what others say... it's admirable. I wish I'd done that."

I don't know what to say. Nobody has encouraged me before. I've second-guessed coming to Tokyo for years now, spent sleepless nights wondering if I've made the right choice because so far, nothing in life has given me a sign that this was the right thing to do. This stranger just offered me more self-assurance than anyone else in my life, even my own parents.

And again, he's offered hints about himself and implied

that he wants more than the role life has given him.

"Your grandfather wanted you to leave the gang?"

Raiden grunts a yes. "Like it's that easy." His voice is steeped in bitterness. "The yakuza way of life should have died years ago. It's antiquated. All of it. The rituals. The codes and conducts. It should have all disappeared a long time ago." On the wheel, his knuckles have whitened, and a muscle tics in his jaw.

Unsettled by his sour mood, I look out the window at the passing scenery.

Raiden puts the car in park, and the gull-wing doors glide open. The restaurant is across the street from Ueno Park. Raiden leads the way through the crowd of people dressed for a night out. It's April, so the days are warm, but the nights are still chilly enough for a light jacket.

Raiden leads me to the doorway of a restaurant, the windows covered with rice paper to give the customers inside privacy. The restaurant bustles with the chatter of customers, and the aroma of delicious food fills the air.

I join Raiden at the bar. The restaurant is all light cedar-wood floors and furniture, rice paper walls, and dim, cozy lighting. Jazz plays low and soft from the wall-mounted speakers.

"Hey, Tenko!" Raiden calls, waving at the chef behind the sushi bar.

"What can I get you, gentlemen?" the chef asks, sharpening his knives.

"Do you drink sake, Hiro?" Raiden asks.

I almost don't reply right away, unused to my alias. I wonder what my name would sound like in his voice.

"Sure." I prefer beer, but I like sake just fine.

Raiden leans over the bar, excitement bright in his eyes. "A bottle of your best sake."

Raiden bumps his shoulder into mine. "Try the house-made tofu."

Per Raiden's recommendations, we end up ordering a ton of deep-fried, slow-grilled, salty and spicy small plates. Sweat beads on my brow. This is going to cost a fortune.

The sake is good, full-bodied, chilled, and light. I'm on my third cup while Raiden and the chef chat. I need the liquid courage to loosen me up.

Raiden and I get to talking about movies we like. I've always been a big film geek. I could talk about my favorite movies until I'm breathless. Raiden's a fan of big blockbusters, while I prefer more obscure indie films, but we end up talking for thirty minutes about a mutual love for Star Wars.

I can't believe it, but we actually have a ton in common, and Raiden's so easy to talk to, I worry I'll accidentally spill all my secrets to him. Once he stops scowling and opens up, I genuinely like talking to him. Except we can't be friends. This man is a yakuza, and he's kidnapped two people so far. It's likely, anyway, since he was the last person seen with them. I don't actually know for sure that he did, but so far, he's the only lead I've got.

Suddenly overwhelmed, I excuse myself to the bathroom and lock the door behind me. The noise of the bar becomes muffled. I take in a breath and let it out slowly. If Raiden really is behind these disappearances, I'm going to have to betray him. I can't afford to feel anything for him. Not if I want to write the story of a lifetime and prove to everyone back home they were wrong to doubt me.

Suddenly, furious shouting and terrified screams come from beyond the door. My heart drops into my stomach.

What the hell has happened now?

CHAPTER 4

Raiden

Hiro smells like cherry blossoms.

It's a scent I'm familiar with, especially in the flowering months of March and April, but something about Hiro's scent makes me want to roll around in it. He's pretty. With his glossy brown hair that flops cutely on his forehead, his flawless fair skin, and those sweet chocolate-brown eyes, there's just no denying it. And those plush, cupid's bow lips? I'm a damn goner.

He's the opposite of any guy I've been attracted to. Short and slender instead of big and tanky, face soft and boyish. He looks so delicate, and I want to protect him from anything that might break him—including myself.

He's shy, but he's easy to talk to. Most people piss me

off, but something about him makes it easy to open up, and that's just bizarre.

I told myself a long time ago that I wouldn't do the boyfriend thing. Relationships are a headache. Sex is simple. No feelings necessary. Just a moment of explosive passion, intense connection, and then the spark fizzles out. It's enough.

So can someone tell me why I took this man I just met out on a date? He's a human. He can't be anything but trouble. Yet since the second he smiled like a pure ray of fucking sunshine and I caught his cherry blossom scent, I've already broken my no-dating rule... and I want to break more.

I never sleep with the same person twice. But if I had Hiro under me, his face flushed, his hair tousled, if I made him moan my name, I don't think once would be enough. I think I'd be hooked. And that... that's a problem I just don't need.

Damn it. What's *wrong* with me?

And that's when chaos erupts in the restaurant. Four thugs storm in through the front door, shouting like idiots, aggressively rolling their Rs like yakuza from a bad movie as they sneer and mock people in the restaurant. They smell like wolves and Takada-kai. Guess the fucker sent these clowns to make the Namikawa-kai look bad. Enemy wolves in our territory brings out my fangs and claws as I lurch to my feet.

A woman screams as one of the Takada-kai thugs knocks plates of food from the table that she and her friends are sitting at. Another rips a painting off the wall and smashes it over his knee. The third and fourth thugs wrestle customers out of their seats.

"Stop this, please!" Tenko shouts from behind the bar, but he's forced to hide as a thug throws a mug of beer at him.

A Takada-kai with a bald head tries to stomp on a man he hurled on the floor. I seize Baldie by his thick neck and yank him away from the prone man. "Get the hell out of Namikawa-kai territory, you piece of shit!" I snarl.

"You see, people?" A Takada-kai leers, baring yellow teeth. "The Namikawa-kai are so incompetent, they let us disturb your meal. If Saito Takada were in charge, the Namikawa-kai wouldn't have been allowed to put one foot in the door!"

Grabbing a glass mug off a nearby table, I hurl it at Yellow Teeth. He yelps as the glass explodes against the side of his head. People run out the door, leaving behind partially eaten food in their haste to escape the chaos.

Yellow Teeth, Baldie, and the two others advance on me. Their growls rumble like thunder in the air, nails sharpening into claws. I roll out my neck and put my fists up. "Come on!" I bark through my fangs, my blood boiling for a fight.

Baldie charges and swings. I grab his fist and slam my

hand down on his elbow. The bone cracks, but he barely has time to scream before I swing him around and hurl him into the wall. Yellow Teeth roars in fury and rushes at me. He's faster than Baldie, and I take a hit to the stomach that folds me in half. The wind gets punched out of me, and my stomach tries to heave up what I just ate.

Taking advantage of his proximity, I wrap my arms around him and haul him in close, slamming him into the bar and pinning him there. With a swing, my fist connects with his face once, twice, and then he crumples to the ground.

"Watch out!" It's Hiro's voice.

I spin around in time to be knocked on my back by the third Takada-kai member with a crooked nose that looks like it's been broken twice. Crooked Nose draws back his foot. I pull up my knees and absorb the hit that would have gone into my stomach, but the fourth guy plows his foot into the back of my head. Stars explode before my eyes.

"Leave him alone!" Hiro shouts, and something shatters against Crooked Nose's back, making him yelp.

Distracted, he and his friend storm around me and go straight for Hiro. "You wanna fucking go, pretty boy?" He bellows and lunges, grabbing hold of Hiro's arm and squeezing. Hiro yelps as Crooked Nose tugs him close.

My wolf roars to life within me, and a red haze clouds my eyes as fury like nothing else I've felt before possesses me.

Mine, the wolf snarls.

In seconds, I'm on my feet. I seize Crooked Nose and his buddy by the backs of their necks and tug them away from Hiro. They stiffen as my claws dig into the skin of their necks. "Put your hands on him again, and I'll fucking kill you," I growl. The scent of their fear and sweat makes my mouth water to taste their flesh.

I yank them apart and then together, cracking their skulls against each other. Groaning, both men flop to the floor at my feet. Hiro stumbles back, clutching his arm to his chest. Is he hurt? Can't be hurt. Have to make sure he's okay. Scent him. Lick his wound. Make him smell like me and mine so no other wolf can touch him.

"Are you okay?" I ask, my voice barely more than a growl.

Hiro nods, but I grab his arm anyway and tug up the sleeve. There'll be a bruise, I can already tell. The fuckers. They dared to come into my pack's territory. They dared to touch what's mine—I give my head a shake. Seriously, what's with my wolf tonight? He's never this possessive of anyone.

"Get out, both of you!" Tenko suddenly snaps. He slams his hands down on the bar.

"Tenko—"

"What the hell is the point in paying your damn protection fees if you let those Takada-kai thugs do whatever they want? First you let them kill Aida, then you allow them to abduct people, and now this! Out!"

Shit. This is the last thing our organization needs. If the people under our protection question us, we can lose face.

Gnashing my teeth, I throw some bills on the bar to cover our meal. "Sorry for the trouble."

Fury boils within me as we step out onto the sidewalk. A crowd has gathered around my ride. Oh, fuck, no. I shove my way through the crowd and curse. Those bastards slashed my tires and bashed in the windows! Hiro gasps when he sees the wreck. Growling, I yank a pack of *Seven Stars* from my pocket and light up a smoke. "Fucking hell." I take in a deep drag, then blow out smoke. Beside me, Hiro rubs his arm. I can't look away from the bruise already forming there.

For a while there, tonight almost felt like a normal date. Then, those Takada-kai bastards showed up and dragged Hiro into the violence and chaos of my world. He should be out tonight with a nice guy, someone with a normal job and a safe life. Not some yakuza thug like me.

"Sorry about that."

Hiro just shakes his head. "It wasn't your fault."

A cloud of smoke billows from my lips. "Where do you live? I'll take you home."

"Home?" Hiro's face falls. "Already? It's only six PM."

How can he still want to spend time with me after that shitshow of an evening? "You should go home. This was a mistake."

Hiro winces, and I immediately want to punch myself in the throat. Damn it. I'm no good at this at all.

"I only meant—" I bite back a groan. "You're not a mistake."

Hiro actually laughs. "My parents would have to disagree with you."

He means it as a joke, but my wolf growls deep within. Reaching out, I take his hand. "I had fun tonight. With you."

Finally, Hiro's features light up. "I did, too."

There it is. There's my sunshine.

I jerk a shoulder toward the bar. "Sorry those bastards showed up and ruined dinner."

"It's okay. Sorry about your car. Hey! Did you see me? I threw a plate at one of them!" He grins. "And you... you were so badass." His voice gets oddly gravelly, and lust spikes his scent. "I mean, you were terrifying. But it was... kinda hot."

A pleased rumble escapes me. I want to lean in and breathe in the sweet scent of his arousal, bask in it. "The night's still young. How about we stay out a while longer?"

"I'd like that."

I put in a call to get my car towed off for repairs.

"Tenko said something about abductions," Hiro says.

"Yeah." I bite down harder on the cigarette between my teeth. I wish he hadn't heard that.

"He thinks the Takada-kai are behind it?"

"Help me!"

The memory of a woman's scream pierces my brain.

"Get off me! Help!"

"Raiden?"

Hiro's voice makes me jump.

"Are you okay?" His doe eyes are wide with concern.

What *was* that? I haven't harassed any women for protection fees lately. Oddly breathless, I fill my lungs with smoke and give a dazed nod. "I'm fine."

"I asked you a question."

"You did?" I must not have heard.

Why did that woman's voice sound familiar?

"About the disappearances—"

"Fuck that." Wanting to change the subject, I ask, "Was it scary?" I want to swallow the question right away.

"The fight in the bar? Oh, yeah. I almost pissed myself!"

"I meant leaving it all behind. Striking out and doing your own thing?"

Hiro hums thoughtfully beside me. "The scariest thing I've ever done."

"But you did it anyway."

"I had to. There was no other option. It was either I leave it all behind, or... I spend the rest of my life trapped."

My chest squeezes with an unusual rush of anxiety at the thought. "This life... it's gonna be the death of me." I look away before Hiro can meet my gaze. Taking a drag on my smoke, I exhale. Why can't I keep my mouth shut around him? What's this human doing to me?

"So, change it." Hiro says those words as if it's as easy as breathing. "It's going to be hard. And scary as all hell. But if you want to change your life, change it. Nobody can do it for you."

"You think I could?" I finally look at him.

Hiro laughs breathlessly. "Honestly? I think you could do anything you set your mind to, and anybody who tries to stop you better watch out."

Warmth blooms in my chest and my heart does some weird skipping thing. I touch the center of my chest and rub, wondering if it's something I ate or if the damn cigs are finally getting to me. It feels nice, having someone who believes in me. I've never had that before. I take his hand and squeeze.

"Thanks, Sunshine."

Suddenly, I have an idea. I don't know why, but I want to show him one of my favorite places in the city. It's not something I've ever done with anyone before. It's a sacred place, full of bittersweet memories I'd rather no one knew about. I guard it like I guard all my other scars.

But for some reason, if it's him, I don't mind. My wolf's instincts are telling me to bare my very soul to this man who's little more than a stranger to me, and I don't understand why.

For so long, I carried the burdens of my past just fine, and now... it's like all that weight I've been carrying around is too heavy to bear on my own.

I want someone to know these burdens and scars. To know *me*. And my wolf needs it to be Hiro. It's weird, but my instincts have never led me astray before.

"You like surprises?"

"No. I hate them. They give me anxiety."

I roll my eyes. "This won't. Come on."

He gives me a fond but nervous look. "Are you going to get me in trouble?"

"Probably."

Hiro blushes. "Why do I like the sound of that?" he mutters, scent spicy with lust. "Fine, lead on. But if we get chased by yakuza, I'm not going down with you."

"What's in Shinjuku?" Hiro asks as we roam the dark streets together.

"It's the ward where I was born." I've tried to stay away for that very reason. Too many bad memories, but I've let them poison the good memories I still have.

Hiro rocks back on his heels. His brown gaze is up-turned to the dark skies above. "What are we doing here?"

I glower at him. "I said it's a surprise. I bet you're the guy who asks what's in it? when someone hands you a present."

Hiro pokes his tongue out between his teeth. I want to suck on that tongue. "Okay, okay, I get it. Show me this place already. It better not be a tree stump."

I grab his hand and tug. Not sure why I keep grabbing his hand. It's not like he can't follow me. It's just... instinct, I guess. I want him close and in my sights. "Just shut up and follow me."

I lead him through the streets. As we walk, the scenery gets more and more familiar, stirring memories I haven't revisited in years. The gates of Shinjuku Gyoen National Garden bring back a rush of nostalgia. I came here all the time after school to do my homework, or just watch the carp swim around in the lake, or lie in the grass and stare up at the sky.

"Man. It hasn't changed at all," I say, leading Hiro deeper into the garden. The further we walk, the quieter the world becomes, like we've entered a whole other planet.

"Is that a smile I see?" Hiro teases.

I realize I'm smiling. It feels good being back here. "I came here all the time when I was a kid," I explain, leading him beneath rows of flowering cherry blossom trees. "No matter how shitty things were, I'd come here and feel better."

Hiro's eyes soften. Damn it, he's feeling sorry for me.

"It was an escape. You know? Somewhere I could forget about stuff at home."

"Like?"

A wooden bridge creaks beneath our feet. I lean on the railing and watch the koi fish swim, free and untroubled.

"Life at home wasn't easy. My parents were dirt broke. They fought all the time about anything and everything. When it got to be too much, I'd come here." I try to lift my heavy lips so he doesn't think this still hurts as much as it does. "I remember one time, I hid here for hours. I thought maybe they'd get worried and come looking for me. They'd work together to find me, and maybe..." I pause, realizing how stupid this all sounds.

"What?" Hiro sidles up beside me and bumps his shoulder into mine, eyes kind and inquisitive.

I shrug, averting my gaze to the koi below us. "I don't know. Maybe they'd work together and remember they still, what? Loved each other?" I flick a leaf off the railing, annoyed at myself. "Anyway, I didn't bring you here to bitch and moan about my past. The past is the past. It won't change just because I wish it would."

"Why *did* you bring me here?" Hiro asks.

I turn, leaning on my elbow as I face toward him. "I don't feel like a lost boy or a yakuza grunt when I'm around you. I'm a different person."

A little smile hooks the corner of Hiro's mouth. "Yeah? And who is that?"

Reaching out, I curl my fingers in the soft material of his sweater and pull him close. I lean down, touching our foreheads together, and close my eyes. I breathe in the sweet, clean scent of cherry blossoms emanating from him.

"Raiden," I answer. "Me. Just me."

Hiro hums, a soft, happy sound. "I'm thinking I like Raiden, surly bastard that he is."

I can see it so clearly. If I let him, Hiro could be my sanctuary. I'll never be free of the yakuza. I'll never have a normal life. Since I was eight, Namikawa has owned me, body and soul. My whole life has been dedicated to serving him, protecting him. I've never had something, someone, that's mine and mine alone. I want Hiro to be that person for me. My port in the storm. My first taste of a normal life.

This is... dangerous. I've never felt this way around anyone. It can't last. This thing between us could bloom bright and beautiful, but it will inevitably die. I know that. Nothing good ever lasts. People leave, or die, or betray me. Hiro could do any of those things, especially if he finds out about the beast lurking beneath my skin. The smart thing to do is to get my fill of him, then let him leave.

And yet, a darker part of me snarls at the idea. Thinks that if he even tries to leave, I'll do whatever it takes to keep him. Even if he hates me for it. I lock that dark, animalistic urge in a box with all my other demons. It scares and thrills me... the things I want to do to him. The things he might let me do to him.

"You shouldn't." The words come out a low growl, and I have to clear my throat.

Hiro sticks out his chin defiantly. "Yeah? Why not?"

Squeezing his forearms, I turn him so his back is against the railing. "I'm not a good person."

Something dark must have crossed my face because unease twists across Hiro's features. "Because you're a yakuza?"

Bracing my hands on the railing, I pen him in, trapping him against my body. "If you knew half the fucked-up things I'm thinking about you, you'd run screaming."

Hiro leans back, tipping his head up to gaze at me. The column of his throat is exposed. All that smooth, pale skin, the pulse fluttering like the wings of a butterfly, it calls to every predatory urge I have. "Try me."

I swallow hard, trying to rein in my fangs. The urge to mark that soft pale skin with my teeth, to claim him as mine, burns within me. Willing my claws to stay blunt, I lift my hand and curl it around his exposed throat. Hiro's breath catches in his chest. His pulse races beneath my thumb, and oh, how I hunger for him.

"I want to put my teeth in your skin and bite until you bleed for me." I press the words into the hinge of his jaw. People cross the bridge behind us, too lost in their own world to notice us. They don't get to hear this confession. It's for Hiro and him alone. "Cover every inch of your skin with my mark so everyone knows who you belong to." A shiver runs through Hiro as I lean in and trace the shell of his ear with my lips, then nip his earlobe. "You'll leave, eventually. Everyone does. But I want you to try anyway, so I can hunt you down and catch you."

"And, when you catch me..." *When*. Not if. Fuck, my blood's on fire for this man. "What would you do to me?"

I hum, thinking long and hard, fantasies twisting through my head. "I'd ruin you for any other man."

Hiro's breathing hard, heart hammering beneath my thumb. At first, I think I spooked him... until the spicy notes of arousal seep into his scent. "And if I..." His throat works beneath my hand. "If I wanted all of that?"

Holy shit.

Maybe I underestimated this guy. I lick his neck, enjoying his gasp. "Depends. What is it that you want?"

Hiro grabs my shirt. He hooks his leg between my thigh and rubs up against the most sensitive parts of me. When he leans in, his breath is hot against my ear. "Take me dancing. And once we're alone, put your hand around my neck again, and fuck me."

CHAPTER 5

Jinta

Why did I suggest we go dancing first? My dick is going to fall off before the night is over. The logical part of my brain is screaming at me to run the other way. Not only is Raiden the criminal I'm supposed to be investigating, but he also has a possessive streak a mile wide and no concept of boundaries. He's bad news in every way... and yet I want him so much, I think I'll lose my mind if I can't have him.

This isn't me. I don't do hookups. Once, I wanted the kind of love I read about in books. Hell, I thought I'd found that kind of love. Until it blew up in my face. I haven't wanted another relationship since. I've kept to myself for so long, but in one night, Raiden is making me want things I swore off long ago.

It's fucked-up, but I've always wanted to be desired, obsessed over, wanted. I blame my childhood for that. I was never good enough. I lived my life in the shadow of my family's love while my brother stole the spotlight. He was adored by our parents and constantly praised, and he got into relationships with people who thought the sun rose and set with him. I was jealous, pure and simple. It's horrible, but there's no denying it. Just for once, I want someone who's all mine. I want Raiden, and somehow, this gorgeous, powerful guy who could have anyone in the world... wants me.

Until he finds out my secret. Or until he realizes I'm just not good enough for him. Damn it. What he thinks of me doesn't matter. He's into me? Good. I can use this to my advantage. We'll fuck. I'll get him wrapped around my finger, discover his connection to the disappearances, and that will be that. Everything is going according to plan... although I can't say seducing a yakuza was ever in my plan. Before I know it, I could have enough evidence to pen the story of my career.

Surely after all that, my family will finally stop seeing me as their good-for-nothing son. They'll see they were wrong to turn up their noses at my idea to move to Tokyo and pursue a career in investigative reporting. Maybe, just maybe, I could be a part of the family again instead of the outsider looking in.

Raiden and I wander the streets of Tokyo's gay district in Ni-chome, Shinjuku. There are many varieties of bars catering to bears, butch and femme lesbians, and a crowd of leather-clad men wait in line at the doors of what I assume is a BDSM club. Most of the bars are quite small, and crowds spill over into the narrow streets with their drinks. A rainbow flag waves from the window of one bar we pass. Another club has a torii gate painted in rainbow colors. The population is a mix of both locals and foreigners alike, and I catch snatches of English as we walk.

"Have you been anywhere in Ni-chome?" Raiden asks, looping his fingers through mine as we walk.

"I've tried a few of the cafes."

"This neighborhood... it's special to me."

"Me, too. I felt like I was the only gay guy in the city until I came here."

A bittersweet smile tugs at Raiden's mouth. "I was real confused when I was in my early twenties. I knew I liked guys and girls, but I didn't even know bisexuality was a word."

Empathy makes me bump my shoulder against his. "That's a lonely, scary feeling."

Raiden frowns somberly. "I was sure I was the only

person in the whole country who felt this way until I came here. I came all the way here to go to a gay bar for the first time, and I was too freaked out to even go in." He scowls.

I squeeze his hand. "I get it. I felt the same way my first time at a gay bar."

"I was so pissed at myself. But I came back another night, and some guy noticed me hanging around and offered to buy me a drink inside." He tips his head back, gazing up into the sea of neon lights. "I was too shell-shocked to get his name. But we drank a lot. He gave me a blowjob in the alley, and that was that. Gave me the guts to start finally messing around with guys instead of just girls."

I whistle. "Wow." Raiden's led an exciting life. "I think my first time with a guy was in a bathroom of a bar, and he threw up right after sucking me off. Not because I tasted bad or anything! He just had too much to drink."

Raiden laughs beside me. "Don't think I'll have that problem."

I trip over my own feet at the visual.

We stop outside a bar called *Pixel*. The bouncer lets us skip the line with a nod in Raiden's direction, and in we go. The bar is packed, but there's more seating up the stairs on a balcony overlooking the bustling dance floor. Strippers twirl and spin up and down the poles, their bare skin glistening with sweat and sparkling with glitter.

At the bar, we put away a couple of ice-cold *Sapporo* drafts between us.

Raiden asks, "What's your favorite song?"

I drain the last gulp of my beer. "Uh... I have no idea?"

"Off the top of your head."

"To dance to, or just to listen to, or—"

He groans. I'm lucky if I'm getting laid at all later. "Doesn't matter. Whatever."

"I guess... 'Somebody to Love' by Queen." We both enjoyed that song earlier.

Pulling out his phone, Raiden shoots a text to someone, fingers flying over the keypad. Up on the stage, the DJ smoothly transitions to the very song I just mentioned. Raiden yanks me against him, and I all but pull him onto the dance floor. The temperature climbs as we're surrounded by dozens of bodies, growing almost humid. I can't dance for shit, but I don't care, not with Raiden's big body flush against mine.

Lights swirl over our heads, dyeing Raiden's jet-black hair shades of blue, pink, and red. He pulls me close so we're chest to chest, hip to hip. Without thinking, I sink my hand into his hair, guiding him closer. Hungry lips nip and suck on my neck while his big, graceful body moves against me.

Then Raiden leans in, and his mouth crashes against mine.

Everything else fades away, and it's only Raiden's lips, surprisingly soft against mine and so warm. I make a sound that has my cheeks burning, and he answers with a low groan that has my blood stirring, liquid heat flowing south. He's all I can feel, smell, and taste. Raiden's hand curls in my hair. That same hand gripping, squeezing, tipping my head back so he can press that sweet, hot mouth against the hinge of my jaw and—*fuck*.

I've been kissed before. Good kisses. Bad kisses. Even the best of them were never like this. My breath was never stolen. My heart never felt like it would rupture. He kisses me, and I understand the difference between being kissed and being seen, wanted, *needed*.

The crowd disappears, and he's all I can see. I reach for him, needing him close again. My fingers sink into his hair, pulling him to me, and we kiss until I think I'll die unless we stop.

The hard line of his cock digs into my hip, and my own arousal is evident. All I want is to grind on him, his body eager and warm against mine. But the roar of the crowd tears me from this fantasy. We aren't alone. It would be so easy to just let go with him.

Raiden's lips leave mine hot and aching. His eyes are dark, pupils expanding almost to the edge of his irises. His tongue darts out to caress his lower lip, swollen from our kiss. I did that to him. Made him look so wild and turned on. He's always been so put together until this moment.

His Adam's apple bobs when he swallows, and I want to put my mouth there, anywhere he'll let me. I'd worship at the temple of his body and never stop. With a single kiss, this man ruined me, and I won't be satisfied until I've tasted him again, everywhere.

"How many songs can you get through in this state before you ask me to take you home, Sunshine?" Raiden murmurs into my ear.

I'm so worked up, I'm panting, but like hell am I going to make this easy for him. "Bet I can make you say it first."

Raiden glides his teeth over his lower lip. "Give it your best shot."

Turning so my back is to his front, I reach up and hold the back of his neck. I push my hips back against his groin and swirl them, grinning when he tenses and grabs my waist hard. When he hardens against my ass, I can't hold back my triumphant grin. I got him hard for me.

"Fuck, this ass of yours..." He growls against my neck, teeth sinking in. I'm grateful the music is so loud it hides my groan of pleasure. His fingers curl around my throat, and when he moans in my ear, I know he felt the sound I made.

His canine teeth are sharper than they should be, dimpling my skin to the point of pain, only to draw back before he can break my skin. Gripping his hair, I urge him on, and his lips scorch a path up my neck, kissing, biting, sucking on the marks he leaves behind.

Gripping my wrists, he hoists my hands up and over my head. "Keep them there," he orders, and then he runs his hands down my front. My head falls back at his touch, heat scorching through the barrier of my clothes to my skin. I've never despised clothes so much. Raiden dips his fingers past my belt.

"Enough," Raiden snaps in my ear. I'm whirled around and plastered to his front. "Can't take this anymore."

I'm more than in agreement. "There's a bathroom over there if—"

Gripping my chin, he pulls me in close to nip my bottom lip. "If anyone but me sees you naked, there will be a bloodbath."

"Possessive, aren't you?" I suck his lip into my mouth, fingers bunching in his shirt.

His palm lands on my ass with a meaty smack through my clothes. "Yes. I am. Now start walking, or I'll carry you out."

"Doesn't sound so bad when you say it like that." I kiss the hinge of his jaw.

Raiden loops his arm over my shoulder, like he's staking his claim on me.

Tonight is going to be amazing. I can already tell.

Since we've been drinking, Raiden calls for a taxi to take us to his place. I didn't expect the car ride to be such torture, especially with Raiden's leg pressing against mine. I just want my dick to chill until we get to his place. Raiden's gaze burns over my skin, and I swallow hard when his eyes land on my obvious arousal.

His breath hits my ear when he rumbles, "Wanna suck your dick. Right here."

My pulse skips. The idea is both horrifying since the driver could so easily overhear us, and so sexy that it makes my balls ache. "We don't have condoms, do we?"

"Do we need one?" Raiden's hand is warm on my thigh.

"I haven't been with anyone in a while, and I tested negative the last time I slept with someone, so…"

Raiden shrugs. "It's fine by me. Hey, can you turn on some music?" he asks the taxi driver. The driver flips through a few stations and settles on some J-Pop station. I watch the scenery fly by, willing the arousal heating my blood to abate for now. Any hope of that happening disappears when Raiden glides his hand over my thigh. I squeeze my hands into fists, heart in my throat as he pets the hard line of my dick through my trousers.

"It's fifteen minutes to my house from here. Think you can last that long before you cum?" he asks, voice low and rough in my ear. When he unzips my fly and strokes me through the silk boxers I'm wearing, I stop worrying about anything else.

"Love how soft these are on you. That pale green color against your pretty skin? So sexy. And damn. You're so hard already," he teases, swiping a thumb over my leaking head. "When's the last time anyone's touched you like this?"

"D-don't remember." My hips jerk into his touch. I bite my lip as moans try to spill out. When Raiden sucks on his fingers, then wraps them around me, stroking in earnest, I almost bite through my lip. "Oh, fuck."

Lips to my ear, Raiden whispers, "Like that, Sunshine? Don't hold back. You sound so sexy when you moan for me."

I rest my head against the window, breath fogging the glass as I pant. Everything feels too hot as I turn my face away. I'm horrified we'll be caught like this, but I'm so damn pent up, I think I'll break if I tell him to stop.

In my peripheral, Raiden bows his head, leaning over my lap.

I have to bite down on my knuckles so I don't shout when he takes me in that hot, wet mouth and sucks. My toes curl, and my balls draw up. I grab at his hair, driving my nails into his scalp. "Fuck, fuck, fuck," I whimper, breath steaming up the glass.

Raiden kisses my slit, then pushes his tongue in, and I whine. Loudly. The driver's head twitches, but he doesn't look all the way back.

"Don't cum yet," Raiden says, breath hot against my aching cock. "Ten minutes to go."

It's only been five minutes? *Shit*. I'm going to embarrass myself in a few seconds.

"Can't. Can't hold back." I'm horrified I'll be too loud. How can I stay quiet? I can't. Tears prick my eyes, and shame heats my cheeks.

"You can last a little longer for me, can't you?" He strokes me in his hot, tight fist. "You really can't wait until I get you home, can you? You want to be stuffed full of my cock that badly? I want you so pent up you blow your load the moment I shove my cock inside, feel your tight hole clenching around me while I fuck you."

I grind my teeth until my jaw aches as a sudden orgasm barrels through me. He didn't even have to touch me. All he had to do was talk dirty to me and that was all it took. *Fuck!* The humiliation has me hiding my face against the seat while I pant and shake.

"Sorry, I'm sorry," I croak, too embarrassed to look at him. Tears sting my eyes, making everything worse. He's going to mock me for this, I'm sure of it. "It's been a while. That's why I—damn it!"

He grips my jaw and tilts my face toward him. A streak of cum is smeared across his cheek. "What're you apologizing for?"

My eyes cloud with humiliated tears I try to blink away. "For being stupid and finishing too quickly."

Raiden's eyes narrow. "You're not stupid." The vehemence in his voice surprises me, as if I somehow insulted him. "You losing control like that, being unable to hold back—that's exactly what I wanted."

"Really?"

When he nods, big hands coming up to frame my face, relief brings a smile to my face. "Was that what you wanted, too?"

Cheeks heating, I nod. "And if it made you happy, then... that's even better."

Raiden leans in and claims my lips in a kiss that makes my head spin. Against my mouth, he murmurs, "You did good, Sunshine. So good for me."

A moan escapes me, muffled against his dizzying kiss. Pleasure blooms bright and warm in my chest. I can't remember the last time anybody praised me, and it feels so good, especially coming from him.

"You like that?" Raiden nips my bottom lip. "You like being my good boy?"

A delighted shiver runs down my spine. "Yes."

He lifts his thumb and wipes my cum off his cheek, then holds his thumb out to me. "Love the way your cum tastes. Go on. Taste how fucking sweet you are."

My spent cock twitches. Swallowing hard, I lick my own cum from his skin. I meet his gaze, hoping I've pleased him, and his eyes are nearly black with lust.

"Fuck," he growls, then lunges in, devouring my mouth with his. "You are so fucking sexy."

The car pulls up to the curb. I'll be amazed if I can walk to the front door.

"Thank you," Raiden says to our driver, as if he didn't

just make me blow my load in the back of the poor guy's car. Not that the driver is any the wiser. I'll never look at taxi cabs the same way again.

I don't know why I'm surprised when I step into the lobby and it's immaculately gorgeous. There's a concierge desk, marble walls and floors so polished they shine, and a water wall I would stop and admire if I didn't have a hot, horny yakuza on my arm. Raiden waves innocently at the lady behind the desk, and we almost look like we aren't going to do dirty things to each other as we wait for the elevator.

The doors open with a ding. There are sixty floors total, with a few penthouses. Raiden presses the button for PH3, the final floor. "Of course you have a penthouse," I say, smirking at him. "Sheesh. Crime really does pay, doesn't it? Maybe I'm just wasting my time on this photography gig—"

I'm slammed against the wall, caged into place by Raiden's body. Eyes dark and face deadly serious, he rips open my belt. When his hand curls around my sensitive cock, my knees all but buckle. Raiden smirks. "Hard again, already?"

How is this even possible? My refractory period is usually much longer than this. "Shut up," I croak, my hips moving of their own accord into his strokes. The way he touches me... like he knows my body as well as I do. *Fuck*. I won't last much longer this time.

"Bet I can make you flood my mouth before we even get to the penthouse."

I curse because he's probably right, the bastard. "Everything's a competition with you."

He grins as he sinks to his knees. I suddenly realize there's a camera pointed right at us. Someone's going to get a show.

"Don't worry about it. Nobody watches them this late at night."

"Maybe we should wait until—oh, fuck!" I cry out as he swallows my cock down to the root, nose buried in my pubes. All I can do is grab onto his shoulders, gasping as he bobs his head up and down my length.

He pulls off and takes me in hand, stroking up and down my foreskin. "Still want me to stop? Or do you want me to make you cum?"

"Don't," I groan, squeezing his hair. "Don't stop. Oh, fuck. Please don't stop."

With a throaty growl, he swallows me back down. Just the sight of this powerful force of nature on his knees, worshipping my cock, has me ready to blow. My stomach muscles clench deliciously and my thighs are shaking as he swirls his tongue around me.

"Fuck my mouth, Sunshine," Raiden rasps, then kisses my cock. "Wanna see you let go. You can cum again for me, can't you? Wanna taste you again so badly."

His sweet, sensual words, followed by the perfect heat of

his mouth, makes me moan. I watch the floors and curse myself. This elevator is slow, and we're only halfway there. I can do it. I can hold back. I can, I—Raiden tightens his lips around me, sucks me from the base to the tip so hard, his cheeks hollow. I can't hold back and snap my hips forward, groaning as my cock glides in and out of his mouth faster and faster. My pants become ragged gasps and moans, growing louder the closer I get to my release. I tear at his hair, my hoarse scream filling the elevator as I shoot down his throat.

Just as I think my legs will give out, Raiden's on his feet, arms around me. The earthy tang of my own cum in Raiden's mouth makes me moan.

"You taste so damn good. Can't get enough," Raiden purrs against my lips. Our mouths part with a smack and I gasp for breath, lips tingling and hot. Raiden shakes his head, looking at me the way I must have been looking at him all night. With awe. Reverence. "Such a good, dirty boy for me." The caress of his fingers along my cheek makes my eyes flutter.

Shit. I think I like being his good boy a little too much.

The elevator doors ding open. Hands locked, we step into the private vestibule. His penthouse is styled after ones in the west. The stunning view of Tokyo almost distracts me from the high of my orgasm. Raiden unlocks the door, and we take off our shoes in the entryway. A panoramic wall of windows wraps around the living room.

The space is sprawling, clean, and reeks of pure luxury.

"How many bedrooms?" I ask.

Raiden comes up behind me, arms looping around my waist. He bites my neck. "Four. We should fuck in all of them."

I thought my dick was spent from two orgasms in less than an hour, but I was wrong.

"What does a guy need with four bedrooms?" I muse, marveling at all that space. I'd be lost in a place like this. And he lives alone, too. "You don't ever get lonely in a place as big as this?"

I turn around and yelp when he shoves me. I go crashing onto the sofa. Raiden peels his shirt off over his head, and I'm breathless as he bares all that tattooed skin to me.

"You're here, aren't you?" He pops the button on his jeans and shoves them down to pool at his ankles. Stepping out of them, he advances on me like a beast on the hunt. With his vibrant tattoos and rippling muscles, this man is a work of art. I swallow hard as he crawls over me in only tight black briefs that hide absolutely nothing. "So no. I'm not lonely."

I squirm out of my clothes, but he stops me before I can pull off my underwear. He takes them off himself slowly, like he's unwrapping a present he wants to savor. I've never been the object of such slow, careful worship before. Lifting the underwear to his face, he breathes in deep, exhaling a growl.

"Fuck. You smell good."

A gasp escapes me when he latches onto my neck, nipping and sucking at the bruises he's left there. I wrap my arms around him, clutching him to me. Finally, we're skin to skin. His body is hot and hard against me. It's the most amazing feeling.

I palm the firm globes of his muscular ass and pull his briefs down. Reaching between us, I grasp his hard, heavy cock. He's like iron, and I want him inside me more than I've ever wanted anything else.

Raiden reaches over and opens the end table. He tears open a pack of lube and drizzles it all over our dicks. Taking us both in hand, he strokes. My eyes roll back, a whine tearing from my throat as our cocks slide together with slick, wet noises.

Raiden's eyes are dark, and he stares at me with his lip between his teeth as he rocks against me. "Fuuuck," he groans, long and drawn out. "Can't believe you're hard again. How many times have I gotta make you cum before it's enough?"

"Guess we'll have to find out," I say, panting as I snap my hips up into our stroking fists.

Lunging down, Raiden captures my mouth with his, thrusting his tongue inside. He slides his lube-slick hand down my body and circles my hole. When he presses inside, the stretch has me gasping. He pumps his finger in deeper, curling it until he strokes my prostate. The sensation's uncomfortable at first after neglecting that part of my body for so long, but the burn slowly fades into something mind-numbingly good. When he adds another finger, forcing me open wider, I rock my hips and chase the fullness inside me.

"So fucking tight for me." Raiden pants against my mouth. He stretches me open until he's four fingers in, and the pleasure is on the cusp of pain. My body's so needy, so desperate to be filled and fucked. All the while, our cocks grind together, elevating my pleasure until I'm dangerously close to finishing again. If it happens again, that will be it for the night. There's only so much my body can take.

"Raiden," I gasp.

"Ready for me, Sunshine?"

"Yes," I say around a groan.

"I'm not convinced." He curls his finger over my prostate again. My dick's so hard, it's leaking all over both our cocks.

"Please. Please, fuck me."

He smacks a kiss to my lips, fucking my mouth with his tongue while he fucks me with his fingers. "Good boy." He rolls me over suddenly and smacks my ass. "Grab onto the back of the couch."

I comply. On his knees behind me, he shoves my thighs open. With a hiss of pleasure, he lubes his cock up and presses his hips to my ass. I'm breathing hard like I've been running as he snags my hair in his fist and yanks my head back, mouthing at my neck and shoulder. The blunt head of his cock presses against me, then into me. He's thicker than his fingers, stretching me wide and filling me just the way I wanted.

"Don't go slow," I rasp, voice slurring as I surrender to the feeling of fullness. "Fuck me hard. Please." I try to plead for more, and he rocks his hips, sinking even deeper into me. "Yes! Like that. Give me more!" Every nerve in my body tingles as he drives into me faster, harder. It's so hard I have to grip the couch so I don't collapse.

"Taking me so good, Hiro." He snaps his hips, thighs slapping my ass hard enough to bruise. "That's it. Fuck! Love the way you grip my dick. So hot and fucking tight. So perfect for me."

His honeyed words are like a balm, soothing pieces of my heart I didn't know were aching. Finally, if only for tonight, I'm enough for someone.

My mouth goes slack, and I can no longer hold back the shameless moans he forces from me. The pleasure makes everything hazy around the edges. There's only his hand around my throat, his teeth sinking into my shoulder as he pants and growls like a beast in heat. His cock pounds in and out of my clenching, needy body. I squeeze around him, trying to keep him there, right there, deep inside me.

"Fuck. Do that again. Yes!" Raiden snarls, slapping my ass with approval as I tighten around his cock once more.

My balls draw up and I'm close, reduced to nothing but whimpers as my body shakes and shudders. "B-bite me," I beg. "Put your teeth in me."

The sound that escapes Raiden is positively feral. He bites down on my shoulder so hard I scream as I start to cum, spilling over his hand as he jacks my dick. His teeth are painfully sharp, sharper than they should be, but the pain sends me to highs I've never been.

A strangled shout escapes Raiden as he grips my hips so hard, I wonder if I'll always feel his touch there down to my bones. Deep inside me, his cock twitches with every pulse of his release.

He crumples, sweaty forehead to my shoulder, breath huffing hotly against my skin. The vulnerable gestures make my heart squeeze in my chest, even if it means nothing. His arms go around me, and we fall onto the couch together. He's still inside me, twitching and throbbing.

"Stay there?" I ask.

"Nowhere else I wanna be," he rumbles, kissing the bite he left on my shoulder. He runs his fingers over the broken skin, and I wince. "Sorry. I didn't mean to make you bleed."

I look over my shoulder at him. "It's okay. I liked it. Really liked it."

He grins and fuck, he's gorgeous. His sweaty hair is tousled and clings to his forehead, his lips are red and swollen, and some of my blood smears his chin. He looks debased, ruined, and I was the one who did it to him. "You're beautiful," I tell him.

His eyes go wide, and I think the flush kissing his cheeks deepens. *Fuck. That's cute.*

Cute? God. I'm going to be in over my head if I'm not careful.

"You're the one who's..." He grimaces. "Going any-where?"

"No way. I want you to stay inside me all night."

"Good." Grinning, he curls close to me and kisses my shoulder. "Get some rest. I'm not anywhere near done with you." He plants a lingering kiss on my lips that I'd almost call gentle, despite everything we just did.

Wrapped in his arms, sleep comes for me.

I remember I'm supposed to snoop around his apartment after he's asleep. But as his arms tighten around me, and I feel him thick and warm inside me, I realize that my investigation will have to wait for tomorrow because I can't bear to leave his arms.

Shit. That can't be good, can it?

Chapter 6

Waking up with the man I slept with curled against my chest, his body warm against mine is... different. I always give people the boot after sex, or go to my own bedroom and leave them to sleep in the guest bed. I've never literally slept with someone. There's so many firsts I've never had that I'm now having with Hiro.

I don't like it. If I'm not careful, this thing between us could get complicated fast. But I can't bring myself to pull away, even if I should. Not with my cock cradled against his plump ass, and his body so warm and soft against mine. The bruises my teeth left on his shoulder have colored so beautifully, like I claimed him as mine, inside and out.

Ours, my wolf whispers, shocking me. My wolf rarely

ever speaks to me.

No. *No.* I didn't claim him in some stupid fated mates destiny way. I claimed him in a way that's tangible and real. Only two supernatural creatures can claim each other as mates. The couple has to mark each other, and there has to be consent.

Fated mates *can* be humans and they can feel the bond, but they can't reciprocate with a bite. A strange tingling around my finger makes me grind my teeth. And then there's all the orgasms I wrung out of Hiro. Supposedly, only a fated pair can go round after round without tiring like that...

Fuck it. None of this matters. I stopped believing in that stuff a long time ago. *But this is... it's nice.*

Even after I've made him cum and scream my name, arousal still heats my blood. I've got to have him again before we go our separate ways for the day. Carefully, I try to rise. Hiro's face pinches in discomfort as I leave the warmth of his body. I don't like that.

Leaning down, I press my lips to his cheek and smooth his hair back from his face. His handsome face relaxes, soothing something heavy in my chest.

What the hell is this man doing to me?

Shaking my head, I pull my jeans on, not bothering with underwear. In the kitchen, I scoop some rice into the cooker, crack and whisk some eggs that I mix with green onion, and get a pan heated up. The stove has a grill perfect for cooking fish, so I grill up some leftover mackerel.

The rice cooks quickly. The fish grills to flaky, tender perfection. I roll the eggs carefully, then cut them into thick fluffy rounds. By the time I've finished reheating some leftover miso, Hiro yawns behind me. He's sitting up on the couch, still wrapped in the blanket, his hair askew.

"Morning," I say, surprised when serenity dances through me. It's hard not to feel like all is right in the world when he looks so damn good.

"Morning." He rubs his eyes and rises, the blanket wrapped around him like a towel. He winces a little when he gets up, rubbing his lower back. "Damn. Think we overdid it."

"Are you okay?"

"Yeah, yeah. Just... been a while since I was used so thoroughly." He grins lopsidedly, and my heart kicks in my chest.

"Hungry?"

"Starved. Where's your bathroom?"

"Back down the hall to the left."

I plate up our food and finish preparing coffee for me and Hiro. The toilet flushes down the hall and Hiro returns, sitting at the table with me. He winces when he hits his foot on the table leg. The table shakes ominously. His eyes widen. "Uh. Think I just broke your table."

"Nah. This thing's falling apart. I'm getting another one."

Grabbing some egg between his chopsticks, Hiro takes a bite and moans. "So good."

Something loosens in my chest, and for a moment, I forget about my food and watch Hiro tuck into his meal. My mornings are always so routine. I wake up, go for a jog, have a quick meal, and then I'm out the door.

I never realized how quiet my home really is until now that Hiro is here filling in all the quiet spaces with the soft clink of his utensils against his plate and his little happy sighs. Sitting across from someone and sharing a meal together is nice. Peaceful.

My life is chaotic with each day being unpredictable and dangerous. As I share this quiet moment with Hiro, it feels like I've found a port in the stormy sea that is my life. I like this feeling. Even if I know it can't last, I wish it could. I wish I could have more mornings like this.

"Where'd you learn to cook like this? This is amazing."

I pluck some mackerel off my plate and take a bite. "My grandfather owned a restaurant when I was a kid. I lived with him for most of my life, so I came to his restaurant with him after school. I'd study there mostly, but I'd also visit in the kitchen with him and watch him cook."

Hiro's eyes brighten with surprise. "My family are all cooks. I loved cooking. Always thought I'd make a career out of it."

"But you didn't?"

Hiro shakes his head and takes a moment to chew his

food. "I loved cooking. Just not with them." A note of sadness touches his voice. "It was obvious I'd have to change myself if I wanted to be a part of their lives. Date women. Have kids." He shrugs and looks away, lips sinking at the corners. "So I decided to go my own way and didn't look back."

"Yeah, my family was shit, too. I get it," I say, surprised by how easily I can be honest with him. "I don't have many good memories from my childhood, but the days I spent with my grandfather make up for all of it. Watching him cook was like magic to me. He'd make the most incredible things out of a few ingredients. Eating his food always brightened my day."

Delight springs across Hiro's face. "And now, you've brightened mine."

Something flutters through my heart. Not butterflies. That's a stupid analogy. Maybe, I don't know… moths. Or wasps. Something cool. Ah, fuck it. I have to roll my lips in so I don't beam at him like a damn sap. What is with me? Somehow, making him happy and hearing from his lips that I've brightened his day—it makes me want to smile.

For once, I did something good for another person. I wish I could do that more often. That I could be good for someone. A better man. Who the hell am I kidding? That's never going to happen.

I scoff. "It's just food. Mine's nothing like his."

Why is it that every time he says something sweet like

that, my impulse is to ball myself up like a porcupine and show my quills? Or hiss like a damn alley cat?

"Nobody's made me breakfast before. So hush and let me savor this." He takes a big bite and sighs dreamily.

Nobody? I find that hard to believe. Yet the wolf side of me preens at that.

We provided. Made him smell happy. Pleased our—

Shit. Things are getting too sappy. I need to get back into familiar territory.

Grabbing my plate, I walk to his side of the table. "Tried the mackerel yet?"

"I'm not the biggest fan of fish."

I place a piece of fish between my lips and cock a brow at him.

With a long-suffering huff, Hiro parts his lips. When our lips meet, a fire starts beneath my skin, burning me up from the inside. Our tongues tangle and I swallow the quiet moan that tries to escape Hiro. All his sounds of pleasure are mine. Twisting my fingers through his hair, I yank his head back to kiss and lick his throat.

Ours. Ours. Ours.

My wolf loves it when he bares his neck like this, when he submits.

"Hard already?" I squeeze the tent protruding through the blankets. He gasps and squirms. "Should we do something about that?"

Hiro whimpers against my mouth.

"Want me to fuck you again?"

He nods frantically, fumbling with the blanket covering him.

"Then ask me nicely."

Color blooms in Hiro's cheeks. He's a lot more reserved than before I've made him cum twice.

I tug on his hair. "Ask me nicely."

Screwing his eyes shut, Hiro whispers, "Please."

"Please, what?" I nip the hinge of his jaw, palming my hand over his straining cock.

"F-fuck me. Please."

I groan against his skin. "That's my good boy. Since you asked so nicely..." In a couple of swift motions, I shove his plate aside, then I haul him up and over the table. I tear the blanket off him, biting my lip when his rigid cock is revealed to me. He's already so hard, jutting up toward his stomach, the tip dewy with pre-cum. Bowing before him, I lap the length of his cock and suckle the tip.

"Fuck," he yells, grabbing at my hair. He throws his head back, eyes closed in bliss.

"Eyes open, Sunshine." I rub his thigh, and Hiro whimpers. "I want those beautiful eyes on me when I give you the best damn head of your life."

Hiro bites his lip, his eyes hazy as I take him in deeper. Every time I meet his gaze, sparks sizzle down my spine straight to my dick. I'm so hard it's a wonder I don't bust through my zipper, and I've only sucked him so far.

Panting, he rocks his hips, pushing his cock deeper down my throat. "Fuck. Raiden. Fuck. Feels so good." Trembling fingers grab at my hair as he wraps his ankles around the back of my neck, urging me up and down his length. "God. How are you so good at this?"

Around a mouthful, I tilt my head.

Hiro grimaces. "Oh. Right. Yeah. Let's not even go there."

I pull off his cock, ignoring his disappointed gasp. I kiss his leaking head. "Jealous?"

Fuck, that's too hot.

Ripping down my jeans, I slather my cock in lube, then march back between his thighs. Grabbing his legs, I spread him open. We both shout when I slam inside. I don't wait. He's still nice and loose from last night, so I let go, snapping my hips into his needy little body.

"Fuck, Sunshine. You have such a perfect, tight little hole."

Hiro thrashes beneath me, hands grasping at the flat glass tabletop. He cries out in bliss as I fill him again and again. Each thrust makes the table rock and creak, inching it across the floor.

I know it's about to snap. I can hear it coming. Without thinking, I lunge, wrapping Hiro in my arms and hauling him against me. Hiro gasps, legs locking around me, nails biting into my back. The table leg gives out, and the table falls to the side. Glass shatters on impact.

"Holy shit," Hiro gasps, clutching at me. I'm still buried snugly inside his body. "Did we just break your table?"

My legs are trembling, hips still pulsing even through the momentary panic. "It's fine. I'll order another one." I yank his mouth back on mine and carry him to the counter. I lay him down on the marble-wrapped counter carefully, then yank his hips so he's half hanging off. I fuck him like we never stopped, and the angle is even better. I have the perfect view of my cock slamming into his hole and can watch the way he stretches around my dick.

"Taking me so good." I groan, unable to tear my eyes away as I disappear in and out of his body, faster and faster. "Love how you beg. Love how insatiable you are for this dick."

"More!" Hiro moans, and I love how utterly shameless he is. I love that I've made this shy, reserved man fall apart. "Harder. Please!"

My hips smack the back of his ass, and I hope it bruises. I want my marks all over his skin. "Fuckin' love the way you squeeze around me, gripping my dick so good. How hot and tight you are. You like taking my cock?"

Hiro latches onto my shoulders, nails biting into my flesh. "Y-yes! God, yes!"

I lunge down to capture his lips, rewarding his honesty by fucking his mouth with my tongue. Our teeth scrape, lips get cut, and when I taste his blood, I start to unravel.

"You know what you do to me? Gonna breed this tight

little hole."

"Raiden!" He keens, breathless and hoarse, wrapping one hand around his cock and stroking. "So close! Fuck, I'm gonna cum."

"Give me what I want. Cum for me. Milk my fucking dick."

Hiro's eyes roll back, and he bites his lip. "Yes. Fuck. Yes. Fill my hole. Claim me."

I knew he was filthy. I knew beneath all those sweet blushes and shy, sunshiny smiles, I could corrupt this man into a complete whore for my cock.

My balls draw up tight and I pound him through my impending release, chasing the feeling building deep inside me. It's never been this intense. I've never wanted to mark someone so much. Sex has never been like this before. I've always chased the end goal, the climax, but it's more than that. I want him to finish, knowing it was me who took him there.

"That's it! Fall apart on my cock."

I know I've taken him over the edge when he clenches around me, abs tightening, head thrown back as he shouts hoarsely. Ropes of cum spill over his fist, spattering his stomach and chest. I lose myself in the tight grip of his body, everything around me falling away. I drive into him mindlessly, using his hole to get myself off. All that exists is his tight, warm body, his arms locked around me, and his lips that somehow found mine. I fall into the kiss, devouring his lips as my release wrings me out.

When I finally open my eyes, all I can see is hazy chocolate-brown eyes gazing up at me, full of the same dazed wonder warming my heart.

"Fucking hell." I breathe. I run my finger over his swollen rim, feeling where we're joined, hot and slick with my release.

Hiro just nods weakly, eyes lidded, mouth slack. I kiss him again, unable to help myself.

"Gonna be thinking about this the rest of the day," I murmur against his mouth.

When his fingers caress my hair, I all but melt.

"Me, too," Hiro whispers, his voice soft and happy. "I hate that I have to go to work."

"Quit your job," I say. "Move in with me. Spend all day naked with me, and I'll pay you by the hour."

Hiro laughs, the sound sweet and bubbly. "Why am I actually tempted?"

"Because it's a good idea." I grip his ass and squeeze.

Damn. I won't see him the rest of the day. If he could just stay here with me...

Fuck. Bite. Claim, says my wolf.

Fucking hell.

All day long, thoughts of Hiro consume me. My damn wolf won't stop grumbling at me.

Boy. Need boy. Find boy. Claim boy.

I wish the bastard would shut the hell up. It takes everything I have not to pull out Hiro's business card and text him. I'd love to see him again tonight, but I've got to meet with Namikawa at the Lotus to discuss how to deal with the Takada-kai. They're getting more and more brazen, trying to make people lose faith in the Namikawa-kai's ability to protect our own. If this isn't stopped, we'll lose face.

Yet all my stupid wolf cares about is getting his knot inside Hiro. He and I really are alike.

The Lotus is packed in the evening, full of people dancing, eating, and drinking themselves into oblivion at the bar. Ren locks eyes with me, then asks the barback to take over before she darts my way.

"Did something happen? The boss is furious."

"Takada-kai attacked one of our restaurants last night. I chased them off, but Tenko was pissed. We'll be lucky if he pays up next month."

Ren lurches to a stop and grabs my arm. "Why didn't you tell me? Did you get hurt?"

"Of course not," I say, tugging out of her grip. "I handled it just fine."

We bypass the bouncer guarding the VIP section and head upstairs into the soundproof booth. Namikawa is already there, stern mouth in a thin line and eyes narrowed. Sitting at his side is my grandfather Hideyoshi, Namikawa's right-hand man, who meets my gaze and tips his head in acknowledgment. The booth is packed with other Namikawa-kai, all tense and scowling.

Namikawa says, "Takada is trying to encroach upon Taito. He has been killing those who owe us money and destroying the businesses under our protection. I believe he may even be abducting people from our territory."

My spine stiffens as I recall that odd memory of the woman's voice from last night. If it even was a memory. Hell if I know.

"If word gets out that we cannot protect our own, we will lose face. We must strike back tonight. We will split into groups and strike all throughout Minato. Destroy his businesses, fight his men. Another group will come with me to his nightclub, Wolf's Den, and confront Takada himself." His eyes land on me, and it's clear where my place is. By his side like a well-trained pup. "Is this clear?"

"Yes, boss!" shouts the gathering of Namikawa-kai.

"Let's move out." Namikawa motions for me to follow as he sets off at a brisk pace.

Myself, Ren, Hideyoshi, and Namikawa pile into a big black *Cadillac*. Hideyoshi starts the engine, and we drive for Minato. A few black cars follow us, while others split off in different directions. My heart starts to race as the prospect of battle looms closer and closer. Cars yield to us as we weave through traffic, and nobody dares to cut us off.

I wonder what Hiro is doing now. I wish I'd called him and heard his voice, but I don't know why. Fifteen minutes later, we're driving through the streets of Minato where Takada and his pack reside. Tokyo Tower glows golden against the night sky as Hideyoshi slams on the brakes outside of a club a few streets down from the tower. People are lined up to get inside the club, dressed for a night of clubbing.

Hideyoshi grabs my arm. "Raiden, sit this one out."

"I can't," I hiss.

"It's going to be dangerous. Stay close to me."

I can't help rolling my eyes. "I'm not a pup anymore. I don't need you to protect me, Granddad."

A fond smile tugs at Hideyoshi's wrinkled mouth. "No. I suppose you don't, and yet I always will."

Sap. I hurry to catch up with Namikawa.

"Boss," I say, trying to grab his attention as we close in on the club. "This place is going to be packed with civilians."

Namikawa's stride doesn't falter. "If they interfere, then cut them down."

My stomach twists. "Boss—"

"He has killed our people. An eye for an eye is the only fair response. He wishes to prove to us that we are incapable of protecting our own! To make fools of us all. We shall prove the opposite is true."

Ren meets my gaze, wide-eyed and complexion paler than usual.

My heart is somewhere in my stomach as we muscle our way to the front of the line.

"Hey, assholes!" the bouncer snarls, and his eyes bulge as he catches sight of Namikawa, shielded in the center of our group. "What are you—"

But with one swift motion, Namikawa pulls a knife from beneath his sleeve and slits the bouncer's throat. The people behind us scream and begin to run.

With a kick, I throw open the doors and my pack streams inside. Loud music throbs in my ears. People dance without a care on the crowded dance floor or laugh over drinks at the bar with friends.

As our scents waft in, the atmosphere changes in an instant. Takada-kai men at the bar leap up and bellow warnings to each other. They rush us in seconds. There aren't many, but I know that will change any moment now.

One of the Takada-kai men pulls out a knife and hurls it over the sea of people. It strikes a Namikawa-kai member in the skull only inches from me. The club erupts in screams. Glasses shatter as people drop their drinks and seek cover or run for the exits.

The lights flash violently around us, making it hard to tell if the ones rushing toward us in the crowd are yakuza or civilians—and I'm not the only one confused. A few of our fighters panic as they pull out knives they've hidden away and start biting and slashing anyone who rushes at us, yakuza or not.

Someone launches themselves at me from the crowd and swings a punch into my stomach. Claws bite into my skin and tear my shirt. With a snarl, I drive my teeth into my attacker's shoulder and tear out a chunk of flesh and clothes, making him scream.

From the balcony above, a throaty growl of a voice bellows, "What the hell is going on here?"

I shove my attacker to the ground and kick him across the face. When I look up, Saito Takada looms on the balcony. Lights flash across his face, which twists in fury. He leaps from above and lands on his feet, claws sharp at his sides. Others jump down and flank him protectively. At the forefront of his protection is Hirano Kasamatsu, Takada's second-in-command.

"Stay behind me, Saito!" Hirano growls.

"Shut up, don't tell me what to do!" Takada barks.

The club has emptied, and nobody stands between us except four injured civilians sprawled on the ground and a few bloodied Takada-kai thugs.

"Noboru, would you kindly?" Namikawa asks, and the command in his voice is one I can't refuse. Going to Namikawa, I stand in front of him, ready to defend him even at the cost of my own life.

Takada curls his lip in a sneer. "Being a subservient little bitch isn't a good look on you, Noboru. If you were in my pack... well. You'd be my bitch, too. But I'd make it so good for you."

Beside me, Ren tenses. Hideyoshi's nostrils flare, and in a rare show of anger, my grandfather unsheathes his claws. "You will not lay a hand upon my grandson again. Filth."

Damn. I forget my grandad can be a badass when he wants to be.

"Enough," Namikawa snaps. "If you take issue with my leadership, then challenge me man to man, Takada!"

With a snarl, Takada charges us with his men. I swing, claws narrowly avoiding Takada's face. He grabs my arm and spins me around, sending me flying across the floor on my back. I'm on my feet in seconds just in time to deflect the punch he throws at me. Inches apart, Takada grins at me. "Join me, Noboru! You know you want to. You'll never be Namikawa's pet again!"

"Shut up!" I snarl and throw a kick into his stomach so hard it sends him soaring back and crashing into the bar.

The club door crashes open. "Boss! Sirens! The police are coming!" someone shouts.

"Shit!" Takada screams, and he shoves one of his men toward us and takes off running toward the back of the club.

"Scatter!" Namikawa orders. "Split up and lie low. Do not let yourselves be arrested or followed!"

A snarl builds in my throat as I watch Takada run away without so much as a scratch, but as sirens get louder, I book it out of there with the rest of my pack.

For the next few days, we follow Namikawa's orders and lie low.

It's boring as shit. I haven't had to go into hiding for a while. Namikawa received a tip-off from one of the police on our payroll, and he warned us that the cops were going to be raiding our hideouts throughout the city.

There were arrests, quite a few, but nothing to lose sleep over. Still, we haven't had the cops come down this hard on us for a long time. Not until Takada started fucking shit up for us.

At the end of the week, Namikawa goes on national TV and to viewers all over the city, Namikawa bows low and long in shame and says, "To the citizens of Tokyo, I extend to you my sincere apology. On my honor, there will be peace between the Namikawa-kai and the Takada-kai."

My stomach goes sour. Peace? Takada deserves to be wiped out for the shit he pulled this past week. But fighting back hadn't done anything good for our image, and the cops are still breathing down our necks.

When Namikawa calls me on Saturday, he says,

"Noboru. Are you safe?"

"Bored stiff." Currently, I'm tucked away in one of our hideouts in an apartment near Senso-ji Temple. "But otherwise, I'm fine."

"This feud with the Takada-kai must end."

I sit up straighter, mouth going dry. "What's the plan, boss?"

"I have reached out to Takada. The police have cracked down upon his gang, as well. He has agreed to meet and discuss terms for a truce."

Dread settles heavily in my stomach. "You know what he'll ask for. Don't you?"

Who he'll ask for.

"We will see."

I squeeze my phone so hard I hear the screen crack. What does that mean? Surely Namikawa wouldn't... he wouldn't...

"Until then, we must work on repairing our public image. The photographer you met with. Are his pictures any good?"

I'd completely forgotten to talk to Namikawa about Hiro's photos. "Yes."

"Call him. I want to put out a story in the upcoming issue, and we'll need pictures for the article."

I agree, and we hang up.

My stomach churns in the sudden silence that hangs over me.

A truce with the Takada-kai. I know exactly what at least one of Takada's terms will be.

He'll want me. Would Namikawa give me to Takada if he felt that was the only way to achieve peace between our packs?

CHAPTER 7

Raiden

It's been a shitty week, but as Hiro comes out of his building, my day suddenly feels a lot better. He looks adorable in a bright white top layered with a striped sky-blue shirt. And the way those beige chinos hug his sexy thighs? Damn delectable.

My wolf gives a pleased rumble. *Sweet Hiro. Our Hiro.*

I roll down the window and wave. "Hey."

Hiro's enthusiastic grin ambushes me, making my heart leap. "Hey." He sounds amused for some reason.

"What?" I ask, unlocking the door so he can climb into my car.

"Nothing, just... it's been a while."

"Sorry."

"Yakuza stuff?"

I blow out my cheeks. "Yeah."

"I watched Namikawa's speech. I think that's the first time I've seen him on TV. There was some big fight with a rival gang?"

I steer us away from the curb and drive toward the next traffic light. "It was a mess."

Concerned eyes comb over me. "Were you hurt?"

He was worried about me? That's cute. I clap my hand on Hiro's thigh and squeeze. "No. I held my own just fine. Had to lie low for a few days, though. It sucked."

Hiro runs his fingers over the back of my hand. His touch is like a jolt of electricity, kick-starting my heart. "I missed you."

He did? I can barely swallow the pleased rumble as my wolf expresses his delight. The beast has never been so vocal before. "Had a lot of time to kill in hiding. I was bored outta my mind. But if I thought about you, I'd get hard as a damn rock in seconds."

Being away from Hiro was torturous. He'd been on my mind almost 24/7 as the minutes dragged by. I'd jerked off more than once to memories of our explosive night together, spilled so hard at the memory of the tight, hot grip of his body around my cock and the sounds he made as he came against my stomach. My dick threatens to plump up just remembering it all.

Hiro clears his throat. "I, uh... thought about you, too."

A smug grin tugs at my mouth. "Nice thoughts?"

He squirms in his seat, laughing breathily. "Not at all."

A low growl escapes me as I creep my hand up his thigh, stopping just a few inches from his crotch. If I didn't have to drive, I'd get him off here and now. "You'll have to tell me about those naughty thoughts of yours sometime."

In a few minutes, we're at the studio where we normally shoot photos for our various fan magazines. We enter the elevator and ride it up. The sweet scent of cherry blossoms soothes something in me. As we near the top, I reach out and grab Hiro's arm. His quiet gasp is muffled when I claim his mouth with mine. Then he goes lax against me with a quiet moan. I nibble his bottom lip, so soft and bitable, then give his chin a bite.

Ours.

How did I miss him so much? It's almost like a part of me was missing. My wolf was so restless, aching to run somewhere. To... run to Hiro? But why? Why is my wolf so fixated on this man?

The elevator doors open, and Hiro lurches away from me and wipes his lips, his cheeks pink. I chuckle at his embarrassment, and we roam the halls until we find our studio. Hiro's scent shifts from aroused to anxious, and his heart is loud.

"Don't be nervous."

Hiro gawks at me. "Don't be nervous? If I get his bad side, he'll probably cut me up and stuff me in a garbage bag!"

I snort. "No way."

"Oh, good."

"It's too messy," I clarify. "It's much easier to just dump a body in the river."

"*What?*" Hiro squeaks, eyes bulging in horror.

Not liking that he's nervous, I reach out and tug the edges of his mouth to force him to look cheerful. "Chill, Sunshine. I'll protect you." When he blushes, I know my efforts were worth it.

Inside the studio, the crew has arranged lighting and various equipment. The journalist who usually writes articles for the pack is engaged in conversation with Namikawa. At the sight of me, Namikawa holds up a hand to quiet her. Hiro stiffens beside me. "Oh, shit," he whispers. "He's even scarier in person."

Namikawa is old, but he's got a cold, mile-long stare, a stern mouth that always seems stiff on his face, and a tall, straight posture that radiates power. My wolf wants to show his throat, but I stand my ground.

Hiro bows long and low. "I'm Hiro Watanabe. It's a pleasure to meet you."

Namikawa gives a shorter bow. "Noboru has told me you take fine pictures. Let's get started."

Hiro exhales shakily when he straightens up. Namikawa sweeps past him and goes to sit in his chair, surrounded by expensive lighting equipment. The shoot begins, and it seems to go well. I stay back and observe as Hiro's social awkwardness disappears, and he assumes a professional air, snapping photographs of Namikawa from different angles. The director pauses the shoot a few times so Namikawa can inspect the pictures. He only seems to ask for one photo to be reshot. That's good.

The shoot only lasts an hour, then Namikawa announces he's ready to start the interview. The crew packs up equipment, and Namikawa approaches Hiro. "Those were good photos."

Hiro's face goes bright red, and he bows his head in thanks. "Thank you. I'm glad you liked them."

Namikawa says, "I'd like to hire you for a long-term project."

Hiro's mouth goes slack in surprise, but he quickly composes himself. "Sure!"

"Noboru has said that you wish to do a photo book about the yakuza. Now more than ever, the public needs to see a side of our organization that the biased police and the media refuse to show. You would be allowed access to our organization that no outsiders are granted. Every photo you take will be heavily scrutinized. You will not publish any photos we deem unfit for public viewing. Is this clear?"

Hiro nods seriously. "Yes, absolutely."

"Can you start tonight?"

My heart skips. Tonight? We're meeting with the Takada-kai tonight. I don't want Hiro anywhere near Takada.

"Boss—"

Namikawa's sharp look silences me at once.

"Of course," Hiro assures him. I gnash my teeth in frustration.

If anyone gives Hiro trouble, I will rip their throats out with my teeth.

"A bathhouse?" Hiro asks after he swallows a bite of his sashimi. "Why there?"

"It's hard to hide a knife in a bathhouse," I answer, polishing off the last of my rice bowl.

Hiro noticeably pales. "Does the other yakuza group know I'll be there?"

I nod. "Namikawa would have passed the info along to Takada."

"He's a boss?"

"Yeah. Our groups have been rivals for years."

Hiro pauses in chewing. "So why is Namikawa meeting with them?"

I bite my tongue before I can say another word. It's scary how easy it is to talk to him. There's an instinctual pull urging me to spill my secrets, but I swallow it all down. Our affairs are none of Hiro's business. Knowing could mean his death.

"Namikawa thinks an alliance between our clans could be beneficial." My stomach sours at the idea, but Namikawa doesn't pay me for my opinion.

"Doesn't sound like you think this is such a good idea."

"I don't." The words come out a growl. "Our clans used to be one, but Takada was exiled, so he formed his own clan. We've been fighting over control for Taito ever since."

"Ah. I've heard about that," Hiro chimes in. "The gang wars are all over the news."

Hard not to be. A few years back, one fight was so bad, an entire neighborhood got shut down. Residents had curfews at night for when the fighting got really bloody.

"Is this Takada guy bad news?"

"Could be." He's always been bad news to me. "I know him better than Namikawa ever could." And how I wish I didn't. "He won't offer something for nothing in exchange."

And I know just what, who, he'll ask for when Namikawa asks him for a deal.

"So this meeting could be the end of the gang war between your clans."

I nod stiffly. At what cost? Dinner with Hiro was just the distraction I needed, but there's no hiding from the inevitable now. Nothing is predictable in this life.

I ask for the bill when the waitress stops by. She brings us the check and two complimentary glasses of hot green tea.

"Hey, you paid last time," Hiro says, trying to take the check. "I have money, you know. I'm not a starving artist."

I hold it out of reach. "I've got it." I count out some bills and leave them on the table.

"You don't have to pay all the time."

"It's a matter of pride."

"Wasting money on me?"

I hold his gaze. "Taking care of what's mine."

Hiro's cheeks color. Scoffing affectionately, he squeezes my knee beneath the table. "Thanks. I'll have to pay you back sometime."

I smirk and lean in. "I can think of a few ways. Like with your mouth around my—"

Hiro kicks me beneath the table, and I chuckle.

We leave the restaurant together, and I drive us to the bathhouse. I turn the music up louder—Queen's *Bohemian Rhapsody*—and I allow myself to laugh as Hiro sings along. Looks like I've successfully made him a Queen fan. I drive us through Tokyo's neon-streaked streets until we arrive at the bathhouse Namikawa owns. The scents of other wolves in my territory rankles me, and I have to fight back a growl so Hiro doesn't hear.

We arrive in the changing room. I already see a few of my fellow Namikawa-kai brothers getting ready for the meeting, full-body tattoos on display as they change. I find my usual locker and start stripping down, hanging my clothes inside.

Fully naked, I grab my towel and turn around. Hiro hastily looks away, only half out of his clothes. I have no doubt he was checking out the black wolf tattoo on my back.

"I meant to tell you before, but your tattoos are amazing," Hiro says softly, sweeping his gaze down the thematic works of art that cover my body from my shoulders to my ankles. "Did it hurt getting them done?"

I'd bitten down on a wooden block and screamed until I thought I'd pass out. "Namikawa insists we all get our tattoos done the old-fashioned way."

"Why? Isn't that supposed to be painful?"

"To prove we can endure pain. To prove our devotion."

"That sounds horrible." I don't like the pity in his voice.

"I've had worse." The pain at that time had been the worst pain I'd ever felt. But I'm twenty-eight now, and I've been shot, stabbed, bitten, you name it. Looking back, it doesn't feel like much.

My skin prickles under the weight of his gaze. I turn toward him, and my breath catches. Hiro has wrapped himself in a towel, but I've got a great view of his thick thighs and legs. He's got little freckles and moles dotting his shoulders. The tiles whisper over my bare feet as I prowl closer to him, unable to stay away. Hiro takes a step back and bumps into the lockers. His scent is thick in the air, sweet blossoms spiced with lust. My dick threatens to take an interest, twitching between my thighs. Hiro's throat works hard when he swallows.

"You can touch them, if you want."

Hiro's tongue darts out to wet his lips. Eyes wide in wonder, he runs his hand up my arm. His touch makes my breath catch and raises the little hairs on my arms. I have to curl my fingers so I don't do something stupid. He circles me, running his fingertips along my skin. I make sure to flex my ass, smirking when he coughs awkwardly behind me.

"I like this one. Why a wolf?"

I barely suppress a shiver as his fingers trace the shape of the wolf's snarling snout. If he doesn't stop touching me, I'll be rock hard in a few seconds.

"Namikawa likes wolves. Ask him yourself." It was chosen for me. Everyone in the gang has a wolf somewhere on their body to pay tribute to our wolf side, but I can't tell him that.

His fingers twitch before they settle in the center of my chest, right over the kanji Namikawa carved into my skin when I was eight years old. "What is that? That's not a tattoo." He rubs the scar tissue, eyes widening in distress. His shyness disappears as he narrows his eyes. "Eternally bound wolf?" He reads the writing on my chest. "Who the hell did this to you?"

There's a protective edge to his voice that stirs something within me. Nobody's wanted to protect me before. As if he could. But still, knowing he feels that way toward me is... different.

"Namikawa."

Hiro's wide eyes find my gaze. "Why?"

Even if I could tell him, where do I begin? There's no point. I brush off his hands and walk around him.

Hiro blinks fast and averts his gaze, eyes fixed determinedly on the wall. "You... you didn't deserve that."

I've never wanted to touch anyone the way I want to touch him. I want to run my tongue over his clavicle, suck on the warm skin beneath my fingers. Want to bury my nose behind his ear and breathe that cherry blossom aroma deep into my lungs like smoke.

I thought nicotine was my only vice, but if I'm not careful, I could see myself getting addicted to him. To his blushes. To the way he opens up like a flower when I poke and tease him. I've never wanted anyone's hands on my skin more than I crave his touch. It's like there's a hook snagged in my chest, pulling me closer, even when my mind's telling me to run far before I detonate in his face.

He's too good, too sweet, too innocent, and if I'm not careful, I'll destroy him.

Once we've showered, I motion for Hiro to follow me to the door leading to the baths. Before we enter, I grip his arm, making him look up at me in surprise. "If you see Takada, stay away from him. Got it?" Even after a shower, my scent still clings to Hiro, faint but unmissable. Takada won't like it if he knows someone else has caught my interest.

"Okay." Concern creases Hiro's brow.

"Stay near me. I'll keep you safe." I can't resist running my hand along his bare hip, enjoying his shiver. "Go on in."

Hiro squeezes past, camera in his hand. Steam clouds the humid air. The room is packed with yakuza, joining their comrades in one of the many baths in the room. I recognize some of them, but not all. Beside me, Hiro starts taking pictures of the Takada-kai and Namikawa-kai men who are shooting each other wary looks and glares. My skin prickles, and my hands are in fists at my sides. Just knowing Takada will be here soon has my hackles rising and blood boiling for a fight.

"Raiden. You've come." My grandfather tilts his head when he notices Hiro. "And who is this? The photographer?"

Hiro gives a respectful bow. "Yes. I'm Hiro Watanabe."

"Hiro, this is my grandfather, Hideyoshi."

"Nice to meet you," Hideyoshi says after a bow. "Try to capture my good side, yes?"

Hiro laughs. "Of course."

"Come. Enjoy the baths. They're very relaxing." Hideyoshi guides him to a bath.

Hiro sputters. "A-actually, I was just going to watch. I don't want to intrude on any private conversations."

"Nonsense. Feel free to relax. As long as the bosses get

to talk undisturbed, there won't be any trouble." A frown creases his already wrinkled face. "At least, there shouldn't be. But you never know."

In a room full of werewolves? No. You really don't.

The door slides open, and he's here. All heads turn as Namikawa enters the room, towel over his shoulders. I fold at the waist, bowing before my boss along with everyone else in the room. Namikawa's tattoos are less vibrant but not less impressive. Temples, dragons, carp, and flowers decorate his skin. I've never seen a wolf tattoo on him, though. Hiro snaps a picture of him.

Then the scent of Takada hits my nose, and I can barely swallow the growl of contempt that rises to my lips as he saunters in, Hirano at his side like a good guard dog. Takada's dark eyes find mine, thin lips curling to reveal sharp canines.

Takada's nostrils flare as he scents the air, and then his smile bleeds into a scowl. He turns a glare on Hiro. Others in the room have started noticing as well, sniffing and looking around the room suspiciously.

Beside me, Hiro frowns. "Does something smell funny?"

I grab my grandfather's shoulder. "Stay with him."

Hideyoshi stands closer to Hiro while I shoulder through the crowded room and come to stand beside my boss and Takada. Namikawa looks as calm as ever. If I didn't know him, I'd think he never got angry, except I've seen him enraged before. It's not something I'll ever forget. "As I told you, Hiro has been allowed to document our lives. The police are cracking down on us harder than ever. It's important to present an image of the Namikawa-kai to the public that shows us in a positive light."

"He's a human," Takada says, sneering, voice low so Hiro won't hear him. "If I'd known you'd fallen this low as to allow humans into your pack, I wouldn't be wasting my time." Glaring at Hiro over my shoulder, he shouts, "Leave. I won't ask twice!"

Fear spikes Hiro's scent. My fangs drop, claws dimpling my palms. A growl escapes me, and I finally look Takada in his dark, seedy eyes. "Hiro is with me. He stays."

Takada barks a laugh. "Found yourself a new pet, Raiden? How cute." He swipes his tongue over his lips. "He's pretty. You wouldn't mind sharing him, would you?"

Just the idea of Takada doing any of the messed-up shit he did with me to Hiro has a red haze falling over my eyes. "Try and touch him, Takada. I'll tear your fingers off one by one and feed them to you."

Furious mutterings and low growls resonate from Takada's men.

Hirano comes between me and Takada. "Watch your tongue, Noboru."

Namikawa's men close in, muscles taut and ready to start swinging. I glance back at Hiro, wondering if I'll have time to get to him before a fight breaks out. Hideyoshi meets my gaze and nods. He'll take care of Hiro.

Namikawa throws up a hand, signaling his men to back down. He stares down his nose at Takada, like he's nothing but an unruly brat in need of a beating. I bet he could kick Takada's ass, even if he's decades older. "That is enough. Raiden, stand down. Takada, calm your men. We are not here to fight."

Hiro hesitantly raises a hand. "Uh. If it's too much trouble, I can leave."

Namikawa's stare is cold enough to freeze the hot springs when he turns to Takada. "The photographer stays. You have no say in this, Takada. Not in my establishment. Not in my territory. You lost all right to an opinion the moment you turned your back on this family. If having an outsider here will be such a problem, then last I checked, the door still worked. See yourself out or stay and cooperate."

I can hear Takada's teeth grinding together. He never did like being told no. I know Takada well, and he's as prideful as they come. Walking away now would be as good as defeat, and he was never one to go down easy.

"Very well. But he leaves once we start the meeting." Takada points to the door.

"Whatever will give you utmost peace of mind," Namikawa says, not sounding like he cares one way or another as he slinks over to the bath and submerges up to his shoulders into the hot water.

Hiro walks past me, camera in one hand. "I'll wait for you." He leaves the room.

I join the Namikawa-kai in the bath, and finally, silence falls over the room. I look everywhere but at Takada, sitting across the bath from us, flanked on either side by two big, glowering guys.

Namikawa says, "Our way of life faces an uncertain future. We can no longer afford to fight among ourselves. It's clear both our families have harmed one another. No one here is trying to deny that. But unless we can find a way to come together, then we risk losing everything we have built to the police. Takada, name your price for peace, and we shall name ours."

Takada's eyes slide over me, like something wet and slimy over my skin. "I have need of a new enforcer. Noboru would do just fine."

I expected as much. Still, my stomach twists into knots.

And Namikawa... says nothing. He wouldn't send me to Takada, would he? Not unless he's still pissed off that I didn't collect the money and let Takada kill Aida. Fuck. I can't go with Takada. I'd rather tear out my own throat than let him touch me again.

Takada slants his mouth smugly. "And what do you think, Noboru? Come on, now. We have a history, you and I. With me, you could be free of your debt to Namikawa."

I know better than to believe a word he says. Leaning

my elbows on the tiled rim of the tub, I level a glare at him. "Bullshit."

Takada's nostrils flare.

"Is that your price for peace?" Namikawa asks, voice giving away nothing. Sweat beads on my forehead, mixing with the steam. I have no idea what my boss is thinking of doing.

"Yes," Takada growls.

Acid rises in my throat. Even my grandfather looks warily between me and Namikawa.

Fuck. He can't. He wouldn't. Would he? I fight to control my panic.

Steam rises between my pack and Takada's.

Namikawa says, "Noboru is mine. His pack owes mine a life debt. Choose something else."

Relief crashes over me, but it's replaced by fury. Why the fuck would Namikawa torment me like that?

"Fine, then," Takada says through his teeth, "I want a share of your profits, and—"

The bosses talk about dividing up the revenue from specific territories we each control, terms, and conditions. It all sort of fades to background noise. I keep thinking back on Takada's proposal. Freedom. From Namikawa, anyway, from my pack's debts to his clan. But not freedom from the yakuza, and especially not freedom from Takada.

I don't know why I keep thinking there's a way out. Why haven't I just accepted it already?

Namikawa's voice snaps me out of my brooding. "Very well. Here are my terms. Stop abducting people from our territory."

Takada's lip ticks up over his teeth. "What did you say?"

"I know you're the one responsible for the missing people in Taito. That ends with this truce. Am I clear?"

Growling, Takada leans forward in the bath. "That's one hell of an accusation to pin on me with no evidence, Namikawa."

"Is that understood?" Namikawa snaps.

A muscle twitches in Takada's jaw. "Fine."

"Then these terms are acceptable. There will be peace between our clans. Thank you for your cooperation, Takada." He bows his head, and Takada bows back, but his eyes remain locked on me, black with fury at being denied what he wants; his favorite toy.

This ceasefire hasn't solved anything.

It's the start of something much worse.

I can't wait to get out of here. When the bosses rise, I'm climbing out of the tub and grabbing my towel. When I step out into the changing room, my heart lurches when I meet Hiro's gaze. I almost forgot he was there.

"What happened?" Hiro asks.

"The bosses came to a decision." I rake my hands through my wet hair as I shower.

"So, there'll be peace?"

A bitter laugh escapes me. "I guess we'll see. Takada's never been good about letting things go." Especially not where I'm concerned. "Show any pictures you took to Namikawa so he can approve them." One side of my mouth lifts. "Get any good angles of me?"

Hiro laughs, the sound soft and fluttery. "I think so. I'll have to check."

"Not bad today. You survived a room full of yakuza. Didn't know you had it in you."

A grin brightens his face. "Hey, I've got you wrapped around my finger so far, don't I?"

I flick some water into his stupidly handsome face. "Watch it. "

"Maybe this will be my calling. Just call me the Yakuza Whisperer."

"The fuck I will." I splash him with some more water.

Sputtering, he flings some soap at me.

People are staring. My neck warms. I glare at them until they get the good sense to mind their own business—all except Takada. He sweeps his gaze from me to Hiro as he cinches his towel around his waist. When he glares holes in Hiro's back, I move without thinking, obscuring Hiro from his line of sight by standing between him and Takada.

Across the room, we stare each other down.

My lip curls away from my teeth.

Mine, the wolf within snarls.

With a sneer, Takada shakes his head. He turns his back on me and walks away.

I don't look away until I know he's gone.

Outside the bathhouse, I see Takada, and my smile falls off my face. "Go wait in the car," I tell Hiro. He looks worried, but he makes for my vehicle. Eyes fixed ahead, I walk past Takada. He lunges and grabs my arm in a vise-like grip. A snarl tears from my throat as he yanks me until we're inches apart. Takada's nostrils flare. "I thought you smelled... different."

"Let go." My voice is thick with fury and disgust.

Takada ignores me and squeezes harder, cutting off the blood flow in my arm. "Almost like... a human."

My claws pop out, fangs sharpening. "Don't make me say it again!"

Takada smiles, but there's a nasty curl to it. I've seen it before. I know his tells well enough. He's jealous. "Your own kind isn't good enough for you now, Noboru? You've got to stick your dick in a human?"

"It stopped being your business who I fucked years ago," I spit in his face, then rip my arm free. Takada's claws tear through my suit jacket and bite into the skin.

A vein pulses in Takada's forehead. "Come and join my pack. I can protect you from Namikawa."

"Get fucked. I don't need a damn thing from you."

"I get it, you know. For a human, he's pretty." Takada bares his fangs in a predatory leer.

Fur ripples over my arms, and my fangs lengthen to points. "Stay the fuck away from him."

Takada smiles. "You really think he won't run for the hills when he figures out what you are?"

"Of course he will. He'd have the right idea." The thought twists like a knife in my chest, but I won't reflect on why. It's unimportant. "It doesn't matter."

"Oh? So you wouldn't mind if I taught him a lesson about stealing another wolf's prey?"

My hand shoots out and grabs him by his scrawny neck. A grin splits Takada's face even as I squeeze. "You lay a finger on him, Takada, and not even Namikawa's truce will be able to save you."

Takada's words fill me with fury and something else. *Dread.* I won't let him touch Hiro. He tries, and it'll be the last thing he does. Namikawa can be as pissed as he wants, but I don't care if it starts a war between our packs.

No one touches Hiro.

He's mine.

Chapter 8

Jinta

I bring my bike to a stop as I reach the top of the hiking trail and lean it against a tree. I've never had a bike stolen, so I leave it without a care and book it through the woods toward the crowd of police officers and ropes of yellow tape stretching from one tree to another.

As I near the crime scene, the cop I recognize as Kenichi ducks beneath the tape. "That was fast!"

"Thanks so much for calling me," I say, panting as I stumble to a stop beside him. I've got my press badge on and my camera in hand. Kenichi has always been a reliable source of information. "I really needed a big story."

Although big might be an understatement.

"Where are the witnesses?"

Kenichi motions toward two women in hiking gear. "We've already questioned them."

I approach the witnesses, and although they appear unsettled, one of the women, Hana, opens up to me about what happened. "My friend and I were hiking. I felt something snap under my foot. At first, I thought it was an animal bone. But then my friend found a skull protruding from the dirt. There were more bones. I've never seen so many. It was so creepy!"

My pen flies over my notepad, writing down her every word. There's a whole team beyond the tape carefully unearthing... bones. And more bones. My stomach churns as one of the forensic workers puts a skull inside a bag, then what looks like an arm bone.

What the *fuck*? Why are there so many human remains here?

"What happened here?" I ask as I return to Kenichi, thoroughly disturbed.

Kenichi lowers his voice, "Don't put this in your report, but... I think it's the remains of the people who went missing back in 1924."

What? That would make these remains a hundred years old! I turn to him in shock. "People went missing?"

"My great-grandfather was a cop back then. He told my dad stories. People started disappearing. Kind of like they are now. Same pattern. Nobody could figure out a motive or where they were." He expels a bitter breath. "It always ate my grandad up that the victims were never found."

"What about the culprit?"

Kenichi shrugs his shoulders. "Never caught."

My mind is *reeling*. This happened before, and nobody was ever caught. Unless the person behind this is literally a vampire, there's no way it's the same person abducting all these people. This makes no sense. Is there any way this is some weird coincidence? Or maybe even a copycat?

My stomach twists at the idea that the copycat could be Raiden. The idea just doesn't sit right with me. The more I spend time with him, the less I believe he could be responsible. *Fuck*. My feelings are getting in the way of my job. Anger rises in me. This is a huge story I'm onto here. If Raiden is responsible, I've got to be subjective. Maybe I should have thought about that before I let him fuck me.

Unless... maybe the person behind the kidnappings is Takada? I still remember when the owner of the izakaya accused the Namikawa-kai of allowing people to be abducted from Taito. Takada would do anything to incriminate the Namikawa-kai. It's a possibility, one I shouldn't ignore.

"Was there a shrine here?" I ask. There are ruins of some kind looming over the mass grave, overgrown with moss and weeds.

"Looks like it."

A shiver runs down my spine. Could these remains have been part of some bizarre ritual?

An idea comes to me as I leave the crime scene and bike back down the trail, wheels bumping over the earth. If this has happened before, then is there a chance there were any survivors? It's a slim chance in hell. Most of them would be dead by now or close to it, but if there's any chance I could speak to a survivor, or maybe the relatives of a survivor, that would be hugely beneficial. If these disappearances are connected, then to understand what's happening in the present, I may have to dig into the past.

Once my shift is over, I stop in a convenience store to shop for dinner. While I'm shopping, my phone buzzes. I smile when I see Raiden's name, then quickly wipe it off my face. I've got to get a handle on my feelings.

Raiden: *Miss you. Can I come over?*

Once I've taken my case map with his picture on it off the wall, then sure.

Me: *Aww. That's adorable.*

Raiden: *Shut up. I'm not adorable.*

Me: *Let's agree to disagree. Do you like katsudon?*

Raiden: *Who doesn't?*

Me: *I know right?? See you in a few. <3*

Did I just heart-emoji him? Oh good god. So much for keeping my feelings under wraps. I want to throw my phone across the store. I bury it in my bag and focus on shopping. My phone vibrates against my leg, and my heart trips all over itself. Great. What did he say? Did I freak him out by emoji-ing my feelings all over him? I can't look.

I buy the food and walk home from the store. At the final traffic light before my house, I finally cave and check his text, prepared to wince.

Raiden: <3

I stare at the screen for far too long and end up missing the light. He heart-emoji-ed me back. I feel like I'll melt into a puddle of goo. When's the last time a guy made me swoon?

Oh, no. This is awful. I'm crushing on my conflict of interest.

Wait a second. Is my conflict of interest... my boyfriend? He did say we were exclusive, but I just thought he meant that in a fuck-buddy sense.

I can't think about this right now. I jog across the street and walk the final stretch to my house.

The streets are dark and empty. The streetlamp outside my apartment is burned out. I still jump when I hear a noise behind me. A glance behind my shoulder reveals nothing but the empty street, but I thought I saw someone dart out of sight. Unless maybe I just imagined it.

Nerves tangle in my stomach, so I quicken my steps and arrive at my front door. Opening my bag, I fumble around for my keys. Footsteps stampede toward me, making me jump. I whirl around just as a fist comes flying at me. Stars white out my vision as throbbing pain explodes across the side of my face. I crash into the doorway, and my cry of alarm gets choked off when a thick hand wraps around my throat.

My attacker is big and bald, and he only has four and a half fingers on the hand around my neck. A yakuza, and he's not alone. Another yakuza, scrawny and with a crooked nose, sneers at me from over his buddy's shoulder. The big guy hurls me to the ground.

"Wait, stop! Who are you, what do you want? I have money, I'll—"

A foot flies into my back, knocking the breath out of me. Another kick cracks across the back of my head. When one of the thugs presses the dirty underside of his boot against my cheek, the pressure feels like it will crack my skull. A strangled scream escapes me as he grinds my face against the pavement.

What the fuck do these guys want? Who are they? Terror squeezes my lungs until I'm panting. They haven't even tried to rob me. Are they going to kill me? A whimper escapes me.

My shirt presses into my throat as the thugs drag me toward a car at the curb. Shit. Are they abducting me?

Where will they take me? Panic claws at my chest, and I struggle to break free. I can't let them take me away!

Across the street, a huge shape melts out of the shadows. Brown eyes glow in the dark. Claws scrape over asphalt. One of my attackers shouts a warning, but it's far too late. A black wolf, the size of a damn horse, slams into the guy pinning me, and bowls him off his feet. I'm frozen, unable to make myself run, unable to even look away as the monstrous wolf grabs the yakuza by the arm and hurls him into the wall so hard, I hear his bones crack.

"I'm s-sorry!" the yakuza screams as if the wolf can understand him. "L-let me go!"

The other yakuza clutches his bloody arm. He grabs a broken bottle off the ground and throws it. The glass shatters against the wolf's head, giving the yakuza's buddy time to get up and run. They split up. The wolf looks back at me, and those whiskey-brown eyes make my breath catch. There's something so off about those eyes.

They almost remind me of...

With a snarl, the wolf whirls away from me and pursues the yakuza down the street and around the corner.

I can't move. My knees shake, and I fall back to the pavement. I rest my back against the door, panting as my heart races.

Did I... did I really just see that?

That was a wolf. The biggest wolf I've ever seen.

What the *fuck*.

Twenty minutes after I've managed to pick myself up and go upstairs, I'm still in shock. My mug of green tea cools in my hands as my mind churns. Wolves. Yakuza. A mass grave full of remains going back one hundred years. What the hell is happening in this city? I can't make it make sense. Maybe I'm in over my head. None of this makes sense anymore. I can't do this.

I guess Raiden isn't coming. Maybe he decided things are too weird between us after we slept together. I don't even know, but it doesn't matter. I can't focus on him. I've got to investigate the disappearances from all those years ago.

And yet all I can think about now is that damn wolf. Am I sure it was a wolf? It couldn't have been a dog. But it makes no fucking sense. I open up a search engine and start typing. There were two wolves endemic to Japan, the Honshu Wolf and the Hokkaido Wolf, and both were exterminated during the Meiji Restoration period.

So why was one running around Tokyo?

Unless I imagined the whole thing. I'm about to crawl into bed and forget about the day, when a headline grabs my attention. I almost laugh.

WEREWOLVES SPOTTED IN JAPAN?

Good grief. I have to see this. I click the link. Shitty as the website is, whoever wrote it genuinely believes the government is trying to cover up the existence of werewolves. And then my eyes snag on something about disappearances. The writer of this article believes that werewolves are behind it. After all, the disappearances only pile even higher in the week before a full moon. That's not true, though. The abductions are completely sporadic.

I think about all those bones in the mountain and shiver.

No. No way is any of this true. I've got to hand it to this person, they've managed to connect these disappearances to werewolves in a way that's almost believable.

God. I'm seriously scraping the bottom of the barrel if I'm turning to werewolf conspiracy theorists for answers. My father would laugh his head off and tell me I should have just joined the family business. And maybe he'd be right. I don't always second-guess my choices, but tonight, I'm just drowning in self-doubt.

I'm searching the cabinets for sake I can spike my tea with when the intercom buzzes.

Could it be—I rush to the door and ask, "Who is it?"

"Let me in, Sunshine."

Oh, shit. Raiden's here, and I look like I just got the shit beaten out of me. I run around my apartment, tidying up. I tear my case map off the wall and cram the pictures into a box in my dresser where I keep the rest of my reporting gear like my press I.D. I close the box and cover it with a pile of shirts. Then, my doorbell rings.

Raiden's appearance is the one bright spot in my night. Although, he looks... off. His clothing is rumpled, and his hair is disheveled. Those eyes make me shiver. Their whiskey-brown hue is the exact same as that huge wolf's. It's freaky.

"What the hell?" Raiden growls, eyes going wide as he takes in my appearance.

I avert my gaze. "It's nothing. Just—"

"That's not nothing, Hiro." A scowl slips into place as Raiden reaches out. His fingertips brush my cheek, and I wince. He touches the bruise on my cheek from where the bastard hit me. Raiden's jaw tightens, eyes narrow in anger. "Who did this to you?" The low, furious rumble of his voice makes me shiver. I've never heard him so pissed before.

"I don't know. Some guys. They attacked me just as I was going inside." I wince as he touches the scrape on my cheek where the guy ground my face against the pavement.

"Fuck..." Bristling, Raiden stomps into the bathroom and returns with a first aid kit. "Sit down."

"It's just a few cuts."

"Hiro, just sit down and let me take care of you."

I'm a grown man, and I've been looking after myself for five years. I don't need help... but that doesn't mean I don't want it. "Yeah, okay. Sure." Exhaustion weighs on me. I collapse on the sofa.

Raiden kneels before me, and I'm struck by the sight of this man, strong and powerful as he is, on his knees before me. "This'll sting," he warns me, dabbing some disinfectant on a cotton ball. I wince at the burn when he rubs the cotton against my cheek. The discomfort fades once the wounds are clean, then he takes out a few Band-Aids.

He presses one of them to each of my injuries, gently smoothing them down against my skin. His touch is so... careful. It's the tenderest touch I've known in such a long time that my eyes actually start to sting. Fuck. I didn't know I needed this so badly. Someone to take care of me, to touch me like I'm made of glass. I shouldn't like that it's him in my hour of need. I should wish it was someone else, someone less complicated and dangerous. But I don't.

Without thinking, I touch my forehead against his, closing my eyes as his soothing scent of aftershave and clean clothes caresses my nose. "Thank you."

A pleased sound rumbles from Raiden's chest. He runs his big warm hands up and down my arms. "I'll always take care of you, Sunshine." He leans in and slants his mouth against mine. He kisses hard enough to bruise, yet so sweet my body goes slack against him, surrendering to his consumption. "No one is laying a finger on you again. I promise."

I don't like that look in his eyes. Okay. I do. Some fucked-up part of me really likes the idea of committing violence on my behalf—okay, my dick likes the idea.

"What are you going to do?"

Raiden squeezes the nape of my neck. "Find those bastards and make them regret touching what's mine."

"Don't get hurt on my behalf," I say breathlessly, surprised by how painfully the idea of him being hurt twists in my chest.

His flushed lips lift in a cocky smirk that gets my blood rushing. "I won't. Have a little faith in me." He pats my cheek.

We microwave our convenience store katsudon and eat side by side on the sofa.

"Did the guys who attacked you take anything?" Raiden asks, plucking a pork cutlet from his bowl and offering it to me.

"No. They didn't have time to." I eat the food off his utensils. Surely he'll think I'm crazy. Yet I can't resist confiding in him. We've already been intimate physically. It's hard for me not to bare myself in other ways, too. "There was this... this wolf."

Raiden stops eating. "Really?"

"Yeah. I'm not crazy, honestly. It was a freaking wolf." I drink some green tea, my throat dry from nerves, but the green tea makes that worse. "I think it... saved me? It attacked the guys, then chased them away." I shiver remembering those eyes. I need to stop thinking like this. Werewolves do not exist.

"Huh. You sure it wasn't just a helpful dog?"

I shake my head. "Definitely not. I've never seen a dog that looks like that." I reach out and flick some rice off his cheek, making him jump. "Hey, want to watch a movie?"

"Sure."

Since we both like *Star Wars*, I find it on a streaming service and play it. Heart racing, praying he won't push me away, I scoot closer to him ever so slowly. Finally, I'm close enough to lean my head against his shoulder. When he tenses, breath hitching, I think he's going to push me away. Instead, he slips an arm around me. He turns his body so he's sprawling on the couch, and I end up lying between his thighs, my back to his chest.

My face warms pleasantly as he wraps his arms around my waist, chin coming to rest atop my head. He buries his nose in my hair with a slow inhale, arms squeezing me tight. We don't speak. We don't have to. I've always hated sitting in silence. There's too much room for self-reflection, or in my case, self-deprecation. But with him, I'm okay with it. I don't feel like I have to say anything interesting or try to be someone I think he'd like.

It's okay if I don't have anything interesting to say. It's okay if I prefer silence to wasted words. I can just be me, quiet as I am, and that's all right. Raiden doesn't pressure me to talk.

I wonder if this is what it's like to finally be enough for someone.

For now. Until he decides there's someone better for him out there. Someone more handsome. More charismatic.

Like my brother, Katsuki.

It's happened before. What's stopping it from happening again?

Squeezing my eyes shut, I hide my face in Raiden's chest and try to stop anticipating the worst.

CHAPTER 9

Raiden

I throw open the door to Namikawa's office. The old man behind the desk doesn't even jump, just regards me with cold indifference behind his glasses.

"Boss, I sincerely apologize!" his guard shouts, trying to pull me back out of the room.

I swing around and sock him in the jaw. The guard crashes into the wall.

"It's far too early in the morning for this behavior, Noboru," Namikawa says, as if he's scolding a bratty kid.

Damn straight it is. I should be back at Hiro's apartment, waking him up with my mouth around his dick. Instead, I have to speak to Namikawa.

"Takada's guys attacked Hiro." Fury makes my fists

tremble.

"Oh?" Namikawa arches a brow, but he takes an un-bothered sip of his water.

"He did it to get back at me because he's a jealous ass. Hiro is a guest in our pack. He's under our protection. Harming him is an attack against us."

"Is it now?" Namikawa's indifference makes me gnash my teeth.

"Yes!" I snap.

"I do not see it that way."

My fingers curl at my sides.

"Regardless of your... interest in him, he is human. What happens to him is of little concern to me. As much as his little project would benefit us, he is not worth risking Takada's wrath by confronting him about this."

I didn't expect anything from him, but I'm still pissed.

Namikawa sets down his glass of water hard. His hand shakes, like just lifting the glass cost him great effort.

In the light, his face looks hollow and gaunt, like the skin's stretched too tight. "What would you have me do? Punish Takada's men? Evoke his fury, risk starting yet another fight between our clans? Over what? A human?"

The disdain that colors the word human makes me growl. "I can't let this attack against Hiro go unpunished. Takada has to pay! Just... let me target the ones who hurt Hiro. That's all, that's it, I—"

Searing pain carves into my chest, lighting my scars on

fire. I try to hold back the scream, but I can't. I crumple to the floor and succumb to the pain tearing my chest open, stabbing hot needles into my heart. I tear my shirt open, desperate for relief as my chest tightens so painfully, I'm sure I'll go into cardiac arrest and die on the spot.

The scars carved into my flesh are red and angry looking, like they were burned into me with a hot poker. And damn, does it feel like it.

I almost beg for him to stop. Almost. I bite my lip so hard, my fangs pierce the skin.

Violent coughs rack Namikawa's body, and he grips onto the desk.

Everything stops. I gasp for breath, heart pounding so hard I'm afraid it will rupture.

Through watery eyes, I pant up at Namikawa as he comes to stand before me. I almost shifted completely to my wolf form; fur's thick on my body, my ears are pointed, and my claws have gouged the wood floor.

Namikawa fists my hair in his hand and rips my head back to meet his glare. "I must have allowed you too much freedom as of late, if you truly think you have any say over your own destiny. You are mine, Noboru. Your father decided your fate the moment he chose to betray me."

Baring his teeth in a smile, Namikawa pats my cheek. "When I have need of you, I will summon you. Until then... do nothing to drive a wedge between Takada and this pack, Noboru. I don't care if Takada abducts the boy and pulls off his fingernails one by one. If you evoke his anger... you will wish I had killed you."

He leaves me panting on the floor, in too much pain to move.

Fuck him. I still have free will.

Those bastards won't get away with hurting Hiro.

If Namikawa doesn't like it, well... there are worse things than being dead. Like being his bitch for the rest of my damn life.

The club bustles with activity as salarymen drink themselves under the table with their boss, and scantily clad women twirl on poles beneath swirling lights. I take a seat at the bar and grab a glass of Hibiki. The bartender eyes me with suspicion but serves me anyway. From where I sit, I have eyes on the door, so I'll see if anyone comes in.

Takada owns this club. I'm risking pissing him off by prowling around his territory. His men frequent the bars they own, and I got a good look at the faces of the ugly fucks who attacked Hiro. Goro Takahashi was one of them. He should be coming here tonight.

"Look," Ren says after a swallow of beer. "I get it, Hiro is cute and nice and all. But is his bubble butt really worth getting in trouble with Namikawa?" Her worried brown eyes stare right through me.

I don't know how to answer. Sure, I've defied Namikawa every once in a while, and the punishment has never been worth it. So why am I risking it for some guy I've known for just a week?

This isn't just anger flowing through me. If I hadn't been there to stop them, they could have killed Hiro. The thought makes me spiral down into something black and suffocating.

Maim. Kill. Protect Hiro. Our Hiro.

My wolf has hungered for blood since last night, and only vengeance will silence him.

"Takada targeted Hiro because of me. I need those bastards to pay for hurting him."

"He will hurt you if he finds out." She grips my arm.

"So, he won't find out."

She rolls her eyes. "Raiden—"

"My wolf needs this, Ren."

"I knew it," she whispers, and I bristle at her words.

"Knew what?"

She takes a drag on her cigarette and blows out smoke. "You know, this whole denial thing you've got going on is really something. It's almost admirable how stubborn you are."

I snatch her cigarette and suck on it, ignoring her growl. "I'm not denying shit."

She bats her eyelashes. "So, you do admit he's your fated

mate?"

Ren thinks Hiro is my mate? No. *No.* "He isn't my mate." I whirl around to face her, needing her to understand this. "He's not."

But it would explain a lot. Like how all it took was a look into those chocolate-brown eyes, and he'd burrowed himself into my brain. How his scent soothes the wolf's primal rage. How furious I become whenever he's even slightly threatened.

No. Fuck. *No.*

"Raiden," Ren begins gently, but I pull out of her reach.

"That mate bullshit isn't real."

Maybe when I was a kid, I believed that the red string of fate brought two destined souls together. It was like a fairy tale to me whenever my mom told me the story of how she and my dad met.

"I saw him, and I just knew that from that moment on, the sun would rise and set with him. He became my whole world. A light in the dark. I knew there'd never be anyone else for me."

Bile rises in my throat. She'd looked so happy, so in love. Life was hard back then, but I'd thought that as long as we were a family, everything would be okay. My parents loved each other, and I loved them.

Until my father tore the red string of fate from his finger and severed his connection to my mother. And then, everything had fallen apart.

If I concentrate... really focus... there's a tightness around my pinky finger. A tugging at my skin. Something warm glowing around my finger like candlelight. Normally, people can see it right away. The red string of fate materializes the moment we're close to someone we're meant to be with.

I closed my heart and mind to fate's influence when I was a kid. But If I wanted to, I could reveal the thread around my own finger. If I wanted, I could follow where it leads and see who it leads me to.

But I don't want to. I don't care. Fate, destiny, mates... none of this shit matters. Fated mates or not, love never lasts. It's a lesson I learned a long time ago when my father tore apart our family and broke my mother's heart.

I don't know what Hiro and I are. I'm not ready to examine it. That shit is going in a box where I store all the other things I don't let myself brood on. Like severed red threads. A little bronze coin, pressed into my hand.

I promised myself if I ever found my fated mate, I'd reject them with everything I had.

And yet here I am, risking Namikawa's punishment for a man I've only recently met.

I'm spared from arguing with her when the doors to the club open. A guy I recognize as one of Takada's boys walks in. He's an ugly fucker, dressed in all white with a yellow dress shirt, a bald head, and a goatee. One of the men who attacked Hiro. Goro Takahashi. He and his brother are going to pay for putting their hands on Hiro.

Ren wrinkles her nose. "That's him, but it doesn't look like his brother is with him. What's the plan?"

"He's got a thing for guys. I'll talk to him, get him to follow me outside. You sneak up and get the drop on him."

She frowns. "Shouldn't we be stealthier about this?"

"He won't see your face if you come up from behind."

"But he'll identify you, idiot! He'll report you."

I shrug. "If he cries to Takada, let him. I'm not Takada's property anymore. Maybe this'll finally teach him not to fuck with me." Or to touch what's mine.

Snubbing out Ren's cig and ignoring her grumbles, I pop a few buttons on my shirt to expose my chest and cross the room. My eyes lock with Takahashi's, and the lust in his eyes makes my stomach clench.

Still, I sit with him and have a few drinks. Let him touch my thigh even if I want to bite his hand off. I even return his touches until I can feel how hard he is.

"Want to follow me outside?" I ask.

Takahashi leers at me. "Lead the way."

Just as planned. I let him follow me outside the club, then take a detour around the side of the building where it's more secluded.

There's only a chef there, taking a smoke break, but he stomps out his smoke and goes back inside. We have the alley all to ourselves.

Takahashi slams me against the wall, forces his thick

thigh between my legs. My entire body tenses up. Memories I've locked away try to come crawling in. When his goatee scratches my neck and his dry lips bite my skin, bile crawls up my throat.

No. I'm not a victim. I'm not a helpless, naïve little kid anymore. Fuck this asshole. Fuck Takada.

Takahashi suddenly squeaks, eyes bulging. There's a knife against his throat. "Hands off," Ren snarls in his ear, eyes blazing. Takahashi takes a few steps back, throat bobbing as he swallows hard.

I wipe the smear of his spit off my neck, a shiver of revulsion racking me. I grin at Takahashi through the disgust making bile rise in my throat. "Where's your brother, Goro?"

"D-don't know," Goro whimpers. "Let me go."

I click my tongue. "Goro, Goro, Goro. That's not the answer I wanted to hear."

I swing my claws across his face, slashing his eyes. He yells in horror, and Ren and I tackle him to the ground. There's a pothole filled with rainwater next to him. I make a mental note of that.

Goro's scream is silenced when I wrap my claws around his thick neck. The smell of his blood has my fangs sharp and claws out. The bloodlust rises like a tide within me, vision running red at the corners. I'm sure my eyes are glowing, and fur prickles all over my body as the wolf roars for blood.

All they did was punch and scratch Hiro, and I'm livid. If they'd done anything worse... I want to tear his entrails from his body and feast upon them until I bloat. "Where. Is. Your. Brother."

"W-with his girlfriend."

"And where is she?"

He mumbles out an address.

"Got that?" I ask Ren.

She smiles pleasantly from the shadows. "Yup."

"Good."

Goro swallows thickly, blinking blood out of his eyes. "Let me go. Okay? I told you everything."

"I don't think I will."

His eyes bulge, face going pale. "Why? What did I do?"

"You hurt what's mine," I growl, voice infused with the fury of a wolf.

The wolf snarls, *Bite. Kill. Protect!*

"How long can you hold your breath, Goro?"

"Huh?"

"Let's find out!"

I roll him onto his front and slam his face beneath the water overflowing from the pothole. It's deeper than it looks, submerging his whole head. He thrashes, and air bubbles break the surface of the filthy brown water. I shove my clawed hand beneath the water and tear out his throat.

The streets are empty, so we carry the body to the trunk of my car and dump it in without anyone seeing us.

Ren whistles. "Damn. That was kind of badass."

"Now for brother number two."

I don't care about the consequences. Nobody harms Hiro and gets away with it.

CHAPTER 10

Jinta

I put the finishing touches on my article about the mass graves and send it off to the editor. Exhaling, I lean back in my seat. It's a pretty good article and this could be a huge story. It could even be my first one to make the front page since I started writing for Jiji.

I'm smiling as I take my lunch break. As I scroll social media, I chow down on an egg salad sandwich... and almost choke when I see a photo of Katsuki and his girlfriend. They're on vacation in Hawaii, the sunset behind them, and Katsuki's girlfriend is proudly showing off the ring on her finger.

My brother is getting married. Here I was excited about some stupid article while my brother just got a promotion *and* engaged to the love of his life.

There's more I should be doing. I've been at this for five years but meanwhile, my brother is leaps and bounds ahead of me. Maybe he always will be, no matter how hard I try. Nothing I do ever feels good enough.

My phone buzzes.

Raiden: *Hey. Can you come over?*

My heart leaps, and happiness chases away my dour mood. He wants to see me, and I want to see him.

Shit. This isn't good. My feelings are spiraling out of control for this man. I can't go there. My stupid feelings, whatever they are, are going to detonate in my damn face. He's a source of information. That's *all*.

After work, I meet up with Raiden at his apartment. He leans down and gives me a kiss, and then we go up to the penthouse together.

Once we're inside the penthouse, Raiden leads me to the living room. "Want coffee? Matcha?"

"Either is good."

"Just a second."

I'm wondering what he called me here for.

Raiden brings our drinks to the coffee table. I thank him

and take a sip, humming my approval. He even frothed the milk. "You should quit this yakuza stuff and make coffee."

Raiden suddenly puts his hand on my knee and holds my gaze. My throat goes dry. Shit. What's he going to say?

"The men who hurt you are not a problem anymore."

His words ring in my ears. What does he mean? "The guys who attacked me? You found them?"

"And they won't be bothering you again."

For a moment, my mind goes blank. I lean back against the sofa, staring at him. "You killed them."

A stiff nod is my only answer.

Raiden killed them… for me? Two people were killed in my name. It should bother me, but considering they were yakuza, it's probably for the best they're gone. "But. Wait. You said they were Takada's men. Won't you get in trouble?"

"If Takada finds out. Which he likely will." He doesn't sound like he cares at all. Has this guy got a death wish?

"Then why did you do it?" I snap. My heart starts to race as the realization of what he's done crashes down on me.

He cocks his head, brows furrowing. "What gives? Why're you pissed at me?" He glowers, though it looks suspiciously like a pout, and crosses his arms.

God. This fucking guy…

"You—of course I'm pissed at you!" I stumble to my feet and back away from him. "You could get in trouble because of me! And didn't Namikawa just arrange some kind of truce between your clans? You pissing off Takada just put that truce in jeopardy!"

He shrugs. "Good thing I don't give a shit what Takada or Namikawa think."

I groan and hide my face in my hands. "Are you kidding me? Why would you risk starting a war with a rival gang?"

Raiden's slippers slap over the wood flooring. Raiden grips my hands and tugs them down from my face to meet my gaze. "Because they had the fucking nerve to touch what's mine."

A shiver travels down my spine.

Raiden grips my hair at the nape of my neck, squeezing. "You're off-limits. To anyone. I'm not a normal person, Sunshine. I'm not even a good person. But I protect what's mine at any cost."

I'm quiet, letting his words sink in. My disgust and horror has faded. This man risked evoking the anger of his boss... for me. Why? What have I done to be deserving of that?

I shake my head. "I'm not—"

He tugs on my hair in warning. "What?" His voice is low, urging me to choose my words carefully.

"I'm not worth that."

His nostrils flare. "I decide what you're worth to me."

I don't know what to say. Nobody has ever gone to such lengths for me.

"Why?" I croak.

He tilts his head, confused.

I clear my throat. "Why me? Why not anyone else?"

Why not someone like my brother?

Raiden takes in a breath and considers me, stroking his fingers through my hair. "I've dedicated my whole life to serving Namikawa. I never let myself think there could be anything outside the clan, and now... there's you. There's eating meals together and quiet nights in watching movies. This shitty, dark world of mine is suddenly brighter with you in it. I want to keep you for myself, separate from my life in the gang. So if anyone from my world tries to drag you into mine, I'll do what I have to in order to keep you safe." Something sad twists across his face. "I don't know how long I can do that. Maybe I'm just kidding myself. Maybe you'd be better off if I'd just go away. I'm a selfish bastard when it comes to you."

I feel the same. For all that darkness inside him, he's brightened my world, too. I don't want to lose that.

"Be selfish," I beg him, then I yank him in, and when his lips crash against mine, the sound that comes out of me is feral and unhinged. Somehow, we end up on the sofa, leather squeaking beneath me as I scoot back to give him room to sprawl between my legs.

I want all of him. All of his dark, all his light, for however long I can have him. Any moment together could be our last. This greed for him doesn't feel like it will ever be sated.

There's so much I want. I want to beg him to touch

me, to possess me, body and soul, but I can't because Raiden just won't stop kissing me. He lavishes my mouth, sucking on my bottom lip, breaking the kiss only briefly to nip my chin. My eyes roll back, and I practically melt from the attention. I've never been kissed like this, like I'm somebody's whole damn world.

Fuck. I don't want to lose him.

We only stop kissing long enough to get my shirt off over my head. I sit up on my knees and crush my mouth to his, groaning when his tongue tangles with mine. I fumble with the buttons of his shirt, clumsy in my eagerness to feel his hard, warm body. With a roll of his shoulders, Raiden slides his shirt down his arms. The sight of his scars makes my chest ache. Splaying my fingers over his hot, firm pecs, I kiss the scars carved into the center of his chest.

Raiden's chest hitches beneath my lips. Gripping my arms, Raiden falls backward and tugs me down atop him. When he bucks his hips against mine and the hard length of him grinds against me, I have to bite my lip so I don't curse as I grind back down against him. Our chests touch, rising and falling faster as we pant for breath between hungry kisses. I give his plump lower lip a bite, then the column of his throat. One hand comes up to grip my hair, stroking as I flick his hard nipples with my tongue, then kiss my way down his quivering abs.

When I reach his waist, I undo his belt and he lifts his hips up so I can slide his pants and underwear down in one go. My mouth waters as his thick, hard cock curls up toward his stomach, the tip already dewy with pre-cum. "Fuck. You're so beautiful," I whisper, leaning in and kissing his hip. I need to show him what this means to me.

"Hiro," Raiden groans as I suck the wide head of his cock into my mouth.

Suddenly, I'm aching to hear my name, my real name, tumbling from his lips. All my life, I've hated being Jinta Onodera. Jinta Onodera was never good enough, never fit in, never belonged to anyone. I want to be Jinta. Raiden's Jinta.

"Fuck, Sunshine. That's so good," Raiden says, stroking my hair as I take him in deeper. When he moans as I swirl my tongue around the head, lapping at the pre-cum dribbling from his slit, satisfaction soars through me. I did that. Pleased him. Made him feel good. "Look so fucking sexy swallowing my cock."

I bob up and down, and, moaning, Raiden rocks his hips to fuck my mouth. His brow creases, and he bites his lip. "That's my good boy. Can you take more? I think you can."

I've never been good enough for anyone else, but if I can be good for him, then maybe that can be enough.

Moaning around the thick, hot cock in my mouth, I suck him hard and deep. Raiden thrusts, and for a split second, he hits the back of my throat. My throat prickles, and I gag around him.

"Good, that was so good. Think you can take it again?"

I nod and swallow around him when he bucks up into my throat, eyes watering when his thick length briefly fills my throat and cuts off my airflow. My heart trips, but the thrill of choking on his cock is worth it. Reaching down, I cup his balls and squeeze, loving how hard they are already. If I keep this up, I'll make him spill down my throat.

"Your lips look so damn pretty around my dick. But I'd rather fill up that tight, perfect hole of yours. You want that?"

I moan around him, cock jerking in my pants. I'm already so close just from servicing him. If I don't get him inside me, I'll lose my mind. Pulling off his dick, I sit up and wrestle my pants off. Raiden cracks a grin, and I laugh hoarsely, knowing I must look as frantic as I feel.

"Lube's in the end table."

I find a bottle in the drawer and lube up his hard dick. Panting, I reach my fingers around and between my cheeks. Raiden growls his disappointment, but as I moan when I stretch myself open, his eyes darken with longing. Curling an arm behind his head, Raiden watches me like I'm a god of sex as I finger myself open.

When I'm ready, I straddle his hips and reach back to grab his cock. I sink down, breath catching as the wide head pushes into me. Raiden grabs my hips, fingers dimpling my skin. Gasps and pants escape us as I slowly lower myself onto his dick. The stretch is so intense, and the pressure inside me is so all-consuming that I forget how to breathe.

"That's it, beautiful," Raiden says, eyes lidded as he squeezes my hips. "You're taking my cock so well."

My dick jerks at his praise. I love pleasing him. I love how he fills me up, and not just in my body. He fills my soul, too, fills a space in me that was empty for so long.

"You feel so fucking good," Raiden groans beneath me, palming my ass cheeks in appreciation.

I start to move up and down, head falling back and eyes closing in bliss. Raiden bucks his hips to meet me, pelvis smacking my ass. A pleasured groan punches out of me.

"Like that?" Raiden asks, a self-assured tilt to his full lips.

"Yes. Fuck. Do that again!"

He snaps his hips as I sink onto him until he's buried as deep as he can go. The leather couch creaks beneath us as we move faster and faster. "Fuck. Hiro!" As Raiden moans my name, head back and eyes dark and lidded, euphoria surges through me. I did that.

My cock bounces up and down between us, and Raiden grabs it in a tight fist and strokes. It's too much. I can't take any more. My balls are so hard and tight, so I know I've only got seconds. "Say it. Please," I whimper. "Tell me I'm yours."

A low growl escapes Raiden as he curls a hand around my throat and squeezes protectively. "You're mine, Sunshine. And I protect what's mine. Don't I?"

"Yes," I whine, eyes rolling back as I bounce on his cock, mindless in my desire to cum. "Y-yours. I'm—I'm—"

My orgasm erupts, and I shoot off like a geyser, painting his chest and abs with my cum. I squeeze so hard around his dick that his every ridge and curve caresses my inner walls. He pulses inside me as he starts pumping round after round into me.

Gasping, I collapse into his arms, and he catches me. I roll off him so my back is to his chest. The couch isn't big enough, especially since Raiden's damn huge, but we make it work.

"Damn, baby," I whisper, then freeze, face going hotter.

Raiden groans his agreement into my neck, then drops a kiss against my shoulder, not protesting the pet name.

"I did good, didn't I?" I smile, knowing his answer.

Raiden grunts breathlessly and runs his soft fingers through my hair. "You were damn perfect, Sunshine." He kisses my temple, and I laugh, feeling warm inside and out from his praise.

Rolling over to face him, I pepper kisses over his tattooed shoulders, tracing my lips from a temple on his shoulder to a dragon that runs down his biceps. "These are so sexy."

Raiden chuckles. "You should get one. You'd look hot."

"Yeah? Where?"

Grinning, he nips the shell of my ear. "My name and get

it on your dick."

I bark a laugh and smack his chest. "Only if you do yours first."

We lapse into quiet, exchanging slow kisses and caresses. Rain sluices the windows and thunder rumbles, but being in Raiden's arms is like I'm wrapped in a cocoon nothing can penetrate. A question comes to my mind. "Raiden?"

"Hm?" He runs his hand lazily down my side to pinch my butt.

I drag my fingers up his wrist, noting the delicate veins that twist beneath his fair skin, to play with his fingers. "Have you ever thought about leaving the yakuza?"

For a moment, he's quiet, hand running over my chest thoughtfully. "All the time." His voice is so soft, I might not have heard it over the rumble of thunder outside. "But it's just not possible."

"Do you want to?" I'd like to hear him say it out loud.

I feel him shrug. "I can't. I have a debt to Namikawa. And even if I didn't, the moment you get your tattoos, you're in this for life. I'll never get work anywhere else, not when my past is tattooed all over my skin."

"In Japan, maybe. But what if you went somewhere else? Like America?"

Raiden sighs, breath tickling my hair. "I've killed people. There's no normal life for someone like me."

I squeeze his arm. "But if you could?"

"No." His voice is a warning, but a half-hearted one. "I

can't."

"Okay. Then can you tell me about your debt to Namikawa?"

"You wouldn't understand."

I roll onto my side, facing him. Our noses are inches apart, his breath warm against my lips. "Try me."

He parts his lips, and the longing in those dark brown eyes takes me by storm. "You wouldn't get it."

I clench my jaw against the frustration. He won't even try to tell me. Every time we're getting close, there are still so many secrets keeping us apart. My secrets. His. I'm sick of it.

"If you tell me, maybe I could help you?" I feel silly just saying that, but I mean it. I would help him, if I just knew how.

Raiden strokes my hair from my face. "I'd go away with you if I could."

Something in my heart eases at his confession. I fold him into my arms and hold him tight. At first, his arms are stuck at his side, then, ever so slowly, they wrap around me and draw me into the warmth of his body.

"I know," I tell him, and I don't let him go, even after his gentle snores fill the quiet of the room.

When I wake up, Raiden is gone, but he's left a blanket draped over me while I sleep. The rain has stopped and in the quiet, I catch the faint sound of Raiden's voice coming from the bedroom. He's talking to someone. My heart crawls into my throat. Quietly, I get off the couch and wrap the blanket around me. My bare feet whisper over the floor. Raiden's voice gets clearer, and I realize the door is ajar.

Holding my breath, I peer through the slit in the door.

Raiden paces in front of the window, phone in hand.

Namikawa's weathered voice asks, "Is the prey prepared?"

Prey? My heart skips at the unusual choice of words.

"Yes, boss," Raiden answers. "It will be a good hunt."

A hunt... the word sends a shiver down my spine.

"Excellent. Will you be there? It's been some time since we all ran together."

"I'll join you soon."

Raiden hangs up. I dart into the bathroom across the hall and linger long enough to flush the toilet and run the faucet so he thinks I was actually doing something instead of creeping around his house.

"Hey," I say, keeping my tone light as I approach him in the living room. He's pulling on his jacket. "Going somewhere?"

"Yeah, Sunshine. Gotta work. Make yourself at home. I won't be back for a while."

That's a lie. He just lied to me. Why?

"Okay…" My stomach churns when he drops a quick kiss on my cheek and walks out. Silence rings in my ears.

A full moon. A hunt. Prey.

Oh, god. The missing people. Bile rises in my throat.

So, all this time, Raiden really was…

Tears nip my eyes.

I've got to follow him. I'm close to something huge. I just know it.

If only I knew what.

Chapter II

Mount Kumotori is the perfect place to shift and run. It's a long drive, but there's nothing like the crisp mountain air, so it's worth it. Here, we can be ourselves.

One by one, we leave the vehicles and follow Namikawa into the woods to a spot in the clearing. The excitement in the air is so palpable I can smell it. My own heart races, skin itchy and tight. The moon's glow is like a caress against my skin, stirring lust deep in my soul. The lust to shift and run and hunt, as powerful as the drive to fuck.

Namikawa faces us, arms open. "Shift, my sons and daughters. Out here, we are wild and free."

Except Namikawa has never shifted around us. I have no

idea what his wolf looks like. He's a shifter. I can smell it. Why doesn't he show us his wolf?

"Going to join us, boss?" I ask.

"Not tonight. I am feeling unwell." I remember his coughing fit yesterday. How can he be feeling sick? Werewolves don't get ill.

Ren peels off her tank top, her tattoos bright. "This is going to be awesome."

My grandfather sits on a log nearby. "Enjoy yourselves."

I discard my clothes and let the change flow over me. Fur sprouts as I drop to all fours, my body rattles, reforming into that of a wolf. When I open my eyes, the colors of the world are different. A thousand different scents command my attention. Beside me, Ren's white wolf prances up to me and hits me in the ribs with her head. I snap at her, and she growls back.

Then, I smell it—sweat and body odor, fear ripe in the air. Wolves growl all around me as from the shadows, a line of dirty, disheveled men and women are led in chains to the center of the clearing, surrounded by wolves.

Namikawa smiles coldly. "Welcome, humans. Tonight is your last night alive."

The men and women begin to panic. Someone tries to run, ankle cuffs rattling, but of course doesn't get far. A wolf tears forward and pounces. The man screams as the wolf rips into his flesh, terrified cries ending in a wet, bloody gurgle.

Namikawa tuts. "Did no one tell you not to run from wolves? Wait until the cuffs are off. Then, run as fast as you can."

The prisoners are escorted ahead of the wolves, facing deeper into the trees. The guard undoes their cuffs. The prisoners shake and whisper prayers. Namikawa leans forward and smiles coldly. "Now... run."

The prisoners tear into the trees, whimpering and crying. The smell of their fear and their sudden movements awaken a prey drive in me that can't be stopped. Not until the prey has been caught, thrashing in my jaws. With a snarl, I leap after the prisoners and the pack follows, the air filled with furious howls.

My paws slam the earth as I give chase, fangs snapping inches from a prisoner's ankles and making the prisoner scream. A wolf body-slams me out of the way and pursues the prisoner. Snarling, I rise and shake myself free of dirt. The winds blow toward me, and then I smell it. Cherry blossoms. But there aren't any in these mountains.

I whirl around, my night vision piercing through the shadows of the woods. Something moves, a pale face in the dark. Brown eyes wide in terror find mine.

No. No. No. Shit!

Hiro. How is he here?

How much did he see? Does he know what I am?

The moment our eyes meet, Hiro hides back behind the tree. The scent of his fear is so strong, I can taste it. If I can smell him, so can the others. He has to get out of here. Now. Snarling, I tear toward the tree. Hiro gasps and closes his eyes as I round the trunk, pressing himself flat to the tree.

He's scared of me. That's not something I ever wanted. I fight the urge to lie down and expose my stomach, to make him understand I'm not a threat to him. I'd never hurt him. My mind can't even fathom the idea.

Then, Hiro chucks a rock at my head. I yelp as the stone smacks off my head and instinctively try to paw away the pain. Hiro tears into the woods, and I can't fight my instincts. I give chase, but not to hurt or kill. I will catch him and when I do, I will claim him where he lies. Mount him. Bite him. Tie him to me so no one can take him away from me.

I will make him mine.

With a pounce, my paws leave the ground and slam into Hiro's back. Hiro crashes to the dirt with a breathless cry. He gazes up at me, my snout inches from his face, paws on either side of his head. I drag my tongue up his neck, to bite his ear. A pleased rumble escapes me as I focus on covering him in my scent. If he smells like me, the pack will know he's mine. They won't be able to smell him or hurt him. But there's only so much I can do in this form. Besides, I don't think he'd like it if I just started humping him.

I pull back my shift, but it's hard to go back to being human. The shift fights against me, wants to keep me on all fours. With a snarl, I tear free from my shift. Mostly. I'm still wreathed in fur that covers my lower body. But I have hands, clawed as they are, and a mouthful of fangs.

"R-Raiden?" Hiro whispers, eyes wide and full as the moon.

"Sunshine," I say, my voice practically a growl.

"What the... hell are you?" He's breathing harshly, and he squirms beneath me.

I seize his shirt in my clawed grip. "You can't move. I... I'm still caught in my shift. My instincts are hard to control. If you run, I'll chase you."

"S-shift?" Hiro echoes, throat bobbing when he swallows. My eyes latch onto the movement. Fuck. I want to put my teeth in him. Want to bite down while I slam in his writhing, willing body. Spill inside him as his blood fills my mouth.

"Yes," I snap out. "I'm a werewolf."

Hiro's chest hitches. "A... a fucking werewolf."

I nod.

A sound escapes Hiro. I realize it's laughter. He's... laughing at me.

"Of course you're a fucking werewolf!" Hiro wheezes, head thrown back as he laughs. "Nothing in this world makes any damn sense anymore." Tears gather in his eyes, chest hitching as he starts to... cry? Laugh? I can't tell.

Shit. He's having a mental break or something.

"Hey," I growl, patting his cheek hard. "Stay with me

here. Yes. I'm a werewolf. Werewolves are real. Humans hunted our kind to near extinction back in the 1900s. We went underground, fell in with gangs to survive, and rebuilt our numbers."

Hiro's lower lip quivers. "You were hunting those people. Raiden. I saw you. You were going to kill them, weren't you?"

Ah, shit. I close my eyes tight, willing my panic to go away. "I can explain that."

"Save it!" Hiro shouts, voice breaking. "You're... you're a fucking monster. I knew this about you, but I thought... Fuck! I thought—"

He shoves at me. He's trying to run. To leave me.

A furious snarl escapes me. I grab his wrists and slam them above his head, pin his hips down with mine.

"You're right. I am a monster. But I'm the monster other monsters fear. Those prisoners? They were fucking scumbags who escaped the justice system. Or enemies from rival gangs. Scum nobody is going to fucking miss."

"Yeah, right," Hiro spits. "Your clan, or pack, or whatever, is behind all those disappearances!" Huh? What's he talking about? A tear leaves a track down Hiro's cheek. "I... I can't believe I actually thought you were different."

"Hiro, listen!" I snarl, horrified that he'd think that. "Listen to me!" I grip his jaw in my other hand, mindful of my claws. "I couldn't tell you what I was." I wipe away the tear on his cheek. "Whatever you want to know, I'll answer it."

Hiro swallows hard. "Those people… they're really not innocent?"

I scowl. "Far from it. You saw the tattoos. They're from rival gangs, criminals the world won't miss. The others are fucking pedos. Rapists. Murderers. People who have harmed civilians in our territory or raped the women at our host clubs and bars. We're doing the world a service, trust me."

"I'm just supposed to believe you?"

Scowling, I straighten up as the sound of frantic footsteps approaches. The tattooed man screams at the sight of me, then I grab him by the throat and force him onto his knees. "Look at him and tell him what you did."

"Wha—"

"Do it!" I snap.

Whimpering, the tattooed man looks down at Hiro. "I… I r-raped one of the bitches at the hostess club. Namikawa found out and b-banished me from the clan."

Hiro's face twists in disgust.

I shove the bastard and he takes off running, disappearing into the dark. He screams within the woods, and wolves snarl hungrily.

"Believe me now?" I ask.

Hiro exhales slowly. "Y-yeah. I… I think so."

I kneel in the grass before him and prostrate myself, forehead to the earth. Shame churns my insides. I feel like such an asshole for frightening him. I hate that he found out like this. "I'm sorry I kept this from you. I swear, I'm not going to hurt you, or let anything happen to you. I'd never hurt you."

"I know," Hiro croaks, breath quickening. "You saved me. You were that wolf."

"I was. Takada was pissed, so I wanted to be near you."

"Why was he mad?"

I hesitate. Because he knows what Hiro means to me. I don't know how to say that out loud. "He was jealous. Smelled you on me. He sent those thugs to beat you up to get back at me."

"So he's your ex?"

I grimace. "Something like that. Rather not talk about him right now."

"Raiden, on the news, there was a story about hundred-year-old remains in a mass grave."

I'd heard about that. "I know."

"Were, um... werewolves behind that, too?"

I open my mouth, but the words are trapped. I physically can't speak. The scars on my chest begin to burn like they've been set on fire. "I... I can't—" I grip my chest, shocked as burning pain eclipses everything else.

Hiro's brows furrow. "What's wrong? Are you hurt? Holy shit. Your scars!"

They probably look as horrible as they feel.

"Raiden, what's going on?"

Sweat breaks out on my body. I give up trying to tell him what I know, and the minute I stop trying, the pain recedes. Panting, I lean back against a tree. Hiro scoots over and sits beside me, taking my hand.

"Those aren't ordinary scars, are they?"

I shake my head. "It's a curse."

"Like... as in a literal curse?"

I nod, body relaxing as the pain slowly fades. "Yeah. Namikawa hired a witch to bind me to his service."

"A... witch? Hang on." Hiro blinks those wide eyes at me. "How many supernatural creatures are there?"

I shrug. "Demons are real. But they only appear if summoned, usually. Werewolves, of course. Vampires, too, but they haven't been in Japan in years since wolves kicked them out. Witches are even rarer."

"Oh, my god..." Hiro slumps back against the ground, gazing up at the stars. "You're telling me there's a whole world of supernatural creatures right under humanity's nose?"

"Yes. I know, it's a lot to take in."

Hiro laughs softly. "Actually, a lot about you now makes more sense."

I arch a brow. "Seriously?"

"Yeah. Like how crazy possessive you are. All the biting during sex. The growling."

I squeeze his thigh. "You really are a freak if all that really does it for you."

Hiro chuckles. "I blame you for this. I was an innocent boy until you corrupted me. Anyway, tell me more about this curse. Why would Namikawa do that to you?"

I trace the kanji carved into my skin. "To punish my father for running off on the pack." That's the simple answer. I'm dangerously close to spilling all my secrets to him, but I can't get into that with him tonight. It's too much.

Hiro leans his cheek on my shoulder. "That's horrible."

I roll my shoulders. "It is what it is."

"Is there any way to break it?"

"Only Namikawa's death can free me."

Hiro exhales softly beside me. "God. I'm so sorry, baby."

I shake my head. "Don't be."

"Are other werewolves behind these disappearances?"

"Don't know. Our pack doesn't target humans. It could be another pack. Sometimes people just disappear."

Hiro shakes his head. "Not like this. These disappearances are exactly like the ones that happened back in 1924. There's a connection. Has to be."

Why does he care so much? "Some things are better left unknown."

Hiro sighs like he's disappointed, then he asks, "Is it lycanthropy? Like, a disease? Can you spread it to others?"

Snorting, I tousle his hair. "No. It's not a disease, and it can't be spread through biting. We're born this way, and it's passed down through the generations. I'm not a lore expert, but the stories go that back during the time of the Tokugawa Shogunate, there was a clan of samurai who served a fierce lord who domesticated wolves and unleashed them upon his enemies. The clan admired wolves so much, they summoned shape-shifting yokai to possess their warriors and turn them into wolves, gifting them with superior strength in battle. That clan was Namikawa's ancestors, or so he claims."

"Are all yakuza werewolves?"

"Nope, and not all werewolves are yakuza. Plenty are regular citizens. But Takada's clan and ours are the only werewolf yakuza clans in the city."

"What is Takada's beef with you guys?"

I shake my head. "It goes deeper than the current feud between our packs. Takada believes that his pack are the true descendants of the first-ever werewolves, and that this gives him some almost divine right to rule over Tokyo. But Namikawa claims the same thing, that our pack is the one with the deepest roots. It's all just some glorified territorial dispute."

Hiro whistles. "Shit. This is all super complicated. What about magic? That's a... thing, right?"

I nod. "I'm no witch, but my understanding is they also get their powers by making deals with spirits. I'm not sure of all the details."

Softly, he adds, "Were you ever going to tell me?"

"Probably not. It's risky for humans to know about us.

Historically, humans have been nothing but trouble for our kind."

Suddenly, Hiro crawls into my lap. He cups my face in his hands. "I won't tell anyone. I promise."

A smile tugs at my mouth. I love how serious he is. "Good. Otherwise, I'll have to hunt you down and eat you." I bite his chin, and when he moans, I claim his lips with mine.

Hiro squirms on me, rubbing his hips against my aching cock. Is he doing that on purpose?

"You okay? You aren't scared?"

"At first," he admits, then reaches up to stroke the tip of my furred ear. "But this is... kind of a hot look on you."

Relief makes it easier to breathe. "You aren't going to run?"

"Isn't it a bad idea to run from wolves?"

I chuckle, the sound more like a snarl. "Yeah. Especially when it's a full moon, and they're horny as hell." I grind up against him, primal satisfaction making me snap my teeth when he groans. "Besides, if you did run, I'd hunt you down like the prey you are."

"Yeah?" Hiro rasps, breathing harder.

I drag my tongue over the crook of his neck, then bite his ear, enjoying his gasp. "Shred the clothes from your body. Fuck you right where I catch you." A moan escapes Hiro when I snap my hips against his hardening cock. "You like that, don't you? Like the idea of being my prey?"

"No," Hiro says, then rocks his hips against me when I grab his clothed cock and squeeze. "F-fuck. Raiden…"

"How about we play a game? You run as fast as you can. If you escape, you win. If I catch you, I'll fuck you on the forest floor like a damn animal. Does that sound good?"

Hiro nods frantically. "Yes."

I release his wrists and stumble off of him. "Then run." I crouch, digging my claws into the earth to hold myself back.

Hiro scrambles to his feet, cock straining his jeans. He throws a heated look over his shoulder that makes my cock swell. Then he runs. A snarl rips through me, and I tear at the forest floor to keep from chasing him. My mouth waters. Every instinct screams at me to hunt, to run, to catch and bite and fuck.

I wait as long as I can bear until he's hidden within the trees. I can still smell him, cherry blossoms mixed with the scent of arousal. My control unravels. I howl to the moon above, telling him I'm coming for him. Then, I run. The shift consumes me, turning my clawed hands to paws. The forest blurs around me as I run, following the scent of my prey through the woods. His scent gets stronger, closer, and I can practically taste his arousal.

I don't know if I'll fuck him or kill him—tear him apart with my cock and with my teeth, bury myself inside his body and live beneath his skin. Ahead of me, my prey weaves between the trees, arms pumping, feet slamming the ground. He looks back, our eyes meet, and his scent mixes with lust and fear.

Yes. Fear me.

Yes. Want me. Only ever me.

When I know I'm close, I pull the shift back so I'm human again. My paw becomes a clawed hand, and I seize his ankle.

Hiro yelps as he falls, but I'm there to catch him, wrapping him in my arms, twisting us so I take the brunt of the fall.

We roll, tumbling over and over, and then I pin him beneath me. We gasp, breathless as if we've just fucked. His eyes are wide, pupils blown out until there's just a rim of color at the edges of his iris.

"Mine," I snarl, and then I devour his lips.

Hiro moans into my mouth, arching beneath me. He's so hard, and I can smell his pre-cum, his lust for me. I yank his head back, claws in his hair, and sink my teeth into his neck, biting down.

"More," Hiro gasps. "Oh, fuck. More! Cover every inch of me."

I break the skin, relishing in his hoarse cry, and lap up the blood. It's not a mating bite, but the intention is there; to claim him, mark him as mine and nobody else's. But all these damn clothes are in the way. I tear open the buttons on his shirt and sink my teeth into his soft pec, snarling around his flesh when he cries out in pleasure and pain.

Hiro's blunt nails drive into my back, and I growl, loving that he's trying to mark me, even if the marks will fade. I rake my claws down his chest, leaving angry red welts as I bite my way down his body. He's pushing at me, urging me down, down, down. I flip him onto his stomach and yank his pants down to expose that perfect, plump ass.

I squeeze his cheeks, dimpling the skin with my claws, then pry him apart so he's exposed. I'm going to wreck this hole. I can't speak, too lost in the beast. Only growls and grunts come out of me as I shove my face between his cheeks and inhale. Hiro's panting, writhing beneath me, chanting, "Right there. Raiden. Fuck. Please. Yes. Please."

I bite down on his ass, and his scream of pleasure and pain goes straight to my aching cock. Growling. I spread him wide and spit, then shove my tongue inside his tight heat.

"Oh, god!" Hiro cries out, tearing at the dirt, humping the ground as I burrow inside his body and lick. I snarl my pleasure, his taste, his moans and cries feeding my primal lust. He's so perfect. I could spend all night devouring this tight hole. I might have to. I don't have any lube. I've got to get him good and wet and loose for me.

I sheathe my claws and wet my fingers in my mouth, sinking them inside Hiro's body and curling them. He whimpers, rolling his hips back onto my thrusting fingers. I drag my tongue down to his heavy balls and suck on them. I spread my fingers, making him gape open so I can lick inside. Hiro's a whimpering, groaning mess, incapable of words as I worship his hole.

I wrap my hands around his cock and jerk, hard and fast as I fuck him with my tongue.

"R-Raiden! Stop. I'm going to—"

That's what I want. I need him loose and relaxed. I lean over his back and bite down on his shoulder, jacking his cock while I thrust my fingers inside and stretch him open.

"Oh, fuck. Raiden!" He shouts my name and covers my hand in hot, sticky cum. His ass spasms around my fingers, damn near breaking them from how hard he's clenching.

The earthy tang of his cum in the air makes me snarl, and I lift my soaked hand to my lips and lick at the mess he left. I want to swallow it all, but I need it. I stroke myself, slicking myself up with his own cum. Hiro's gasping and shaking beneath me, but he still arches his hips back, lifts onto his hands and knees and presents himself.

I can't hold back. Grabbing my dick, I press against his loosened hole and push.

Hiro moans in bliss, rocking back on me as I slide easily inside. I go slow, rolling back and forth, letting his tight, eager body get adjusted to my girth. My cock is bigger in this form. And then there's my knot, already expanding at the base. If I don't slam all the way in, he won't even know it's there.

I plaster my body to his back, dig my claws into his hips, and thrust, going faster and faster. He feels so good around my cock, so hot and tight and perfect. Animalistic snarls and growls of pleasure rumble from me as I fuck him faster and deeper. When Hiro starts to moan and pant beneath me, rocking back to meet every slam of my hips, I know he's feeling just as good.

My fangs dimple his shoulder, and I bite down to stifle my howl of satisfaction as pleasure builds and builds. I haul him up and against me, arms around him, pinning him to my body as I pound my hips against his ass. Hiro's head falls against my shoulder, his cries echoing freely into the woods around us. I grab his cock, hard already, and stroke.

"Mine," I snarl into his ear. "Mine. Mine. Mine."

"Yours," he whimpers as I slam inside, again and again. "Yours. *Yours.*"

The thrill that goes through me when he accepts my claim is unlike anything I've ever felt before. I'm so close. Wanna shove my knot inside and breed him, fill his hole with my cum.

"Yes. Please, yes. So close. Gonna cum. Oh, fuck. Please!"

I grab his throat in my clawed hand and bury my fangs in the meat of his shoulder, and just like that, Hiro gives a victorious shout. His tight asshole strangles my cock, and with a howl, I slam all the way inside and let him clench around my knot, wringing the most intense, mind-numbing orgasm I've ever felt out of me.

My grip on him softens. My animalistic features retreat, and I lower him gently to the ground and cradle him to me.

"What... is that?" Hiro asks breathlessly.

"My knot," I explain, voice hoarse from all the growling. "It only happens when I'm in my half shift. Shit. Is it uncomfortable? I can force it down."

"No. No... I... I feel so full. I like it."

A primal rumble escapes me. "Good."

"How long does it last?"

"Half an hour, usually."

Hiro rocks back against me, and we both groan when my knot tugs at his rim. I kiss the bites I left on his shoulder. "Do these hurt?"

"Oh, yeah. But I like it."

"Good."

"That was... fuck. Intense."

I lick the sweat from the back of his neck. "My wolf is a very happy bastard right now."

"Really?"

"Yeah. We're very possessive when we've found someone who speaks to our inner animal."

Hiro reaches around to stroke my hair. "I can tell. You damn caveman."

"Did you mean it?" I kiss the shell of his ear. "When you said you were mine?"

Hiro's throat bobs beneath my gentle grip on his neck.

"Hiro," I growl, propping myself up to meet his gaze. "You can't say things you don't mean. Not to a werewolf. I knew you were mine the moment I saw you. Had to have you." I stroke my thumb along his lower lip. "Don't tell me you don't feel the same." I hate the vulnerability that bleeds into my voice.

Hiro blinks fast. "I... I do. I don't want to share you with anyone else. I hate the idea of you with someone else. Isn't that crazy? I'm a human."

I laugh and kiss his soft lips. "No. It's very normal for us, and even for humans to feel that way."

"Normal..." Hiro mutters, and I slap his butt. For a moment, we're quiet. The stars are bright in the night sky. Distant howls from the hunt echo within the trees, but with Hiro wrapped in my arms, nothing else matters. It's just me and him, and I never want that to go away.

Dawn brightens the sky by the time I arrive back in Tokyo. Hiro is fast asleep in the seat beside me, my suit jacket draped over him. I kill the engine but make no move to wake him up. Silence blankets us and I watch him sleep, fighting the urge to reach over and stroke his hair. I can't believe he just... accepted me. Trusted me with his body even after I showed him what I really am.

I was terrified I'd push him away. I've never been afraid before. Not really. I've learned to compartmentalize so much of my life and the things I do. Locked my soft, weak feelings up tight to do what I have to do in order to survive. Death doesn't scare me, nor does pain.

But if he'd rejected me and run from me... I would have been broken. Just the thought twists like a knife. I wouldn't have been able to let him go. I'm not selfless enough. I'm not a good person. I can never be good enough for him.

Hiro yawns softly beside me. "Are we here?"

"Yeah." I unlock the doors and step out with him. Hiro's stumbling to his doorstep like a drunk, worn out from everything we did. Even I'm sore and tired. I've never been so satisfied before. I hook my arm with his, and we walk to his door together.

"I'll see you in the morning," I say. "We'll get breakfast before I have to go to work."

Hiro smiles tiredly. "Sounds great."

Before he can turn away, I cup his cheek in my hand. He closes his eyes, and I claim his lips with mine. For a moment, everything disappears. All that matters is his body against mine, his sweet scent, how soft his hair is between my fingers.

I've never cared for anyone like I care for him. Already, I miss him and can't wait to see him in the morning.

When we part, I tip my head back to the moon above.

"The moon's beautiful tonight, huh?"

Hiro laughs softly. "Yeah. It is."

My heart sings.

It's a confession. It's not the moon that's beautiful; it's him. It's the way he makes me feel, like the whole damn world is beautiful when I've only ever thought it cruel and cold. It's about as indirect as it gets, but that's what I'm comfortable with. I don't know if I love him. If I ever could after all the shit I've been through. But... I like him. That's all I know, and that's enough for me.

I watch him until he's safely through the front door. I can't wipe the smile from my face as I turn away.

The drive home is peaceful. I'm more content than I have been in a long time. Parking in the garage, I lock my car behind me and turn away, eager for bed.

Something slams into my face. My nose snaps as it breaks. Ears ringing, I crash to the ground. Two men tower over me. I recognize their scents. They're my own pack mates, Namikawa-kai. Before I can stand, a foot collides into my face. The world spins around me as I tumble over, blood blinding my vision.

"Sorry, Noboru. The boss wants to speak with you. You're in big trouble."

I blink blood from my eye in time to see the Namikawa-kai's boot soaring toward my face.

Well, fuck.

CHAPTER 12

Raiden

My head throbs as I come to. I'm in the back seat of a car, lying on the floor where no one can see me. My hands are bound with silver cuffs that sap my strength.

Silver doesn't burn our skin, not unless it penetrates the flesh, so there's that at least. But I know I won't be pain-free for long. I should have figured Namikawa would find a way to ruin my night.

This was coming. Bound to happen. Of course Namikawa would find out I'd gone behind his back. The old man knows everything. I try to calm my racing heart.

I know what's in store for me. It's happened before, but after the last time, I'd started being more careful and obedient. But there was no way I could let that attack against Hiro go.

When the car stops, my heart starts banging against my chest.

The back door opens. One of Namikawa's guys grabs my ankles and tugs, dragging me down onto the pavement. Oh, yeah. I recognize immediately where we are. The warehouse where we interrogate and torture enemies of the gang. And tonight, that's me.

I'm shoved to my feet. I glare at the guy. "Ease up, asshole. I can walk on my own."

At our approach, the doors open from the inside. Namikawa stands in a dim patch of light, hands clasped in front of him. As I enter, something smashes across my face.

Blinding pain erupts throughout my skull, and in my shock, my knees give out. I crash to the ground, squinting up through one good eye at Saito Takada.

"You son of a bitch!" Takada snarls, and he slams his foot into me.

I curl my knees to my stomach, so his foot bounces off my kneecap, and I raise my chained arms to shield my face. That doesn't stop him from kicking every part of me he can reach, making my body ache.

"Takahashi and his brother are dead because of you!"

I crack a grin at him. "They were too easy to kill. You really should have trained 'em better."

Takada's shoe flies toward my face. My nose crunches,

blood floods down the back of my throat, and I choke. The injury heals in seconds, but I'm still coughing on blood.

Takada fists my hair and hurls me to my feet, then shoves me straight into a wall. I bounce off and use the momentum to slam into Takada. We both crash to the floor, and he gets me beneath him. He slings back his fist, and I see white as his knuckles crack across my cheek.

With a strangled snarl, Takada hurls another kick at me. Takada leans down, sneering in my face. "All this trouble for some human cock? How low you've fallen, Noboru. I've had my fill, Namikawa. He's all yours." Takada leans against the wall, ready to watch whatever torment Namikawa has planned for me.

Namikawa comes toward me, his steps calm and composed. "I warned you, you know."

I huff a laugh at the ceiling, tasting blood in my mouth.

"It's clear I've given you too much freedom if you truly believe you can defy direct orders and get away unscathed."

Tendrils of fear wrap around my insides. "Fuck you."

A cold smile lifts Namikawa's mouth as he crosses to me and undoes the cuffs. He tosses something on the ground. A silver blade.

"Would you kindly pick it up?" he says, and his words wrap around my mind.

Against my will, my hand reaches toward the blade. The words he carved into my chest long ago begin to burn.

"Screw you!" I snarl at him, trying to wrestle back control, even knowing it is futile.

I fight as hard as I can, but my fingers wrap around the blade. Shaking, I lift the blade and hold it at the ready, pointing the edge at my chest. Breathing hard, heart racing, I look to Namikawa for instructions.

"You know what to do."

To my horror, my left hand moves to lie flat on the floor, fingers splayed. My other hand positions the blade over the first knuckle of my little finger.

"Do it slowly. I want you to feel every slice."

The blade bites into my skin, and I howl as the flesh begins to smoke and burn. Inch by inch, the blade sears its way through my skin and lodges in the bone. My throat is already hoarse from screaming, and I know deep down that this torment has only just begun.

Blood flows, soaking the palm of my hand. I'm doubled over from the pain, on the brink of passing out, and yet my hand keeps cutting, cutting, cutting until the blade cleaves through bone. I'm vaguely aware of Takada laughing at my pain.

Gasping, cold sweat soaking through my clothes, I squint at Namikawa through eyes watery from agony.

Namikawa leans over, inspecting the severed tip of my finger, floating in a pool of blood. "Good. Good. Now, on to the next knuckle."

I will not beg. Never. I'll bear this torment as I always

have. I may not be able to fight the hold he has over my mind, but I am in control of my own response to it. I'll endure. I'll survive.

And someday... I'm going to kill Kensuke Namikawa.

Even if, in the end, I go down along with him.

CHAPTER 13

Jinta

A day later, and I still can't believe it.

Werewolves are real. The pictures I took sure look real enough, and yet, I can't stop myself from replaying the events of the hunt over and over again.

I barely know Raiden, but I trust him. *Fuck*. I *trust* him. I let him hunt me as a damn wolf and trusted him not to tear my throat out. He had the perfect opportunity to kill me then and there to preserve his pack's secret, but he didn't. Though he sure almost killed me with pleasure.

I have so much to process. The existence of a whole paranormal world, for one.

But I have no time to take in any information. I've got to continue my investigation, so I stay late after work and dig up archived newspapers going back to the 1920s.

For hours, I flip through page after page, taking note of any articles about random disappearances, then cross-referencing the names of the victims identified in the mass grave to see if they're a match. It's a mind-numbingly boring process that consumes my entire day.

With my back aching and eyes bleary, I call it a day. So far, none of the victims are alive, and I've gone through fifty out of one hundred victims. There has to be someone who survived, or at the very least, family members of a survivor who can relay their experience to me. There just has to be.

My stomach growls. I need to eat, get some rest, and resume my investigation tomorrow.

I text Raiden, asking if he wants to come over for dinner.

By the time I get off the train, my message has gone unanswered.

Raiden still hasn't texted me back.

I sent him a text saying good morning, asking if he wanted to have breakfast together somewhere. No response. Not even when I texted him a pic of the bite mark he left on my shoulder. I figured that *surely* would have gotten a response.

Something's wrong, and the anxiety makes it hard to focus as I pour over old newspapers. I hope he's okay. I'm worried I did something wrong, but I can't think of what it might have been.

I spend most of the day piecing together evidence I've already gathered for my story, but around 7 PM, I'm starving and my brain won't function anymore. Still no damn survivors.

I take the train and seek out the Blue Lotus. It's packed with people drinking and dancing the stress of the week away. Just like I'd hoped, Ren is behind the bar pouring drinks. She waves at me, smiling brightly. I slide into the last empty seat.

"Hey!" she chirps. "The usual?"

"You know me so well. And some karaage, too." Fried chicken is the best.

"You got it." She hands me my *Sapporo* draft, and I take an eager gulp.

The beer hits my empty stomach like a truck.

"How're you? Enjoying the weekend?" she shouts over the music.

I shrug. "Sure. Hey, you haven't seen Raiden, have you?"

Ren's brow wrinkles. "I haven't, actually. Not since a couple of days ago."

"Since the hunt?" I ask, dismayed before I realize what I've let slip.

She schools her shocked expression, but it's too late.

"It's okay, Ren. I know. Raiden told me everything, and I don't care. Really."

Tension tightens her shoulders. "Just a minute!" she barks at a demanding customer, then leans into my space. "You know."

"I do."

"How?"

"I sort of followed you guys to the mountains. Then Raiden saw me and... told me everything."

Ren blows out a breath. "You could have been killed, Hiro. What were you thinking? You're brave or stupid, I can't tell which."

"My old man always said stupid, so let's go with that."

Shaking her head, Ren says, "Thanks for being open-minded about it, at least. But you know if anyone in the gang finds out, Namikawa is going to lose his shit, right? This has to stay a secret between you, me, and Raiden."

A grin tickles my lips. "Cool. I've never had friends to keep secrets with."

Ren chuckles and raises a fist. I bump her, and we laugh, but worry forms a line between her brows. "I don't like that neither of us have heard from Raiden. He hasn't been home the last couple of times I've knocked on his door."

My heart sinks. "Do you think something's happened to him?"

She purses her lips. "The last time he disappeared like this..." She trails off, worry plain in her eyes.

"He's done this before?" I ask, mouth going dry.

Ren tucks hair behind her ear and looks away. "There are some things that you shouldn't trouble yourself with. If he's gone, then something is going down between him and Namikawa."

I don't like the sound of that at all. "Would Namikawa hurt him?"

Ren bites her lip.

"Ren!" I press, balling my fists on the bar.

"I'm sorry, Hiro. It's not my story to tell. It's Raiden's, and it's very personal. If he hasn't told you, then he isn't ready for you to know." She offers a half-hearted quirk of her mouth. "Don't worry. Even if Namikawa is mad, Raiden is far too important for him to dispose of."

That does nothing to make me feel better.

The kitchen doors open, and a waiter carries a bowl of karaage to my seat.

"I should see to my customers." Ren moves away from me before I can interrogate her more. She ignores my attempts to grab her attention again.

Could Namikawa have somehow found out Raiden shared the clan's secret with me? Or is Raiden in trouble for some other reason, maybe about the Takada-kai men he killed because of me?

God. My stomach cramps just thinking about the possibilities.

My phone buzzes. It's Kenichi, my source from the police department. I'd asked him for help with my investigation.

Ken: *Hey. Think I found something!*

He's attached a picture. My heart leaps into my throat as I zoom in.

The headline reads: LITTLE GIRL ESCAPES RITUALISTIC SACRIFICE. It's dated April 24, 1924.

He found a survivor!

Ken also sent me an email and attached a transcript of the article. My chicken cools as I read and then reread.

Her name is Yuki Katagiri.

While she didn't identify her kidnapper, she claims to have been abducted with her mother and taken to a shrine along with dozens of other people. Yuki managed to escape, though her mother was killed.

I drop my phone onto the bar, mind spinning. How could one person kidnap so many people? Is it possible there's some kind of paranormal connection? Is the person behind these abductions even human? That's a disturbing thought, one I never would have considered until recently.

Okay. So, the mass grave was discovered close to the ruins of an old shrine in the mountains. That must be the shrine Yuki was referring to.

So, could it be that this next ritual will happen at a

secluded shrine, too? And what will happen to all the missing people? Will they be sacrificed just like last time?

Why is any of this happening? I don't know, but maybe Yuki or Yuki's descendants will have some answers for me.

Before it's too late.

Chapter 14

When I open my eyes, I have no idea where I am. What day it is. How I got here.

I'm lying on something soft. Wherever I am, it's pitch-black. My finger throbs where it was cut off. Damn silver is still in my bloodstream. My healing is slow. A familiar scent fills my nose. I'm in my room. I'd know the smell of my den anywhere. Fumbling blindly, I flick on the light—and stare in horror that turns my skin ice cold.

My hands are caked in blood that's dry and cracked, falling in little brown flakes onto the white sheets. I fell into bed with my shoes on, and there's dirt scattered all over my bed. My suit is ripped and dirty, like I went stumbling through the woods.

"Help me!"

The memory of a man's panicked scream pierces my brain.

"Someone, please! Help me!"

Panic claws at my chest, turning my breaths ragged.

What did I do?

What the fuck happened?

Gasping, I stumble into the en suite bathroom. I tear off my clothes and duck beneath the shower. I rub my hands together beneath the spray and crimson water spatters the tile.

"No! Get away from me! Stop! Let me go!"

I slap my bloody hands over my ears, a pitiful whine escaping me.

What the hell is happening to me?

Are these... memories? Am I losing my fucking mind? How did I get from Namikawa's warehouse to my apartment? My knees buckle. I slide down the wall and collapse, head flopping back against the slick wall. My hands won't stop shaking.

What did I do? Who did I kill? *Why?*

"Excuse me!" A distant voice carries from down the hall. "Raiden? Are you home?"

Hiro. Oh, shit. No, no, no. He can't see me like this. He can't. Before I can do anything, there he is, in the bathroom doorway.

Horror seizes Hiro's face. "Oh my god!" He throws

open the glass door and kneels beside me. Water spatters his clothes and soaks his brown hair. The scent of cherry blossoms soothes my frantically beating heart.

"H-hey, Sunshine. I'm fine." I'd be more convincing if my voice weren't shaking.

"What happened?" He snatches up my wet, bloody hands. When he sees my missing finger, he sucks in a shuddery gasp. His eyes begin to glisten. "Fuck, baby."

"I r-ran into some trouble with Namikawa. Takada was there, too."

Horror widens Hiro's wet eyes. "They did this?"

"I did." I didn't mean to say that. "Namikawa made me."

There's a long, icy pause. To my horror, tears fill Hiro's eyes. "As punishment for Takada's men. The ones who attacked me." His lip quivers and his hands start to shake, so he curls them into fists. Tears sparkle like stars in his thick lashes. He looks pretty when he cries, even if I hate it.

"Sunshine, I'm fine."

"Don't." He snarls the word, sounding as fierce as a wolf. "Just *don't*." He turns away, one hand over his eyes. Water drips onto the floor as he steps out of the shower. He takes in a few deep breaths. "Fuck. I'm such an asshole. I'm sorry."

"For what?" I grab a towel and sling it around my waist, then grab an extra one for him and drape it over his shoulders.

"I had no idea." His voice is thick with pain. "I thought... I thought you were just ignoring me, but you were... oh, fuck, Raiden. I'm so sorry. I knew something was off. I knew it, but I didn't do a damn thing."

"There was nothing you could have done. And why would I ignore you? Like hell I'd just let you forget about me so easily." I try to reassure him, to be the positive one for a change. "Why does this bother you so much?"

Hiro whirls around. His face is wet, his eyes red and glossy. There's a mixture of anguish and incredulity there. "What the fuck do you mean? Of course it bothers me! I care about you, you asshole!"

For a moment, I'm too surprised to speak. Hiro... cares. About me? *Me?*

"You do?" For some reason, my voice comes out all soft and hopeful.

Somehow, this feels different from when Ren says she cares or when my grandad says it. I care about Hiro, but I've never stopped to think he might feel the same way about me.

Hiro laughs softly, shaking his head. The sweetest smile lights up his face, and I think, there he is, my sunshine. Then he launches himself at me. His smaller body collides into my chest, arms winding around my shoulders and hauling me against him.

I freeze up instinctively, waiting for pain. After hours of

agony, something as normal as a hug feels completely foreign. As his sweet scent caresses my nose, my guard comes down bit by bit. My arms wind around his shoulders, and I let myself relax into his embrace. I nuzzle my nose into his shoulder and breathe in his scent, rubbing the bridge of my nose over his skin to make him smell like me.

I like that he cares about me. It's different and weird, and I can think of a thousand reasons why he shouldn't, but I'm a selfish bastard, and I'll never let him go. Even if he deserves so much better than me.

"Why is it such a surprise?" Hiro asks against my chest. He slides his warm hands up and down my back and sways us side to side.

I rest my chin atop his head. "Daddy issues."

Hiro snorts. "In a gang, covered in tattoos—I could have guessed."

I plant a kiss against his soft hair.

"Raiden. Of course I care about you."

I close my eyes and try to think if anyone's ever really said that to me. "My parents didn't."

Hiro presses his lips against my exposed collarbone.

I try to stop them, but secrets I've worked so hard to bury are climbing up my throat. "My father was Namikawa's second-in-command. He was a complicated man. A drunk. Hotheaded. Kind, but only when he was sober. He and my mother fought often. She wanted him to leave the gang, but that life was all he knew. Mom thought she could change him, make him go straight." I snort humorlessly. "But she wasn't enough. One day, I caught him in bed with another woman. He made me promise not to tell, but..."

Memories gnaw at me. I'd been so young, too young to understand what it meant when I found them naked in bed together. I'd felt so confused, and yet, there'd been a sickness in my stomach that told me whatever I'd seen was wrong. That if my mom had known, it would hurt her.

"But I told her anyway." The guilt is still as strong as it's ever been. "Cheating is unheard of among werewolves. So many of us mate for life. Mom always thought she and Dad were soulmates, destined for each other."

Hiro traces circles over my shirt. "Werewolves believe in soulmates? Like, love at first sight?"

"Supposedly, when we find the one we're fated for, we know right away. There's a belief that a red string of fate ties us to the one we're meant to be with, so we'll know when the red string appears or when we catch their scent."

Hiro hums thoughtfully. "But your mom and dad weren't fated?"

"Maybe they were, I don't know. Mom thought my dad severed the thread connecting him to my mother, rejected her bond, and pursued this other woman instead. Me, I just stopped believing in all that soulmate stuff after how badly their shitty relationship fucked with my head."

Hiro makes a wounded noise in his throat. "Raiden..."

"Don't pity me."

He sighs. "That's awful you had to go through that."

"It gets worse, just warning you." I wish I had a beer to get through the rest of the story. I don't even have to tell him. I *want* to. This poison has been consuming me for years. The only person I'm comfortable telling all this to is him.

"My dad wanted to run away and build a new life with his girlfriend. So he stole from Namikawa and ran. Left us behind to clean up his damn mess. Namikawa came to collect from my mother. Among yakuza clans, betraying your boss would be a death sentence. But we're werewolves. When a wolf wrongs his alpha, he must repay him, or offer him something dear to him in exchange. Since my father was gone, Namikawa demanded my mother give him something worth more than what my father stole."

Hiro looks up at me, wide-eyed.

"She offered me to him." I close my eyes tight, trying to forget the fear that had taken hold of my heart when such a cold, powerful man had shown up at our door. His men had torn the place apart for valuables, anything that could be applied toward his debt. I'd gone to my mother for comfort from these strangers invading our home, and instead, she'd shoved me at Namikawa's feet.

"Take the boy," she'd said. Like I was nothing.

"Namikawa told me that if I wanted to live, I would serve him for all of my life," I say, voice like stone. "Of course, I accepted."

Hiro shivers against me, fingers rubbing the scars carved into my chest. "Those scars are a pact. Aren't they?"

"They're a curse," I growl. "Binding me to him for all of my damn life. He didn't cut into my skin. He didn't chop off my finger. I did. I did all of it because I can't refuse him." Fury makes my voice thicken.

"You... can't? At all?" Hiro's voice is full of horror.

I shake my head. "If he put a gun in my hand and told me to kill you, or Ren, or anyone, I'd do it. I'd have no choice but to obey him."

"So it's, what? Magic?"

"Yes." Just the idea that Namikawa could turn me against Hiro fills me with revulsion, and I want to push him away. If Namikawa figures out how much I care about him, he'll use it against me. I drop my arms and squirm out of Hiro's hold. "I don't know how to break it. I've contacted every witch in the city, even some overseas. No one knows how to lift the curse." I slam my hands down on the marble-wrapped counter. "I'm going to be Namikawa's pet for the rest of my life!" The anger drains from me, and all I feel is defeat. I slump, face in my hand.

"I'm so sorry," Hiro whispers, and to his credit, he sounds like he means every word. "I wish I could help you."

"You can't. Nobody can."

Hiro presses himself to my back, arms tight around me.

"This is why you don't let yourself think about leaving the gang, isn't it? Because you don't think you can."

He's right, but I can't find the words.

"Raiden, it's okay to hope that things will be different."

I just grunt and let my eyes close as his hands stroke over my chest.

"If you were free, what would you do?"

"There's no point!" I growl at him, trying to kill off the wants and possibilities and hopes rising within me. Hope is dangerous.

"Just imagine Namikawa's gone. There's no one holding you back anymore. You're free. What's the first thing you'd do?"

And because it's just me and him alone in this room, I give voice to the pointless daydreams I've had over the years. "I'd leave the gang and open my own restaurant like the one my grandad used to own." The words flow out of me before I can stop them.

"That sounds great," Hiro murmurs, resting his stubbly cheek against my back.

"You don't think it's stupid?"

He laughs softly. "Definitely not. What else would you do?"

"I'd do whatever I want, be whoever I want."

But all of this is pointless. I'll never have any of these things. And yet, I say, "Would we live together?"

Hiro squeezes me. "Yeah. I'd like that. We could live

somewhere small and cozy."

For the first time in hours, my heart feels light and warm. "Sounds nice. I'd like that. Waking up next to you every day. Eating and cooking together. Walking around the city with you. I..."

I have to stop. I can't fall in love with this future I can never have.

I can't fall in love with him.

Not when I can't offer him a single damn thing.

Chapter 15

Jinta

I wake up with my body nestled against Raiden's. We're both fully clothed, too tired from how hectic yesterday was. I roll over and find myself mesmerized by him as he sleeps, so vulnerable and unguarded.

Last night, when he opened up to me about his childhood, I saw through the scowling mask he wears. I hadn't realized it was a mask at all. Not until I'd told him I cared about him and watched that mask shatter. I saw the hope he guards so closely, the yearning for a normal life, the normal love he never got to experience.

I'd do anything to give him what he needs. I'd spend every day proving how much I care in actions, in words. I want to be the only one to give him everything he ever lacked.

Shit.

I'm falling in love with him. How can I not? Every day with him is an adventure. He's brightened my world and filled it with color. I like the way I feel when I'm with him. I like who I am, like I'm enough, just as I am.

I don't want to believe that he's responsible for the disappearances. There's no motive, and yet, he was last seen with two of the missing people. I know by now that he's capable of violence, but that doesn't mean he's a bad person. He's one of the best men I've ever known.

And yet... I've been wrong before.

If I'm wrong, and let's face it, I probably am, and he is the one kidnapping these people, then I'm going to have to choose between him and the truth. I'm a damn reporter. I've got a story to tell, the story that could make my whole career.

And all I have to do... is betray the man I'm falling for.

Unless maybe Namikawa or Takada are the ones behind the disappearances. Namikawa can control Raiden, but that doesn't mean he's responsible. What would he have to gain by abducting people? Takada, on the other hand, has a motive to make the Namikawa-kai look weak and incapable. People being abducted on their turf would certainly make them look bad. But then what's Takada doing with them if he's abducting them? Ah, this whole case is making my head hurt.

Frantic breath hits the back of my neck. Raiden makes an odd, panicked sound in the back of his throat. Shocked, I turn around and find his face scrunched up. His chest rises and falls fast, and he whimpers again.

"Raiden?" My heart breaks in two. "Hey. Baby, it's okay. I'm right here." I kiss his jaw, then his cheek.

Raiden jolts awake, gasping. Wide brown eyes find mine. He lurches upright and looks around frantically. "W-where did I go? Did I hurt anyone?"

"What are you talking about?"

Shaking his head, Raiden pushes his hair back and slumps back down to the bed. "Nothing. Never mind. Did I disturb you?"

I shake my head and he envelops me in his arms, dropping kisses over my shoulder.

I wish I could savor the warmth of his arms and this rare display of affection. Our relationship has mostly been purely physical, but it's shifting fast into something else. I don't know when it started or how. I've never cared for anyone the way I care for him.

I wish I didn't have to choose between him or my career.

When he tugs down the collar of my tee and drops warm kisses over my bare skin, I know I need to pull away. It isn't right, what I'm doing. If he knows I'm a reporter, using him for my next big story... it would destroy him.

"I, uh..." I squirm out of his arms. "Need to head back to my place."

"Oh." He frowns, clearly disappointed, and I want to jump back into bed with him and never leave. "I'll drive you."

"It's really okay—"

He glowers at me. "I'll drive you." He swings his long legs out of bed and marches to the dresser.

See, Jinta? He's controlling. That's a red flag. Then there's the fact he's a criminal, which is bad. Really bad. We shouldn't be together. I shouldn't feel bad about ending things between us at all! It's for the better. Right?

I follow him out into the sunlit streets. Raiden holds my hand in his the whole way.

To my surprise, Hideyoshi is downstairs. He darts his gaze between us worriedly. "Namikawa told me you had returned! Why didn't you tell me?"

"Sorry," Raiden says, and he hangs his head in remorse. "Last night was... it was a lot."

Hideyoshi's brow furrows in worry. "Are you well?"

"I am."

Some of the tension bleeds from Hideyoshi's shoulders. "Good. I'll drive you."

"You don't have to—"

"Oh, hush and get in the car."

With a fond huff, Raiden climbs into the back seat.

"How are you?" I ask.

"Good, good." Hideyoshi puts a hand on my arm and leads me away from the car. Surprised but curious, I follow him a few paces away. "I must say, it's been a long time since Raiden has let someone so close to him. He has a guarded heart, you know."

I nod, remembering our talk last night. "Because of his parents and what his mom did."

"He told you?" Hideyoshi looks surprised.

"He did. His parents aren't exactly winning parent of the year awards." His dad was a cheater, and his mom sold him to the yakuza to save her skin. I hate the both of them, and I haven't even met them.

Anger wrinkles Hideyoshi's brow. "My son was a fool. He betrayed the woman who loved him and abandoned his own child. And when I thought things could get no worse, his mother sold him into our gang. I begged Namikawa, you know. I begged him not to bring my grandson into this life. This life..." He shakes his head. "I wanted so much more for him."

"Was there any chance you could have taken him and run?" I ask.

"I considered it, but I knew Namikawa would never stand for such a betrayal. He would hunt us down, and I did not want Raiden to grow up living on the run. I've worried about him for many years," Hideyoshi admits, a pained look on his face. "I worried he wouldn't let anyone in to see the best of him. He has a soft heart. Always has. But he's learned that soft hearts are easily broken." A smile casts away the pain on his face. "But he's different with you. He isn't afraid to be open, to let you see that soft heart he's guarded so fiercely all these years." He places a warm hand on my shoulder and squeezes.

I can hardly stand to meet his gaze, shame sour in my throat.

"Thank you for taking good care of my grandson."

Oh, god. He's killing me here… "I care about him. A lot."

"I can see that. Be patient with him. He wants to be loved, Hiro, but he fears it, as well. It will take time for him to truly bare his heart to you, but he will. I can see it, sure as day. So wait for him."

There's a lump in my throat when I croak, "I'm glad he has you."

"As am I. He is precious to me. There isn't anything I wouldn't sacrifice for him." There's a weight to his words, the way he sort of sighs them heavily. I can sense whatever he's sacrificed by raising Raiden; it's been a lot. And yet, I can tell that to Hideyoshi, Raiden is worth it. How can I disagree with that? Hideyoshi guides me back to the car.

"What's on the agenda for you today?" I ask as Hideyoshi drives me to my apartment.

"I've got a few debts to collect," Raiden says.

Worry makes my stomach churn. "Be careful."

Raiden smirks. "I will. It's easy work. My debtors usually pay right on time. I never have trouble."

"Call me when you're done with your tasks. We can have

dinner."

"Sounds good." He runs his hand along my thigh but doesn't tease me. He touches me without the expectation of anything more. Like he just enjoys having his hands on me. "Want to meet at the Lotus?"

"Sure."

I'm disappointed when he stops the car outside my apartment. "Have a good day," Hideyoshi says.

Before I can get out, Raiden grabs my wrist and tugs me close. I lean over and kiss him. It's slow and sweet, and I never want it to stop, especially not when he tugs on my hair and slips me just a bit of tongue to get my blood heating.

Raiden whispers, "Come over to my place tonight. I'll fuck you just the way you like."

I bite his bottom lip so I don't moan. "I can't wait."

He grins. "Later, Sunshine."

I leave the car on wobbly legs, wondering how I'll focus for the day when all I can think about is Raiden's hands on me, his taste, his seductive promises.

The minute I'm upstairs, I open up my laptop and continue my investigation into Yuki Katagiri. It takes some scrolling, but I eventually find the *Facebook* page of a woman who seems old enough to be Yuki. She isn't very active online, but I find a photo of her taken in January during a birthday celebration. She's 105 years old this year. Wow. She sits in a wheelchair, and beside her, one arm around the chair, is a pretty young woman. Young enough to be a granddaughter. A quick search through her friends list, and I find the woman in the birthday picture.

Ami Omeda. And I was right. She's the granddaughter. I open up her inbox and type a message, explaining that I'm investigating the disappearances and that I'd like to hear her grandmother's story. I hope she'll get back to me soon.

My phone buzzes. I snatch it up, but my smile falls right off my face.

It's not Raiden.

It's my dad. Fuck. I completely forgot my family was flying in this week for Katsuki's birthday.

Dad: *Your mother wants to know if you are coming to Katsuki's birthday dinner on Thursday.*

Right. Mom wants to know. Dear old Dad couldn't care less if he sees me or not. She always was trying to make us get along, but she never shielded me from his callous disapproval. She never stood up to him… then again, neither did I.

I reread the short text. Should I respond? What do I say?

My phone buzzes before I've made up my mind. Damn it! I *hate* it when people answer a text with a call.

"Hello?" I ask, voice clipped.

"Jinta. How are you?" My father's voice is cold and

clinical, even after five years apart. Clearly, absence did not make the heart grow fonder, as my father would actually have to have a heart for that saying to have any ounce of truth. "Did you get my text?"

"I did. You didn't have to call me." I lean on the sink and try to make myself be nice. "I actually need to go to work soon."

"Oh, yes. *Work*." He practically sneers the word. My blood pressure starts to rise. "Are you too busy to spare some time for the people who raised you?"

Surprisingly, I do want to see my parents. I want to see them so I can rub my success in their faces. Maybe I'm not where I really want to be in my career, but I moved to Tokyo all by myself, and I'm surviving all on my own. I bet they want me to beg for their forgiveness, to see me suffering without them.

If that's the case, they'll be disappointed.

"I'll be there. I promise."

He grunts noncommittally and hangs up.

This is going to be a bad idea. Nothing good ever happens when my family and I are in a room together.

By the time I get off work, the sun is starting to go down. As I walk toward the subway through the park, I check my messages and freeze in my tracks. I've got a DM from Yuki's granddaughter, Ami. She wants to meet so we can talk about her grandmother's experience. This is perfect.

> **Ami**: *Yuki is feeling better than usual today, so this evening would work.*

> **Me**: *Wonderful! On my way! :)*

After a quick detour to my favorite bakery around the corner from my job, I run to catch the train and ride the Chiyoda line to Yoyogi-Kōen Station in Shibuya. Ami's grandmother is a resident of an assisted living home. When I arrive, I take the elevator up and search the halls until I find the door with Yuki's name on it.

Ami answers when I knock. "Come in, come in! Grandma, he's here."

Yuki's room is small but cozy. There are paintings on the walls and framed photos of Ami, as well as a handsome elderly man I assume was Yuki's husband. On the faded yellow sofa sits a woman with thinning silver hair and thin hands gripping onto a cup of tea. Her eyes are cloudy and unfocused when she glances in our direction.

Bowing, I say, "Thank you for having me. I brought these cookies for you. I hope you like them."

"Thank you, dear. How sweet."

"Would you like tea, Onodera?" Ami asks from the little kitchen, separated from the living room by an island counter.

"Yes, please."

Once Ami has brought tea and plated up the cookies, we gather around. I sit in an armchair beside Ami while Yuki remains on the sofa. Ami puts the plate in her grandmother's hand. Yuki runs her fingers over the plate, then finds the cookie and takes a bite.

"These are delicious," Yuki says.

"I'm glad you like them. They're my favorite." I take a bite myself, enjoying the bitter matcha flavor combined with the subtle sweetness of the cookie.

"You're a... reporter?"

"Yes, with the Jiji Shimbun. I'm investigating the disappearances for a story."

Yuki's almost-translucent brows furrow. "Disappearances?"

"People have been going missing since January. They are very similar to the abduction you experienced. I'm worried there's a copycat, taking inspiration from what happened back in 1924."

Hand shaking, Yuki drops her cookie onto her plate. "O-oh dear..."

"I know it may be difficult, but anything you can share with me about your disappearance is greatly appreciated."

Ami touches her grandmother's hand. "It's okay, Grandma."

Taking in a slow breath, Yuki is quiet for a moment.

Finally, she nods. "Very well."

Heart skipping, I take out my notepad and pen.

"This was all so long ago. I was just a little girl, but I remember as if it were yesterday," Yuki begins hesitantly. "I had a high fever one night, so my mother took me to the hospital. It was late by the time we left, and my mother carried me home. A car pulled up, and a young man called out, offering to drive us home. My mother declined his offer. These brutes stormed from the car and grabbed my mother. They forced us into the car and took off. I was too sick to stay awake and passed out."

What Yuki describes next is the scene from a nightmare.

When she wakes up, she's being carried in the arms of her abductors. They're in the woods, walking beneath tori gates. It's pitch-black except for the full moon above. Tears slide down her cheeks. Her heart won't stop racing. She's scared. So scared. Her mother calls out, telling her everything will be okay. She wants to go home. Her mother begs them to let her go, saying her husband will worry for her, but the man laughs and tells her, "I'm sorry, dear, but you will never see your husband again."

She begins to weep, struggling in vain against the cage of her captor's arms. A shrine looms ahead with incense smoke thick in the air. At first, she thinks it is a shrine of Inari, the god of harvest and agriculture. Stone statues of foxes stand guard over the shrine, teeth bared. Something dark red is smeared upon the statues. Then she sees talismans swaying in the wind from where they hang on the shrine's eaves. The prayers ask for power, for the blood of their enemies, for death.

Frightened whimpers fill the night. Chains rattle. There are people in these woods. So many people. Their dirty faces are pale with fear or streaked with tears. She's dropped into the dirt, and pain splits her skull as she strikes her head on a rock. A low growl rumbles like thunder, and she can barely silence her scream as a wolf bares its fangs at her. There are more of them, huge wolves as big as horses, that roam among the prisoners. She wants to run, but she's too afraid she'll be bitten. She knows it's not a normal wolf. It can't be. It bares its fangs in a smile as she whimpers, like her fear thrills it. The wolves surround her and the other prisoners, keeping them from running away.

The man lifts a heavy-looking stone from the altar and holds it up high, then throws it to the ground. The stone shatters into two halves. "The time has come," he announces, voice ringing through the woods. "Prepare the sacrifices."

A scream splits the air as wolves pounce upon her mother. They grab her by her flailing ankles and drag her toward the corrupt shrine until she lies before it.

The man pulls a knife from behind his back and slashes her throat. Yuki's scream echoes in the night as her mother's blood gushes down her front. She collapses on her side, a river of crimson flowing from her neck.

"Bring them!" he bellows. "Now! Hurry!"

All Yuki can do is cover her eyes and sob as the people around her scream, as blood gurgles from wounds, as bodies hit the dirt. The wind kicks up, howling through the trees. The moon's bloody glow gets brighter, staining the forest crimson.

The man howls laughter. The wolves sing, and it almost sounds like a song of triumph. His laughter becomes shrill, almost like the cackling of a fox. His body changes as he shifts to something inhuman. The guard holding Yuki is distracted, in awe of what's happening. His grip on her arm is loose. The time is now. She stamps on his foot as hard as she can, and when he screams, his grip slackens. Yuki runs, and she doesn't look back.

She was lost in the woods for days until hikers found her and helped her finally get home.

I don't realize I've been holding my breath as Yuki tells her story. I suck in a gulp of air, hands in fists in my lap. At some point, I stopped taking notes, too spellbound by

Yuki's story.

"What were they summoning?" I croak.

"A kitsune." A fox spirit. Those exist, too? "But not just any kitsune, dear. Do you know the legend of Tamano-no-Mae?"

"I think so."

She smiles, clearly excited to tell this story. "During the Muromachi Era, it is written that an evil lord plotted to kill Emperor Toba. He hired a woman to seduce the emperor and assassinate him. Her beauty and intelligence enraptured the emperor, and she became his courtesan. But slowly, the emperor became gravely ill. He aged rapidly, and no one could understand why. When an astrologer arrived to treat the emperor's ailing condition, he discovered the courtesan's secret. She was a nine-tailed kitsune. Her identity revealed, she fled the emperor's court. The great warriors Kazusa-no-suke and Miura-no-suke hunted her down, but while they slew her body, Tamano-no-Mae's spirit endured. It was believed that her spirit embedded itself in the Sessho-seki—the Killing Stone." A grim expression twists her mouth. "However, the stone was stolen many years ago. Not long before I was abducted, in fact."

Understanding makes my mouth run dry. "So if her spirit was contained within the stone... then when your abductor broke it—"

She nods sullenly. "He released her spirit and allowed her to possess him."

Ami's eyes are wide, cheeks bright red. "I... I'm sorry, Onodera. Grandma, that's not what happened."

"It is!" Yuki snaps.

Laughing with embarrassment, Ami suddenly springs up. "I think it's time that you left, Onodera. I'm so sorry for wasting your time." She all but walks me out the door. Before the door closes, she says, "Grandma! I told you to tell him what you told the papers! He's going to think you're crazy!"

For several seconds, I'm frozen in the hallway. My mind won't stop spinning.

A kitsune.

If I didn't know about the existence of werewolves, I wouldn't have believed this story for a second. I've heard about kitsune from folktales. They're fox spirits who sometimes possess humans, usually women just like Tamano-no-Mae. But according to Yuki's story, kitsune are real, and they're nothing like the folktales. They're worse.

Is there a kitsune among the Namikawa-kai or the Taka-da-kai?

I wanted a big story, well I've got one.

I don't know if I can do this... but I'm going to give it my all.

CHAPTER 16

Raiden

Just as I was telling Hiro about how boring my job is, the universe decides to flip me the middle finger and make my day a pain in the ass.

I had a little fun crashing a shareholder's meeting and humiliating the guy with blackmail about his affair until he paid to get me to leave.

By 5 PM, I'm ready to just say fuck it and go home, but I have one more job to do. I hope it will be easy, but based on my experience at Suzuki's damned arcade, I know I'm in for a headache. In all the chaos of the police raids, nobody ever collected what Suzuki owes. Surely by now, the bastard must have it.

As if today hasn't been annoying enough. All I'm looking forward to is seeing Hiro. I can't wait for us to have dinner tonight at the Lotus. I need to see him, have him beneath me, feel his arms around me, taste his lips.

He's like a drug, and I just keep wanting more.

I pull up outside the arcade and crack my knuckles. Let this be easy, unlike last time. Suzuki better have the money...

The car door slams behind me. I straighten my suit and enter the arcade. Kids scream and cheer as they play. Arcade machines fill the space with their racket. I catch the eye of a staff member. When she sees me, fear freezes her face.

"Hey, sweetheart." I smile coldly. "Is Suzuki in?"

Mutely, she shakes her head.

"No?" I rotate my neck so the muscles pop. "Any idea where he might be? He's behind on what he owes us again, and if he can't pay, Namikawa can't afford to keep protecting this business, you understand? Something awful could happen. Like... a fire. You'd be out of a job."

She wets her lips and whispers something.

"What was that?" I cock my head.

"H-he went to the convenience store. He'll be back any moment. Please have a seat."

"Thank you." I sit on a chair nearby and check the time. Did the asshole forget I was coming? I wait, tapping my feet. The staff eyes me like I'm a shark and there's blood in the water.

The flaps over the door sway as Suzuki walks in, plastic bag in hand. "Momo is running late. Do you mind staying an hour longer?"

I'm on my feet. Suzuki jumps so bad, he drops his dinner. A couple of onigiri tumble out of his bag.

"Yo. Time to pay the piper."

All the blood drains from his face. "S-shit. Is today collection day? I... I forgot!"

"Really? That's what you told me a couple weeks back, too. You know what I smell?" I make a show of inhaling. The smell of his fear makes my fangs sharpen. "A liar."

Suzuki takes a stumbling step back. "Please. Just wait. Okay? I'll get it for you next week!"

"Time's up!" I snap, making him jump. "Pay up now, or you won't like what Namikawa does."

Suzuki's simpering air abruptly vanishes. He sneers and crosses his arms. "And why the hell should I?"

What the hell? When did this guy grow a pair? "What did you say?" I growl.

"The whole neighborhood heard about how you let Saito Takada murder Aida. Then Takada-kai thugs trashed up Tenko's izakaya. Namikawa is supposed to protect our shops from criminals and rival gangs. Sounds to me like you boys have lost your edge. So, no. I'm not paying. Now get your ass out of my store, wolf!"

"Make me," I bite out the words.

Suzuki's eyes widen at the threat. As a woman walks by

with her kid, he suddenly shoves her, hard. She shrieks, and I lunge to catch her before she hits her head. In that brief amount of time, Suzuki has disappeared through the doors outside.

"Fuck me," I mutter, then dash after him.

Outside, the door to Suzuki's car slams, and the engine starts up. He slams on the gas and steers violently out of his parking space, scratching a parked car. Leaping in my vehicle, I floor it and pursue him. Well, at least my day got more interesting.

For a damn hour, I pursue this guy. He clearly has a destination in mind, leading me on a chase all the way down to the waterfront in Minato.

What the hell is he playing at? My instincts tell me to contact Hideyoshi, to request backup, but I bristle at the thought. I can handle this on my own.

Suzuki swerves into the lot of a warehouse and bolts from the car, tearing around the side of the building. Something's off about this. I slam on the brakes and run after him. "Suzuki!" I yell, arms pumping as I run. My prey drive kicks in, the transformation pulling at me.

Hunt. Bite. Kill!

"Stop running! Last warning!" If he doesn't stop running, I'll rip him to pieces, and then Namikawa will be pissed.

It's too late. My claws sharpen, fangs cutting my lip. The wind howls in my ears as I pounce. In seconds, Suzuki is beneath me, kicking, thrashing. Something flies through the air and explodes into the concrete next to us. A bullet. Cursing, I roll off Suzuki just as another shot hits the ground where we were lying.

"Kill him!" Suzuki hollers as he shoves past me and runs. The little shit.

Around the corner of the warehouse, someone pokes their head out from behind cover, metal gleaming in the sunlight. My preternatural instincts kick in, and I'm able to dodge a bullet just as it comes flying at me.

The shot finds its mark right in Suzuki's back rather than my chest. He flops to the ground, twitching as his blood pools beneath him. The shot was fatal.

Someone... claps? I look up, startled to see a woman wearing the furs of a wolf. She marches toward me, pistol aimed right at my head. Four others appear, armed and decked out in wolf furs.

Fuck. Hunters. There aren't a lot of them in Tokyo, and they aren't usually brazen enough to fuck with the Namikawa-kai. I don't recognize the lapel with their clan's crest pinned to their outfits.

They must be new to town. I guess I know where the money I loaned Suzuki went to, plus probably whatever else he squirreled away. He must have paid them an arm and a leg to kill me.

The woman tugs her hood down, ruby-red lips quirking into a sly grin. "The Wolf of Asakusa. It's a pleasure." She gives a mock bow. Her hunters keep their guns trained on me. "I must say, I'm excited! We've been itching to kill Namikawa's famous Wolf for months now!"

I take a step back, never taking my eyes off them. My heart beats faster. I should have listened to my instincts and called in backup. "How many in our racket have you paid to turn on us?"

She grins, twirling her pistol. "Just Suzuki. For now. We heard you'd had trouble with the law lately, that you've gotten the people you're supposed to protect killed. It's not a good look, unfortunately. The good people of Tokyo deserve to know the truth about the monsters they owe money to. Soon, they'll all turn against you, and Namikawa's empire will crumble. It will be a great honor to kill such a legend of Tokyo! Boys, aim!"

I'm not dying. Not here. I can't. Bullets burst from their chambers one by one.

Burning pain explodes throughout my arm just as I dive behind the cover of a shipping crate. I'm completely pinned down. The burning in my arm gets worse, like fire in my veins. The wound isn't healing. As the pain gets worse, I have to gnash my teeth. It's like my arm is fucking on fire. Something's wrong.

Fuck. The bullet was silver. No. It's worse than that, I realize as cold sweat breaks out across my body. Every inch of me is freezing cold except for the damn bullet, burning under my skin.

Aconite. I've been poisoned.

Panic claws at me. I haven't been scared, not in a long time, but fuck, I'm scared now.

I could die. This could fucking kill me. I've got to go. I can't die, not here like prey.

There's no other choice but to run. I can't shift, not at all. The world around me sways and blurs as I run, moving fast for a human but painfully slow for a paranormal creature. I maneuver my way through a sea of shipping crates and lose the hunters behind me as I book it back to my car.

Just as I leap inside my vehicle, bullets dent the metal and crack the glass. Gasping, covered in cold sweat, I slam on the gas and hurtle from the shipping yard.

I've got to get the damn bullet out. Fast. A hospital is out of the question. My pack is too far away.

What do I do?

I rip down my sleeve, revealing the bullet hole oozing blood from my forearm, veins blackening around the site of the injury. That looks bad.

Bile rises in my throat.

My hands shake on the wheel. I don't want to die. I can't. Not yet. I'm not ready. For years, I've wasted my life serving Namikawa. I've done horrible things to people who deserved better. I've been a bad person. Even though I always knew I'd die a yakuza, it's not what I wanted.

What do I do?

Who can help me?

Can anyone? Is there even time? I don't know how much longer I have, but the blackness spreading through my veins up my arm and toward my heart gives me some clue.

The light flashes red, and I'm forced to halt in traffic, gasping through the throbbing pain in my arm. Each throb makes my eyes sting and water, and my stomach is churning like I'm going to be sick.

I'm dying. I'm going to die.

And really, what does that matter? The world will be a better place without me. The Wolf of Asakusa caused nothing but pain to all who knew and feared him and lived his life in servitude to a man he despised. What does it matter if I die?

The realization threatens to drag me down to the depths of despair.

And absurdly, all I can think about... is Hiro.

Damn it. I was looking forward to seeing him.

I want to see him again. I have to.

There's a light in the darkness around me, and I fight to keep my eyes open, fight not to pass out and die in the front seat of my own car. Not before I've held him one last time.

I'm dying, and Hiro is the only person on my mind. Not my grandfather. Not my best friend. Hiro.

As my life's blood flows down my arm, I realize that I've wasted so much time lying to myself.

No more.

If this is my last hour alive on this earth, then I want to spend it with him.

I step on the gas and drive toward where my heart is telling me to go.

To Hiro.

To my mate.

CHAPTER 17

Jinta

I've just gotten out of the train when my phone vibrates in my bag. It's Raiden. After the day I've had, I'm craving his company, even if it's just the sound of his voice.

"Hey, Raiden. What's up?"

"H-hey, Sunshine."

Immediately, I know something is wrong. His voice, usually so cocky and sexy, is weak and strained. Like he's in pain. "Raiden? What's wrong? Are you okay?"

"'M in a bad way. Not gonna lie."

My hands start to shake. I've never heard so much pain in his voice before. "Are you hurt?"

He grunts. "Y-yeah. It's... it's not looking good. Got shot."

Sour acid burns my throat. "Then go to a hospital!"

"No," he snaps. "Might as well walk into a p-police station."

"Call someone who can fix you up!"

"Too far away. Just need... to get the bullet out. Need somewhere safe to do it." He groans, and the sound cleaves right through my chest.

Listening to him hurting feels like I'm dying, too. Is he dying? Will he be okay? Hasn't he been hurt enough by life, by his shitty family?

"Where are you? Tell me. I'm coming to get you."

It occurs to me he might be in the middle of a fight or something gangster related, a situation where I'd be of no use whatsoever. I don't care. I'm ready to run into a damn war zone for him.

"C-can I crash at your place?"

"Yes. Yeah. Anything. But are you okay? Can you drive?"

"Yeah. Almost there. C-can see your place."

Fuck. Shit. Fuck. My heart's beating out of control, trying to escape out of my chest. "I'm coming. Okay? I'll be there in fifteen minutes. Don't hang up. Stay on the line."

"'Kay..."

I'm already running. It's started raining. I don't know what's pounding harder, my heart or my feet on the pavement.

"Raiden? Still there? I'll be there soon." Not soon enough. Every second feels like a minute. "Raiden? Come on, talk to me, say something."

"Mmm," he grunts, panting through the pain. "S-scared." He laughs weakly. "Don't wanna die, Sunshine."

He's *scared*. The strongest, most intimidating man I know, a goddamn werewolf... is scared. My heart's about to break.

"You're not going to die, baby. I promise!" I pant as I run. "I'm coming to get you. I'll be there soon! Keep talking. I'm on my way."

Please. Let him be okay. I can't lose him.

I round the corner so fast, I almost crash into a couple walking arm in arm. There's no time to apologize as I pelt past them. A familiar *Mercedes* is parked outside my apartment building. And there, lying crumpled in my doorway is—

"Raiden!"

He's not moving. God. Is he dead? Please, no.

I kneel on the wet pavement and grab his soaking-wet suit. I haul him upright. His face is ghost-white, and his lips are an unhealthy purple color. When he opens his eyes, I breathe a sigh of relief until I see how unfocused they are.

"Raiden? Hey! It's me." I frame his damp, cold face in my hands, wiping away the rain.

"Sorry... about this. D-didn't know where else to go."

I kiss him, curling my hand in his hair. "That's fine. Hey, you know you can trust me. Right?"

Raiden closes his eyes, chin slumping to his chest.

"Get up. Come on, let's get you inside." I drape his arm over my shoulder, and on the count of three, I stand.

Once we're upstairs, I unlock the door and heave us both through the threshold. My brain is buzzing, chest tight with panic, hands shaking. What do I do? I can't call an ambulance. The police will want to know what happened, and Raiden could get in trouble.

"What can I do?" I escort him to the couch. "Is there someone I can call?" Once he's sitting on the sofa, I take his hand. "Raiden? Hey!" He's on the verge of passing out. And that's when I see it, a black hole in his forearm. His sleeve has been ripped off, bearing the grisly injury. Black veins crawl up toward his shoulder.

"R-Raiden?" I whimper and clear my throat. "Uh. That doesn't look good."

"S'not. Aconite."

"Wolfsbane? Isn't that deadly to werewolves?"

He nods stiffly.

Oh, no. I rock back on my ankles, heart racing out of control.

"What do I do?"

"Gotta get the b-bullet outta me," he croaks. "Or I'm dead."

"Sh-shouldn't a professional do this?"

"No time." He shakes his head. "Gotta be you. Once the bullet... is out... my body will do the rest."

"Way to put that on me!" I throw up my arms and pace. Shakes rack my body. There's no time to panic. I've got a werewolf to save. Shoving my panic aside, I race into the bathroom and tear the room apart until I find what I need. Bandages. Antiseptic. Pliers. Fuck me, man...

There's a crash. In the living room, Raiden has fallen face down. My legs turn to jelly, and I collapse at his side and roll him over. "Raiden? Raiden! Don't you dare fucking die on me! I'm not going to therapy because of you! You hear? Wake up!" Tears sting my eyes. I slap him. Hard.

He jolts, snarling up at me, but it lacks glowing eyes and fangs.

I'm not a doctor. I have no idea what I'm doing. I hope his healing will make up for any mistakes I make.

I pull on some gloves and rest my fingers near the angry wound oozing red and something nasty and inky-black. Raiden's chest rises fast. I grab his hand and squeeze. "This is gonna hurt."

"S'okay," he croaks. "I don't mind if it's you."

My heart squeezes. "Do you trust me?"

He holds my gaze, eyes bright with pain and fear. Raiden nods. "Y-yeah. I do."

I kiss his cold fingers and swallow the lump in my throat. "Remember that before you take my head off, okay?"

Here goes nothing...

CHAPTER 18

Raiden

I trust Hiro.

Even as excruciating pain tears through me and I writhe and claw at the ground with blunt nails, and I grab the back of his jacket and clutch on for dear life. Tears burn my eyes, and I gnash my teeth against the agony.

"I know. I know. I'm so sorry," Hiro says again and again as he hurts me.

I wish I could tell him it's okay, but the pain whites everything out.

I can count the people I trust on one hand. People I've known all my life who earned their spot there. I've known Hiro for such a short time, but I trust him completely.

My life's in his hands, and I'm fine with that. I mean, if

I died, I'd feel bad traumatizing him like that, but I have hope that I'll make it out the other side of this. If I have to die, it's okay, as long as I'm with him. I'm where I'm meant to be.

With my mate. Hiro's my mate.

Why is it only now I'm admitting it to myself?

My mom, she thought Dad was her mate. He thought she was his. Always said they were destined to meet. He even had a lucky coin in his pocket the day they met. The five-yen coin he gave my mom, who gave it to me.

Destiny. I stopped believing in such bullshit when I was a kid. Fate, destined mates, all that nonsense... it wasn't real. If it was, my father never would have cheated. My family would have been happy for all of our lives. Mom wouldn't have left me behind and given me to Namikawa.

So why... why am I only just now starting to believe in fate? How is it that one man can come along and bust through every wall I've ever built around my heart? I forgot I even had a heart until it started beating for him.

I'm drifting away, leaving my body and all earthly cares behind. Nothing exists except the slow, hard pump of my heart, the space widening between each beat. The pain disappears. Darkness comes for me.

I haven't done any good my whole life. I've been a bad man. I've hurt people. Wasted my life serving Namikawa. There was a lot I wanted to do. Things I once dreamed of that now seem impossible the older and more jaded I become.

I've wanted a normal life for so long, but I've accepted I'll never have it. It's fine. I don't deserve normalcy. Or love. I'm unlovable. A bad person. Dying is about as much as I deserve.

"Raiden?" A distant voice calls to me.

There's a little spark, then. A ray of sunlight in the dark.

"Raiden? Open your eyes. Please. Please don't leave me."

I think if I did one thing right, it was taking a chance on a smile like sunshine and a scent like cherry blossoms in the springtime.

"Raiden? Please. Come back to me."

He's crying. Haven't I hurt enough people? Didn't even bat an eye after a while. Compartmentalized all of it and locked it away. Sometimes, when I'm feeling really low, I'll open that box and drown in all of it.

But I don't want to hurt him. Never Hiro.

So I fight. I kick and claw my way toward that light, toward the smell of cherry blossoms and spring. A bond burns to life in my chest, and I grab on like a lifeline. My body comes alive. My healing kick-starts, driving out the poison coursing through me.

I... I'm coming, Hiro.

Wait for me. I'm almost here. Don't cry. I'm coming. I promise, I...

I open my eyes, gasping in a lungful of air.

Brown eyes, dewy with tears. Damp, pale cheeks. Sweaty, raven locks sticking to his forehead. Most beautiful damn man I've ever seen.

A gentle red light shines on Hiro's face. "R-Raiden? What is that?"

I follow his wet-eyed stare. For the first time, I can see the red thread wrapped around my pinky finger. I follow the thread's twisting path up to Hiro's hand. The thread's wrapped around him, too.

We're connected, bound together by destiny itself. I can no longer deny what he is to me—and I don't want to. In fact, I think finally accepting it is what gave me the strength to live.

"It's... complicated," I mutter, grimacing as the wound starts to close.

"I... I did it!" Hiro holds out the source of all my agony—a silver bullet covered in blood. Such a tiny thing, but it nearly stole me from this world. "Look, Raiden! Look, your wound just closed, and that yucky black stuff is all gone." He grins in triumph. It's the cutest thing I've ever seen.

"Knew you wouldn't let me die." I realize my head is lying in his lap. He makes a comfy pillow.

"Well, at least someone believed in me. Geez. I was freaking out! You can't do that to me again!"

I chuckle and squeeze his hand. "Not like I meant to get shot, you know—"

And then he's kissing me, his lips warm and soft and sweet. He breathes life back into me, and finally, I let myself relax. I lean into the touch of his hands, soft on either side of my face. I'm alive. We're together. Relief surges through me, and I find the strength to sit up and curl my fingers through his hair.

Even though I'm exhausted, my cock kicks to life and tightens my jeans. Turns out surviving certain death and being saved by my mate is one hell of a turn-on. "Need you," I growl against his lips.

"Don't want to hurt you," Hiro says, panting breathlessly from the relentless kisses I shower to his lips.

Slowly, I sit up and straddle his lap. "You won't. I'm healed." I rock against him and find him hard and wanting. I growl my approval when he moans.

"Are you sure?" He yelps when I suddenly flip us so he's on his back on the floor beneath me.

"Need you, Sunshine. Thought I'd never get the chance to do this again. Have you beneath me. Hear you moan my name." I shove my thigh between his legs and rub against him, making him squirm.

"I... I thought you were—" Hiro's voice breaks, and tears brighten his eyes.

"I'm here." I lunge down to kiss him, grab his hand, and press it to my chest. "Here. Right here. Not going anywhere."

Hiro fists my shirt and hauls me in even closer. Our lips

crash together. Tongues tangle, teeth scrape, and I try to pull away so I don't cut him with my fangs, but he makes a needy little sound and holds me tighter.

We rock together, too desperate to get out of our clothes. I could finish this way, grinding on him, locked at the lips, hands roaming and squeezing. But I won't fuck my mate on the floor like some careless hookup.

Of all the people I've been with, no one has ever meant more to me than him. Somehow, he's become someone so precious to me. My sunshine in a world so dark and cold. A port in the stormy uncertainty of my life.

"Wanna be inside you. Now," I say, panting against his lips.

"Take me to bed," he whispers, and those are the sexiest words I've ever heard.

I grab the back of his thighs and lift. His arms and legs twine around me. Carefully, I carry us to the bed. I don't change our position, keeping him in my lap where I want him. Tonight, I need him close.

Hiro loops his arms around my neck as his lips collide with mine. I wriggle out of my suit jacket, and Hiro helps me with my buttons. I growl at him, and he gets the idea, ripping the whole damn thing open. Buttons scatter everywhere. Hiro picks a few off of me, laughing against my mouth.

When Hiro yanks down my pants, I lift my hips until my pants are down to my knees. Hiro strips so fast it has to be a world record.

Fuck, he's the most beautiful thing I've ever seen. His skin is so fair, cute nipples, pink and hard. I suck on them, flicking them with my tongue, nipping until he gasps. I reach down and grab handfuls of his perfect ass, squeezing.

"So beautiful. You know that?" I lick a strip from his clavicle to his throat, enjoying the way his voice box vibrates with a moan. "Anyone ever tell you how damn perfect you are?"

He laughs above me, but it's derisive. There's a pained look in his eyes. "Raiden, I hate to be a downer, but I've never been good enough. Not for anyone."

I yank on his chin to make him look at me. "You're fucking perfect."

A choked little noise escapes Hiro.

"You are. Fuck anyone who doesn't see that." All I wanted when I thought I was going to leave this world was to cook katsudon with him, watch his favorite movies, and show him all the hidden corners of Tokyo that I love. I've never wanted to live so much until I met him.

So I'm going to show him just how perfect he is to me.

Hiro yanks open the drawer and grabs the lube. I take it from him and coat my fingers. Reaching back, Hiro spreads himself open for me, groaning softly when I find his entrance.

I circle him, caress him until he whimpers, then push in. He grips my hand, and I moan my approval as he guides my fingers inside. He rocks on them, lip between his teeth, eyes closing as I stretch him and play with his sensitive rim.

He pants against my lips, grabs our cocks, and strokes us both while I curl my fingers inside his blissful heat. We groan together, lips meeting and tongues stroking. The sweet scent of cherry blossoms wraps around me, and the warmth of his slender but powerful body blankets me.

I've never felt safer than when I'm with him. Emotion squeezes at my chest, and I kiss each of his eyelids, his forehead, even the tip of his nose. He sighs sweetly, and I claim that sound for myself with a kiss.

My body aches to fuck him, but I'm determined to take things slow. I'm going to savor every kiss, every sound he makes, commit it all to memory so I never take him for granted again.

"Raiden." Hiro says my name with such reverence. I want to do all I can to be worthy of his devotion. "Need you."

"I know," I whisper, because I do. I need him in every way it's possible to need someone, need him in ways I never expected.

I withdraw my fingers and grasp myself. I look into his eyes as I push in, and I'm rewarded with the beautiful sight of his head falling back, eyes closing, and lips parting. I let myself bask in the realization that, for once, I'm the cause of someone's pleasure rather than their pain. He makes me want to be a better man, someone who deserves him and who can give him all he needs.

Arms sliding around my neck, Hiro touches his forehead to mine, breath coming short and fast. We give ourselves a moment to breathe. Our breath mingles. His body clenches around me where we're joined. His nails scratch gently at the nape of my neck. He's so beautiful and all mine.

I move, pushing into him deeper. He gasps, breath hot on my mouth. Hiro's thighs flex as he moves with me. When I rise, he falls, and we create something all our own.

There's nothing hurried to the way we move together. I want to stay inside him, drown in him, and never come up for air. Cradled in his body, there's no pain. I'm safe. I'm loved. I'm home.

He strokes my hair like I'm something precious. The way he touches me defies everything I ever thought about myself. I'm vulnerable, fragile, yet so fucking strong all at once. Nothing can hurt me, not in this place. This is ours, all ours, and nothing can touch us.

I move faster, urgently, sighs and moans and the slap of skin on skin are the only sounds in the room. Grabbing his hips, I hold on tight and move him with me. I can't look away from his face, mesmerized as he throws his head back and cries out. I can be better for him.

If I can make him happy, make him feel good, then maybe there's hope for me after all. Maybe I can be different. Better.

I kiss my way up his throat and capture his mouth, muffling our moans with sweeps of my tongue as we move faster, harder. I reach between us and stroke him, and he rewards me with a hoarse cry. He clutches me to his body, holding me to him with desperation.

"So beautiful for me," I whisper into his ear. "Come on. Give me what I want, Sunshine. That's it. Let go for me."

"Raiden," Hiro whimpers, moving up and down faster, "Fuck. Yes."

The scent of his hot cum hitting my chest and stomach undoes me.

"So good. That's it. Like that. So fucking good for me." I pound into his clenching heat and fall into oblivion. I hold him to me, burying my face in his neck as I gasp and shiver.

I want to stay inside him forever. Breathlessly, we gaze at each other. I wonder if I look as wonder-struck as he does as I guide him down for a kiss, soft and slow in the wake of our urgency.

I'm gone. So far fucking gone for this sweet, broken man who deserves so much better than me.

"Never letting you go," I whisper against his lips. I grip the nape of his neck and meet his gaze. "Hear me, Sunshine? The only way either of us are walking away from this is if I die or you do. No one else can have you like this. You're mine."

Hiro grips my face between his hands. "Yours," he whispers, and there's no hesitation.

I'm in this. For however long this lasts, I'm in this with him.

After a time, Hiro rolls off me and lies in bed. I get up long enough to grab a washcloth then return to him. We catch our breath as I sweep the damp cloth over his chest and stomach, then down between his thighs. He shivers, and I kiss his swollen lips.

"Is this a red string of fate?" Hiro asks, lifting up his hand. The thread glows around his pinky. "I thought these only existed in stories." He exhales. "There should really be a class for this kind of stuff. Introduction to Paranormal Society one-oh-one, or something." Smiling sweetly, he brushes his knuckles over my cheek. "So... we were destined to meet, huh?"

"Guess so."

He frowns. "You don't sound happy about it."

It's more complicated than that, but I don't know how to tell him.

"This is all so... different for me. I stopped believing in fate after my parents split, and my mom gave me this." I fiddle with the five-yen coin around my neck.

"Do you know why she gave it to you?"

"I can only guess."

"It's five-yen. Maybe she meant it as a blessing?" Hiro touches the coin, smoothing his thumb over the design on it.

Five-yen coins are considered lucky by some people.

I exhale, suddenly nervous for reasons I'm not sure of. "My father... he gave this to my mother as a gift. The day he told her he loved her."

I can't even picture it. My father, smiling instead of drunk and angry, opening his heart to a woman he loved. My mother, accepting those feelings. So happy in that moment, only for it all to go to hell a few years later. I have to force myself to breathe. I'm not my father. Hiro won't hurt me the way my parents hurt each other. I'm not sure I completely believe that, but it's a chance I'm willing to take.

"My mother told me he gave it to her because he had a five-yen in his wallet the day he met her. The day she left, she gave it to me. I never really knew why, but I think she wanted me to have a fortunate life. Despite everything."

I clear my throat as my voice wavers, and I pause, trying to breathe around the ache in my throat. Looking at Hiro is hard all of a sudden. I've never felt so exposed, and I don't know how to deal with it. All I want is to curl up under the covers and hide all my scars and broken pieces in the dark where they belong. But I can't. I'm trying to be better, aren't I?

"I hated the damn thing for years. I could never bring myself to get rid of it, though. It felt like a cruel joke. A curse. Because for a long time, my life was anything but lucky."

Heart pounding, I force my eyes from the coin and look in Hiro's direction. There's no judgment in Hiro's eyes, only a look on his face so soft and sweet, and I would do anything to be deserving of it. "That changed recently, and I… I think it's because of you."

A quivery smile creeps over Hiro's face. He looks like he wants to say something, but no words leave his lips. His expression is sweetly shocked, and I want to commit it to my memory.

My fingers shake as I clasp the rope at the back of my neck. I lift the necklace over my head and lay the coin flat in my palm. I take Hiro's hand in mine, place the coin into his hand, and squeeze, closing Hiro's fingers over the necklace.

"I want you to have it. It's not much. I know." I have to breathe through the insecurities trying to rear their ugly heads and hold on tight to Hiro's hand. "You're the best thing to happen to me. You're my good fortune. My destiny."

Hiro blinks, his eyes wet and glimmering. "Are you sure? It's special to you."

I kiss the back of his knuckles. "So are you."

Hiro parts his lips as if to argue, but he doesn't. Instead, he smiles big and wide. "Okay."

How can such a simple word make me so damn happy?

Hiro adjusts the string so the necklace isn't too long, then loops it over his head. The five-yen settles between his collarbones. Then, my arms are full of Hiro, our lips mashing together in a kiss that's all teeth and tongue and joy. I kiss the hell out of him until we're breathless, and our lips tingling and slick.

I handed him my heart, but he didn't give it back. He accepted it, every crack, every piece.

CHAPTER 19

Jinta

I f I wasn't in love before, then there isn't a doubt left in my head now.

I love Raiden Noboru, and I'm almost positive those feelings are mutual.

But I can't, in good conscience, do nothing about these missing people. Someone is keeping innocent people locked up somewhere, and soon, whoever it is will sacrifice them all in a sick ritual. I've got to figure out who it is and stop them, but I can't do it alone.

I'm not ready to be open with Raiden about my investigation into the gang. Evidence for said investigation is in the dresser beside the bed we're curled up in. I hate keeping such a huge secret from him, but I'm terrified he'll be angry, or even worse, hurt by my secrets. That's the last thing I want, but I've got to come clean eventually.

Noises in the kitchen make me lift my head off the pillow. Raiden's in the kitchen in nothing but his underwear, cracking eggs and stirring them in a bowl. My stomach growls fiercely, so I get out of bed and grab a robe.

"Making something?" I ask, coming up behind him and hugging him around the waist.

He shrugs and leans back against me. "Just eggs. You seriously need to go grocery shopping. How the hell do you survive when I'm not around to feed you?"

I pepper kisses over his tattooed shoulder.

"Come over for dinner tonight. I'll cook."

"You know I can feed myself, don't you?"

"Then act like it," he grumbles, pouring the eggs into the hot pan and scrambling them. The eggs cook slowly. "You still working on your photo book?"

"Y-yes." I almost didn't understand his question. "Why?"

"Namikawa called while you were sleeping. He's holding a meeting and wants to talk about what happened yesterday. He'd like you there to take photos of the meeting. Something about showing our professional side or whatever."

"What time is the meeting?"

"We have time to have breakfast before we head over. Until then..." Raiden turns around and folds me into his arms, holding me to his chest. I melt against him, lose myself in his strong arms and the heat of all that bare skin against mine.

Something's shifted between us. My feelings have changed, but I think his have, too. There was a wall between us before, but after last night, that wall got torn down.

"About last night," I murmur against his warm, bare skin.

Those big, warm arms squeeze me tight.

There's a lot I want to say, but standing in my kitchen with him, his arms around me, early morning sunshine warm on our skin... everything I could say circles back to how much I'm coming to love him. I can't go there.

Despite how affectionate he is and the way he opened himself up to me last night, there's a part of me that's scared that I'm alone in my feelings.

Every time I try to imagine the possibility of him loving me back, all I can wonder is why he'd care for me when my own family shunned me.

"What's wrong?" Raiden asks against my neck, still lavishing kisses over my skin.

"I..." My breath hitches, heart skipping. "There's something I haven't told you. About my last relationship." Maybe if I finally get this off my chest, he can help alleviate these doubts that continue to plague me.

"Just a sec." Raiden takes the eggs off the stove and

plates them. We carry our breakfast to the sofa and sit, his shoulder touching mine. The eggs are good, soft and creamy, but I only pick at them in my nerves.

"What is it?" The weight of Raiden's warm hand runs up and down my leg.

I blow out a breath and stare down at my plate. "So... I've only really dated one person before you."

Raiden glowers.

"Jealous," I tease, unable to hold back my smile.

"Who was he?" Raiden stabs his egg.

"Takahiro." Just saying his name makes something in my chest twinge, even though it's been five years since I last saw him. "We got together in our last year of high school, back when I was still thinking about joining my family's business."

The moment I locked eyes with him, I'd been smitten. I was sure he was the most handsome man I'd ever seen. One day, he'd asked me to take photos for an article he was writing for the school paper.

At the time, I'd been uncertain about pursuing photography and journalism, but I couldn't resist the opportunity to spend time with him. After I shot pictures for his article, he'd invited me out for dinner as a thanks—and kissed me before we'd gone separate ways at the train station.

My world had turned upside down. I'd had my first kiss with a guy who not only had similar interests as me, but he'd also actively encouraged my own passions, as well. I hadn't been so happy in a long time.

I still smile thinking about it, though my heart twinges with pain. "Honestly," I say to Raiden. "If I hadn't met him, I probably wouldn't have fallen back in love with photography."

Raiden frowns as he cards his fingers through my hair. "So what happened? It can't all be sunshine and rainbows, right?"

No. Not at all.

"I brought Takahiro over to meet my family. They didn't know we were a couple. I told them he was a good friend. He was mostly there to support me when I told them that after I graduated high school, I was going to study at a university of my choosing rather than the one they'd wanted. He stood up for me when they got upset. When I moved into my dorm in Tokyo, we decided to be long-distance. Everything was fine at first, but..." The words get trapped. Shame scorches my cheeks.

"What?" Raiden brushes his knuckles over my cheek.

I swallow hard. "Everything fell apart when I went back to Osaka so we could spend Christmas together. Our first one as a couple. I was excited."

Heart racing, I blink fast as memories assault me. I still remember the gifts I brought him from Tokyo, a miniature of Tokyo Tower, and I'd splurged on a new lens for his camera because he'd liked mine so much.

I opened the door to Takahiro's apartment, and immediately, distant grunts and moans had hit my ears. I'd frozen in my tracks, sickness roiling in my stomach. I'll never forget the sight of Takahiro, head thrown back in bliss as he moaned—and my brother Katsuki standing behind him, groaning as he fucked my boyfriend into the sofa.

And that was the last time I saw my brother for five years.

"I guess I should have seen it coming."

"Why?" Raiden's voice is stone cold, lips set in a thin line.

"They hit it off at dinner. Everyone has always loved Katsuki. My parents. The kids at school. Everyone he's ever dated. I understand why. He's so cool. Good at everything he does. He's charismatic and handsome. Hardworking. I thought I'd finally found someone who chose me. Someone who saw me. Accepted me."

Raiden wipes away the tear I hadn't realized had fallen.

Sniffing, I shake my head. "I'm such an idiot. I'm nothing compared to him. I'll n-never be good enough. Not for my family, my brother. Anyone."

"Hey." Raiden's voice is gruff. He grips my chin and turns my face toward him. "You're enough for sake."

"For how long?" I choke out, unable to stop the flood of my worst fears as they pour suddenly out of me. "H-how long before you realize I'm nothing special? A nobody. Some failure who turned his back on his family, and for what? I've accomplished nothing. I—"

"Sunshine, enough." The harsh growl of Raiden's voice makes me jump.

Suddenly, he's pulled me into his lap, my head smacking against his hard chest. He pens me in against him, big arms tight around me. "Do you know why I call you sunshine?"

Hiccupping, I shake my head.

"Because for so long, my world was nothing but darkness until you smiled and it was like all the lights came on. Do you understand what that means? To finally have someone as bright and warm as you in this fucked-up world of mine? It's *everything*. *You're* everything. And I will kill anyone who tries to take my sunshine away. I'm choosing you, Hiro. I will always choose you."

Tears spill from my eyes before I can stop them. Overcome, I bury my face in his chest and let him hold me as every wall I've built around myself cracks and crumbles to pieces.

I've never trusted anyone so much. All my life, I've kept people at a safe distance because I thought that once they got to know me, once they knew how worthless I was, they'd only be disappointed when I failed to measure up. Like my family. Like Takahiro.

But somehow, I'm enough for Raiden. I don't have to prove a thing to him. All I have to do is give myself to him, cracked pieces and all, and he takes me as I am.

It doesn't feel real. What I've found with him is too good to be true, and I'm scared, so damn scared, that I'm going to ruin this.

We don't speak. He kisses and strokes my skin. I wonder at him, how he can be tender yet so strong, sour one moment then sweet the next.

This man of mine has so many layers to him, and beneath all of them is a heart so fragile and soft that I want to cradle it in my hands so it never gets broken. I want to spend years unraveling his every secret until I know him like I know myself.

"You okay?" he finally asks.

I nod. "Yeah. Sorry about that. I'm fine. Really."

"Good." He rubs my back.

A happy laugh escapes me, and I slip my arms around his shoulders. My stomach growls, and Raiden chuckles despite my embarrassment.

"You're gonna need me to feed you."

"Yes, please."

Raiden's grinning. "Can do." I cuddle against his chest while he feeds me bits of egg, stopping only to give himself a few bites. "You're really okay?" he asks, eyeing me cautiously.

"Yeah." And I mean it. Something so heavy has been lifted from my chest, like I've set myself free. "Come with me to meet my family this evening."

His eyes widen. "What? They're in town? Why didn't you tell me sooner? I need time to get my temper under wraps."

I glare at him until he feeds me more egg with a grumpy expression on his face. "I was going to, but then you showed up on my doorstep and collapsed into my arms."

"I did not."

I'm quiet as I chew, trying to put my thoughts into order. "Seeing them again will be hard. But I want to show them what I've accomplished. And I'd love to show you off as my... boyfriend. If that's what we are."

Raiden is oddly still. I chance a glance up and find his lips parted in surprise.

"You're my boyfriend?"

"I was asking you."

Raiden blinks rapidly, as if I've stunned him. "I don't know. I've never been anybody's boyfriend before."

Heat rushing up my neck, I meet his gaze. "Raiden Noboru, you make me happy. Will you be my boyfriend?"

Raiden looks down, but not before I glimpse a pleased smile. "Oh. That's... that's good."

"Well? Will you?"

Raiden sets the plate on the coffee table, then tucks his head beneath my chin, arms winding around me to hold me close. "You sure about this? I won't share. If we do this, you'll be mine exclusively."

I snort. "Uh. Yeah. That's kind of the whole point of being someone's boyfriend, isn't it? I'm sure, baby. I wouldn't have asked if I wasn't."

Joy breaks across Raiden's face, unreserved and bright.

"Yeah, Sunshine. I'll be your boyfriend."

Warmed by his body, happy to the depths of my soul, I smile into his hair.

"You make me happy, too," he whispers, and those precious words heal my heart and break it all at once.

Chapter 20

Raiden

After breakfast, Hiro and I hit the road, driving out of the city and into the countryside.

It's nice to get away from the city, to be alone with Hiro on the open road.

With Hiro beside me and Tokyo behind us, I'm in limbo between my dangerous life in Tokyo and the freedom I never knew I could have, just out of reach.

Someday, this job is going to be the death of me. Yesterday proved that. It's a reality I thought I've resigned myself to.

So why does the idea now make me sick to my stomach?

The thread glows around my finger, warm and full of life. I think of him, of my mate. My boyfriend.

How he opened up to me.

How he trusted me to comfort and support him.

How pretty he looked when he cried, even as my heart broke into pieces.

I want more than my designation in life as Namikawa's lap dog.

I want... him.

But how can I promise Hiro a future with me when I'm bound to Namikawa's service? It's selfish. Unfair. Wrong.

The selfless thing to do would be to sever the thread between us and let him go, let him move on and find someone who can give him the safe, normal life he deserves.

The wolf inside bares his fangs and roars in defiance. I won't give Hiro up. He's mine just as much as I'm his. It would be like tearing my soul in two.

So what am I supposed to do? How can I possibly make him happy when my life isn't safe or secure?

Sure, he was happy this morning. But sooner or later, the rose-tinted lenses will come off and everything will fall apart and—

I make myself breathe around the iron band tightening around my lungs.

Can't think about any of this right now. Or ever.

"Is this his home? Wow. It's nice." Hiro is looking out the window of the *Mercedes* at Namikawa's huge traditional home in the countryside. It's where we often gather for meetings. Just as I step out of the car, my phone buzzes in my pocket.

> **Takada**: *I know what you did, you son of a bitch.*

What the hell is he talking about?

> **Takada**: *you and me need to have a chat. Somebody needs to make you see some damn reason.*

"What's got him so pissed off now?" I growl.

Hiro turns back around, already several steps ahead of me. "What's wrong?"

Sighing, I throw myself back against the car. "Takada's pissed at me for some reason. Wants to have a chat."

A grimace twists Hiro's sweet face. I hardly ever see him angry. It's quite the sight, especially since it's on my behalf. "What gives? Why is he so obsessed with you?"

I drop my gaze to the dirt, suddenly finding it hard to look at him as memories of some of the blackest years of my life claw at my insides. "We were... together for a while. Five years, maybe, on and off."

A pained look creases Hiro's face before he schools his expression. "I thought you said you don't do relation-ships."

Fuck, he sounds hurt. I scratch the back of my neck. "It wasn't a relationship. I don't know what it was. I was... too young to really make sense of it."

"How young?"

"Sixteen." Such a dumb kid I was.

Hiro comes to stand beside me, our shoulders touching.

"Takada used to work for Namikawa, you know? I was a little kid when I joined the gang and I crossed paths with him a few times over the years as I worked my way up. He started getting friendly with me. Gave me my first cigarette. Taught me how to fight."

I remember how he'd touch me during training, always a hand on the small of my back. How strange it made me feel. I wasn't uncomfortable, but I should have been.

"He got more and more touchy-feely with me. Nothing sexual, not really. Not for a while."

Hiro exhales roughly beside me. "Not until you were legal, you mean?"

I fold my arms when my mate's stare burns into me. "I never asked him to stop. I liked it. Liked that someone was giving me the time of day."

"You were a child, Raiden, and someone was showing you affection after you'd just been abandoned. Of course you craved that from someone. How old was he?" Hiro asks hesitantly.

"He was twenty-five. Fucked up, right?"

Hiro stiffens next to me. "What the hell. You were just a kid."

"I was technically legal when we first hooked up." I don't know why I'm still making excuses for Takada.

"In the eyes of the law, yeah, but mentally, you were still a kid, Raiden." Hiro sounds repulsed. "He was old enough to know better. Way better." Anger ignites his voice, and something inside me basks in his protective anger.

I wish I'd known him so much sooner.

I might not have sought out affection from someone like Takada. Wouldn't have let him get his claws into me if I'd just had *someone* I could turn to.

"We hooked up on my birthday. It was my first time being with a guy. He made it feel special. Told me I was special. That he cared about me." I swallow around the sudden ache in my throat. "I believed him. Soaked up all his shit like a damn sponge." How could I have believed a word he ever told me? Why was I so stupid?

"I thought he…" I can't even say the words. I lean my cheek on Hiro's hair and inhale his sweet scent, let it wrap around my heart. "I don't know. Cared about me. I did anything just to get him to look my way, to acknowledge me. Anything he wanted. No matter how much it hurt me, or… or other people." I can barely get the words out as the shame clogs my throat.

"What do you mean?" Hiro asks. Both his arms are around me now, but it's not suffocating. The warmth of his body is a shield, keeping the cold of my past at bay.

I want so badly to tell him, but my heart's racing so fast. He'll hate me. He'll see me differently. This poison has been festering inside me for years, and I just want it out.

Exhaling roughly, I let go, and the words come out of me in a rush I can't stop.

"One day, I went with him on a job. We were just supposed to be collecting fees. This old man, Suwabe, owned a little shop. He was nice to us, all things considered. Always paid on time. But the day we visited, he was strapped. Asked if we could just wait a few days. Takada refused, said he wanted the money now. I felt bad, so I tried to get Takada to lay off the old guy until he could pay, and…" I swallow hard. "Whatever I said just set him off. Maybe it was that I didn't side with him. I don't know."

The memories crash over me. I'm watching as Takada towers over the old man and beats him half to death. Again and again. There's blood everywhere. I can't move. I'm frozen. I can't reconcile the man before me, covered in blood, smiling as he beats a defenseless old man to death, with the man who held me so tenderly last night.

"I couldn't move. I was just frozen as he was laying into this guy. I asked him to stop. I begged him to stop. Finally, I hauled him off Suwabe, but it was—there was so much blood. Takada was covered in it, and he looked at me like he was going to bludgeon me, too.

"Takada put a knife in my hand," I say, feeling my mate tense against me. "And told me to hurt him. He said if I did this, I would be a worthy mate for him. But if I was weak, if I refused, then he couldn't be with me anymore. It was like the mask he was wearing crumbled, and I saw him for who he really was. Not a man, or even a monster, just... a void. This black fucking void full of nothing but darkness. He wanted to drag me down into the dark with him and keep me there, until I was nothing but darkness, too. And I..."

I grind my teeth, hating what I'm about to say. "I wanted to. I wanted to hurt this nice old man who'd never done a damn thing to me. I wanted to do everything he asked of me, be whatever he wanted, just so long as it meant I wasn't alone anymore."

Hiro takes in a slow breath. "Did you hurt him?"

I remember taking the knife, how cold it was. Remember how Takada smiled, how excited he was as he told me where to cut, where to hurt so he'd scream. Remember the pulse beating in Suwabe's throat, fluttering like the wings of a caged bird. How scared he was, the smell of his fear, how trapped he was. How alike he was to me. Trapped like I was trapped. I'd wanted Takada's attention, wanted something that had felt a lot like love for someone so young and messed up. But I'd known if I did this, there'd be no going back. My soul would be as black as Takada's.

"I told you I've never killed an innocent person. I wasn't lying to you. I dropped the knife on the ground and walked out." Hiro exhales against me, and I take a moment to breathe with him. "I told Namikawa what Takada had done. He got Takada kicked from the gang."

"Did you regret it?"

"Not killing Suwabe? No. But for years, I wished things had ended differently between us. Until I got older and realized how he'd used me. Until I realized how much better I felt without him. Like I could finally breathe. I just wish I'd never..." There's a lump in my throat. "I wish I'd never let him touch me."

Hiro kisses my neck. "I'm so sorry."

I suck in a gulp of air, breathing in his scent. "I wish I'd known you sooner."

"So do I," Hiro admits, pulling me into the sanctuary of his arms.

I wish I could tell my younger self that one day, he'd find someone who will hold him and tell him that he cares.

I wish I could tell that broken, lost boy that real love doesn't feel like darkness.

It feels like sunshine and smells like cherry blossoms blooming after the longest, coldest winter.

Love. Is that what this is?

Do I... do I love Hiro? Or what if I've got it all wrong all over again?

"I'm not a good person, Hiro." I whisper the words into his hair. "I was ready to kill an innocent person. I held the knife in my hands. I gave serious thought to hurting him, all so Takada would love me. Even then, I've still got blood on my hands. Blood of other yakuza. Blood of the people I've beaten when they wouldn't pay what they owe. You deserve to know that."

Hiro cups my cheeks. "You were groomed, Raiden. You were a kid, and you were used by a monster. You were forced into a life you never wanted. Yes, you've hurt people. You've killed people. I won't deny that. I know what you've done. But I also know that nobody's ever made me feel as safe as you do. There's no one I trust more than you."

I'm so unworthy of his feelings. I try to look away, but Hiro doesn't let me. He pulls me close so our foreheads touch.

"You're not a monster. Not to me. Raiden…" He suddenly hesitates, eyes wide and full of vulnerability I've never seen before. "Raiden, I—"

Whatever he was about to say gets interrupted when a car honks on the road behind us. Ren waves out the window. "Hey, boys!" She parks and hops out. "I'm not late, am I?"

"Yeah, you missed the meeting. Namikawa's booting you from the pack."

"Ha, ha," Ren intones. "Hiro, come on!"

I linger a moment, needing some space after my talk with Hiro. Hideyoshi's familiar *Cadillac* parks in the driveway, and my grandfather carefully steps out.

"Heading inside?" he asks.

"In a moment." Tilting my head back, I gaze up at the blue sky. "I told Hiro about Takada."

Hideyoshi gives me a surprised but pleased look, though

he doesn't speak. He knows there's more on my mind.

"It was hard, but... I think it helped me realize some stuff."

"Such as?"

I don't talk about deep, personal stuff a lot, so I'm not sure what to say. "Just. I don't know. Stuff. About my relationship with Hiro. How different it is, I guess. How real it feels. Does that even make sense? He's my... my mate. I thought I didn't believe in that stuff, but lately, I don't know. It's all starting to make sense to me."

"Really?"

I nod stiffly.

Hideyoshi's mouth stretches into a full-on grin, and he looks years younger. He grips my shoulders, eyes warm and suspiciously damp. "I'm so very happy for you."

I try to hold back my own happiness, but I can't. He knows me better than anyone, and he was always there to pick me up after my parents and Takada shattered me to pieces time and again.

"I worried so much about you, you know. After your parents abandoned you, then when Namikawa insisted on having you. Then when that *animal* hurt you time and again."

"I'm sorry." I hate myself for making him worry so much after everything he's done for me. "I was a mess."

"You were hurting. Drowning in so much pain and anger. I taught you to cook because, for me, that was my outlet for all my pain and frustration, and while I think that helped, it wasn't what you needed. You needed someone to love you in all the ways you deserve to be loved, Raiden."

I look away, trying to hide from how hard his words are hitting me. "I'm a moron for hanging on to Takada like I did."

My grandfather just shakes his head. "I think we accept the kind of love we believe we deserve. Your parents abandoned you. They failed you in every way one can fail one's child. It's no wonder you felt deserving of the pain Takada inflicted. It's their loss. You have brought joy into my life, Raiden. I hope you know that."

I cough loudly, trying to dislodge the lump from my throat. "Shit. Come on." I squeeze past him and toward the house. I take a moment to wipe my eyes quickly while my back is to him. Is he trying to kill me? Today's been draining enough.

My grandfather grips my shoulder hard just before I can go inside. "Raiden, open your heart to other things. Let yourself dream of a life outside the Namikawa-kai."

I ball my hands into fists. I can't afford to dream about a future. "What am I supposed to do?" Desperation bleeds into my voice. "This is my life. There's no room for anything else."

Hideyoshi grips my wrist tighter. "It doesn't have to be. You could leave. Run as far away as you can. Let me deal with Namikawa."

My heart skips a beat. I rip my hand out of his warm grasp. "Are you crazy?" I hiss, looking both ways as if I expect Namikawa to jump out of the shadows. "You want me to betray Namikawa?"

"Namikawa is not invincible, Raiden. He's a man."

His words make me freeze in my tracks. "What are you saying?"

Hideyoshi's voice is so soft, I can barely hear him when he says, "I can stop him, Raiden. Just give me time. Trust me. Please. You will never be put under his control again, but you must wait a little while longer."

My heart is racing fast. He can't be serious. Has the old man lost his mind? I shake my head and back away. "I can't think about this. And you'd be smart to forget ever bringing this up."

I turn my back on my grandfather and go join Hiro and the others in the house.

Is it possible I could have a future with Hiro far away from this life?

Chapter 21

Jinta

"Excuse us," I call out as we enter Namikawa's home. We remove our shoes, step into slippers, and proceed inside.

Namikawa's home is beautiful. It's a home built in the Minka tradition with sliding walls made of rice paper that reveal dozens of different rooms. Additionally, there are tons of bonsai plants, which add charm to the house.

The first floor is already packed with a mixture of Namikawa-kai and Takada-kai members. Refreshments are provided for us on a low table. Before we sit in the tatami room, we remove our slippers and sit on floor cushions.

The yakuza packs don't mingle with one another and stick close to their own pack, occasionally shooting wary looks around the room. Even after the time I've spent with the gang, being in a room full of yakuza is still intimidating, especially since I know they can all shift into wolves the size of horses.

Camera in hand, I snap photos of the gathering. The atmosphere is surprisingly casual as people talk among themselves in low tones. I don't see Namikawa among them yet.

There's a nervous churning in my stomach at the idea that anyone in this room could be a kitsune. I've done a little more research about kitsune since I found out, but I don't know how much is folklore and how much is fact.

Supposedly, the more tails a kitsune has, the older and more powerful they are. Some stories say they drink blood or shapeshift into women. My gaze lingers on Ren, the only woman in the pack. No. It can't be her. At least, I hope not... Could it be Takada? Namikawa? I wish I knew.

I've got to bide my time until the kitsune makes a move. Then, I can figure out where they are keeping the missing people and... I don't know what I'll do. Call the police? But would they stand a chance against a powerful supernatural creature?

Raiden and Hideyoshi are dressed formally, like they're going to a business meeting, and Ren has on a black dress that shows off her tattoo sleeves. I'd put on my finest threads, as well.

Raiden gives my hand a squeeze. "Gonna go talk to

Namikawa. Ren, watch him."

"Wait," I begin, not liking the idea of them being alone together. What if he tries to control Raiden?

"I'll be fine," Raiden assures me.

Ren pounces on me, hands on my shoulders. "Come on, leave your boyfriend for five minutes. It's been a while since we hung out!"

I scoff. "What does he think I'll do by myself?"

"Play five-finger fillet with a yakuza, obviously," Ren says.

There are quite a few women here with tattoos on display.

"There aren't normally a lot of women in the yakuza," I note as I grab a glass of sake from the refreshments table.

Ren takes a sip. "Not normally, no. Many yakuza groups still believe a woman's role is to be a wife and care for children while the men handle business. But among werewolves, men and women have always been viewed as being equal in strength."

"That must be tough, being one of the few women in the gang."

"It was at first. Most of the men thought I was just a pretty face or started rumors that Namikawa only let me join because we were sleeping together. That sort of nonsense. They didn't know I'd been in and out of trouble with the law for most of my life."

"Oh?" Ren's so fun-loving and warm, so it's hard to

imagine her being so mischievous. I want to ask, but it seems kind of rude to ask about someone's criminal history.

She grins. "You're curious, aren't you?"

"No! Not at all."

"I'm a big kleptomaniac. If it wasn't bolted down, I'd take it."

I instinctively touch my pocket where my wallet is.

Ren giggles. "Relax. I stole stuff I knew I could sell easily. My mom was a single parent, and we were dirt broke. I joined a few years after Raiden did in my late teens. He put in a good word for me. I mostly bar tend at the Lotus, but if the gang needs me, I chip in."

Lifting my camera, I snap a picture of a yakuza and his wife. "Do you see yourself staying?"

"I got the tattoos, didn't I? I'm in it for life. I can't see myself going the civilian route and only bartending for the rest of my life. It sounds boring, but Raiden didn't get to have that option, no thanks to his dad." She regards Raiden, visible through the crowd as he talks to Namikawa.

"He couldn't just... run away, could he?" Longing wraps around my heart and squeezes tight.

She smiles. "If he could, where would you go?" Her voice is low, reminding me we could be easily overheard if we're not careful.

"Anywhere? Everywhere? I don't know." I clamp my

mouth shut before I can get carried away. "You said if he could. He can't?"

She shakes her head. "He tried. A lot of times. Every time, Namikawa found him and made him regret it. That curse Namikawa has on him makes him easy to find. Namikawa will never let him go."

"Then couldn't we just—" Break the curse, I almost say.

"No one knows how," she answers bitterly.

My heart sinks down into the pit of my stomach. I'm falling in love with a man whose loyalty to the yakuza will always come first. He'll never be mine. I'll only ever have parts of him. Pieces of him.

Can that be enough?

She squeezes my shoulder. "But knowing you has been good for him. Besides, if you two truly are fated mates, then things will work out. Destiny wouldn't have brought you together only to tear you apart. That's what I believe."

I exhale shallowly. "At least one of us has hope."

"Makoto," a cold voice growls.

My heart lurches at the sight of Saito Takada, but my dismay morphs into fury. I never liked him, but now that I know how badly he hurt Raiden, I have to grind my teeth so I don't say something I regret.

Ren scowls. "Takada. You didn't happen to stub your little toe on every piece of furniture on your way in did you?"

He smirks. "No."

"Oh. What a pity."

I choke on my sake. Ren's got guts, that's for sure.

"What do you want?" I ask, reluctant to even take my eyes off him. This is the same asshole who had his goons attack me. I'm not dumb enough to think he's just let his jealousy go.

"I only wished to talk to our guest here. Alone."

Ren bares her teeth. "You must be stupid if you think I'm letting him go anywhere—"

"Okay," I say, pushing off from the wall.

Ren grabs my arm. "Hiro," she growls in warning, her inner animal shining through.

I pull free. Takada can rip me in half, but I don't care. My blood's boiling just looking at him, and in my anger, all caution flies out the window. "You want to talk? Let's talk." I stare him down.

Takada arches his lip in a sneer. He wasn't expecting me to do anything other than cower before him, I'm sure. Jaw tight, he jerks his head, motioning for me to follow. I ignore Ren and march after him toward a door at the end of the hall. Takada slides it open, revealing an empty kitchen.

A room full of deadly cookware; the perfect place to be with a jealous yakuza. Not like he needs knives to kill me.

"I'll be out here," Ren says, and shoots a glare at Takada. "Touch him, and Raiden will flay you."

Takada turns away dismissively, yanking the sliding door

shut.

I cross my arms and refuse to look away from him. "Where are the thugs this time, Takada?"

"I don't need them to deliver my message for me this time."

I check my watch. "What do you want? I've got places to—"

"Stay away from Raiden. I won't tell you again."

My jaw clenches. "Not happening."

Takada barks a laugh. "You're no different from any of the other little twinks he fucked. He'll use you until he tires of you, then throw you out like trash."

His words leave cracks in my armor, but I try to ignore it. "If you really thought that, you wouldn't be here."

"I will say, it's odd he's kept you around as long as he has. Got no clue what he sees in someone like you."

"A human, you mean?"

Takada's eyes narrow. "He told you. And you didn't run for the hills."

"Nope. Turns out, monsters kind of do it for me."

A growl rumbles from Takada. My instincts scream to back up and keep distance between us. Takada looks human, but I know that behind that ordinary veneer is a predator that could rip my throat out with a single bite.

"Trust me, I'm as confused as you are, but I think he enjoys being treated like an actual human being. Instead of, you know, a piece of meat."

Takada chuckles darkly, his smile revealing a hint of fang. "He told you about me?"

"More than enough." I reach up and touch Raiden's necklace, needing the coin's coolness to ground me. If I start thinking about what Takada did to him, I'll lose it.

Takada's lips grow thin, nostrils flaring. "You really think he'll ever be satisfied with you? You're *human*. What the fuck do you know about our kind? You will never know how to give him what he needs. You'll never be good enough for him!"

I want to shrink away as he cuts down deep into insecurities I didn't know I had. "And you are? I'll never understand what it means to be yakuza or a werewolf. But I'll never hurt him like you did. You tormented him. For years. He was only sixteen years old. What is wrong with you?"

Takada's mouth splits into a grin. "I made a man out of him. He came to me a broken, lost boy, and I fixed him. You really think he'll ever be happy with you? That he'll settle for a normal life? White picket fences, a normal job, a civilian life. That will never be enough to satisfy him."

His words break through my defenses like water through the windows of a sinking car.

Takada's grin widens. "You don't know him, pretty boy. But I do. And I know that there's bloodlust in him. Oh, he hides it well, but it's there. You think you like him now? You haven't seen the worst that he can do. He'll throw you aside and come running back to me."

"You'd do anything to have him, wouldn't you?" I cross my arms and stare him down.

"I would," he says without missing a beat.

"Even abduct people to incriminate the Namikawa-kai?"

Takada cocks his head. "Now, why would you say that?"

"If people keep disappearing on their turf, the Namikawa-kai will lose face. People will turn on them. The cops will catch on. There will be arrests sooner or later. Once they're gone, you can swoop in and take Taito Ward for yourself. Raiden, too."

A bark of laughter escapes Takada. "Well, aren't you a little sleuth. You've got nothing to prove I'm the one responsible. But I'd look closer to home if I were you. Your boyfriend will get bored with you and come crawling back to me, begging me to—"

I've heard enough. I slam my heel down on his foot and he yelps, stumbling back.

I dart around him, so my back is to the door.

He snarls at me, fangs sharp and glistening with spit.

"Maybe you're right." I force myself to meet his snake-like gaze. "Maybe I can't make him happy. This could all just be one big mistake for both of us. I don't know. But regardless of how things end between us, I will never hurt him like you did." Fury rises in me until I'm shaking with it. "And I swear, Takada, if you ever hurt him again, I'll kill you myself."

Before he can say anything more, I storm back out.

Ren glares at me. "What happened?"

I shrug. "Nothing." My face burns, and my heart keeps tripping. What if Takada's right? What if I can't give Raiden what he needs?

Ren suddenly turns. "Come on. The meeting is starting."

Grateful to have something else to focus on, I follow her back to the tatami room. Namikawa has taken a seat at the table. At his side is Hideyoshi, and Raiden stands behind him. I come up beside Raiden and take a photo of Namikawa sitting calmly at the head of the table.

Namikawa says, "Thank you all for coming at such short notice. I have grave news to share. One of our debtors betrayed us and tried to have Raiden killed by hunters."

I take Raiden's hand, the memory still sharp and painful.

Concerned whispers and outraged snarls fill the room.

"Hunters haven't troubled us in years, but this clan was brazen, eager even to try to kill Raiden. When Raiden described their crest, it was unfamiliar to me. They must be a new clan. We must remain vigilant. I have no doubt they will strike again. Now, on to other matters."

Takada clears his throat. "I have something to say, Namikawa."

Namikawa motions for him to go ahead. "By all means."

Turning a heated glare on Raiden, Takada growls, "Do you want to tell me why Noboru tried to abduct one of my men?"

Raiden's fingers clamp around mine, and the breath hitches in his chest. My own heart skips. What?

Confused whispers rise.

"What are you talking about?" Raiden growls.

"What indeed?" Takada says, a sneer curling his lip. "Kurogiri came to me and told me you'd beaten him bloody and tried to take him somewhere. When he tried to run, you damn near killed him."

Raiden is frozen beside me.

"Explain yourself!" Takada bellows, eyes blazing with fury.

Blinking fast, Raiden parts his lips. "I... I don't know what you're talking about." His hand starts to shake in mine.

"Bullshit! I thought we had settled this when you killed my men for touching that little pet of yours. Kurogiri did nothing to you! Neither did my other men! So where the hell are they?"

"O-other?" Raiden stammers, brows knit in bewilderment.

"Namikawa, where are my men?" Takada snarls. "Several others went missing the night Kurogiri was attacked!"

What the hell? Raiden isn't the one responsible for the disappearances. He can't be.

A furious growl erupts from one of the Namikawa-kai. "You dare accuse our boss of such cowardly tactics? Namikawa is a man of honor, unlike you!"

A Takada-kai whirls him around and snarls, "What the hell did you say? Take it back!"

"Enough!" Namikawa booms, rising swiftly. "Takada, you dare to make accusations without proof?"

"I know it's you!" Takada roars. "You tricked me with this truce! Where are my men? I should have known better than to trust any offers of peace from you. The truce is over, Namikawa. Your pack will never know peace. You will be driven from my city. Your reign is at an end. Mark my fucking words!"

Namikawa stares him down, lips tightly pursed. "So be it."

The tension in the room builds as both packs size each other up, fangs and claws at the ready. For a horrible moment, my heart sinks. I grip Raiden's hand tight, ready to drag him away if a fight breaks out.

With a furious snarl, Takada storms from the room. His pack follows, shoving past people on their way out.

I exhale, heart racing. Raiden's squeezing my hand painfully tight. Before I can catch my breath, Raiden suddenly tugs me from the room and out into the quieter hallway as the Namikawa-kai talk frantically among themselves. The front door slams, bell tinkling as we step out into the woods. Raiden yanks his hand free and leans on his car, breathing hard with his back to mine.

"Gotta drive."

"Where?"

"Anywhere!" He jumps into the car and starts the engine.

I've barely buckled in before he drives from the house. The scenery blurs around us as Raiden drives, knuckles white upon the wheel.

"I knew something was wrong!" Raiden slams his fist down on the wheel. "I... I've been having these flashbacks. They surface sometimes. The night Namikawa punished me, I suddenly woke up in my home. My hands covered in blood. I couldn't remember how I got there, just that I'd been hunting something. Someone."

I feel sick. Just when I was convinced he wasn't responsible, it turns out I was wrong.

Beside me, Raiden's breath comes quicker, and he tangles his shaking hand in his hair. I've never seen him this unsettled. His reaction is all that's keeping me from spiraling. Raiden was responsible all this time, but there's something more to it. *Stay calm. Hear him out.*

"Baby, keep talking. Tell me what's been going on."

"T-there was a girl. At the Lotus. I danced with her. Her name was Himiko. But I don't remember what happened! Just that she was screaming for help."

My stomach turns over. "Himiko is one of the women who went missing."

Raiden's head snaps in my direction.

"I saw her picture in the papers," I clarify.

Eyes impossibly wide, Raiden suddenly swerves off the road and brakes once we're in the grass.

"He's controlling me," Raiden whispers, voice quaking. "Making me abduct people. That son of a bitch! Why would he do this?"

Heart racing, I lean forward in my seat. "You're sure it's Namikawa? Could it be Takada?"

The seat creaks when Raiden slumps back into it. "It has to be Namikawa. He's the only one capable of controlling me. But why?"

Could Namikawa be preparing the ritual? I can't make sense of what would motivate him to do this.

"You aren't killing them. No bodies have been found." Fingers shaking, I reach out and grip his sleeve. "This isn't your fault."

Eyes damp, Raiden blinks fast. "I can't do this anymore. I've gotta get out of this city. Away from him. He's turning me into a fucking monster."

"Then we'll leave!"

He shakes his head. "Not until we figure out where he's taking people. If I'm responsible for these disappearances, I can't be the reason all those people die. So can you wait a while longer? Wait for me?"

I could never refuse him anything. I nod, squeezing his arm. "Always."

Raiden's mouth relaxes into a smile. "Okay... for now, let's get back to the city. Where is your family meeting for dinner?"

Right. My family. I'd almost forgotten.

I give him the address of the izakaya and we drive, Raiden's hand in mine.

Things spiral toward an uncertain conclusion. I'm not ready, but with Raiden by my side, I think we have a chance.

It's late evening when we arrive in Tokyo. As we park outside the restaurant, my stomach twists itself into knots.

"You okay?" Raiden asks as we step outside together.

I nod, but he just scowls at me. "It's been a long time since I've seen my family," I admit after a rushed exhale.

Raiden takes my hand. "Hey. I'm here. If they give you shit, I'll beat their faces in."

"No, you can't—"

He laughs. "I'm kidding, but you bet I'll have something to say in your defense."

Relief blooms warm in my chest. Pushing myself onto my toes, I peck his cheek, then snatch up his hand and lead him inside.

The restaurant is packed. My family rented out the

whole space. There are lots of employees and staff from the hotels my family manages at the venue. A pianist plays a piece from a Hayao Miyazaki movie. I think it's from *Howl's Moving Castle.*

When I see them, my breath catches. I haven't seen my parents in years. Instead of feeling glad, my muscles clench like I'm bracing for impact. We've never been able to sit down to a meal together without drama of some kind. I can't imagine today will be any different.

Maybe it's not too late to leave. That's it. I can just walk out. I don't need their approval.

"Jinta! Over here!" My mom, Fumiko, calls, waving at me.

Raiden looks at me in surprise.

"I changed my name when I moved," I explain, having already anticipated this. "I wanted a fresh start."

He nods his understanding.

I force a smile, wave, and walk over to the empty seat on legs that shake.

"How are you?" Mom hugs me tight.

The familiar smell of her perfume is nostalgic. I hug her, surprised to find that I missed her. "Good, Mom. I'm good."

And then, I see him. Katsuki, my big brother. The sight of him hits me directly in the stomach. Then, old wounds tear wide open. Suddenly, I wish I'd never come. On his arm is his fiancée, a pretty white lady with a diamond ring sparkling on her finger.

"Hi, I'm Katsuki's brother, Hiro."

My mom frowns at that, and Katsuki glowers at me.

She bows. "Nice to meet you." Her Japanese is good. "I'm Dina. Katsuki's told me so much about you!"

My molars squeak together as I fight not to say, *Did he tell you that he's gay and a cheater?*

Katsuki eyes me cooly as he leaves his fiancée's side.

"Hey," he grunts. "Been a while."

I hum my agreement, squeezing my hands into fists in my pockets. "Congratulations." I tip my chin toward his betrothed, then in a quieter voice, I say, "I didn't know you were dating women now."

A muscle tics in Katsuki's jaw. "Not all of us get to run off and disgrace our family. Some of us have obligations."

Tacking on a smile, I say, "I like being in Tokyo. I like my life." By the bar, his fiancée smiles and chats with my mother. Even though I tell myself not to say it, it slips out anyway. "So. I guess you and Takahiro didn't last."

Just saying his name makes my stomach twist painfully.

Katsuki snorts. "Nah. He was good in the sack, though. I could see why you liked him."

Fury boils my blood. "I loved him," I snarl the words through clenched teeth, heart roaring in my ears. "And you knew it. You knew how I felt, and you—" Even though it's been years since then, a lump forms in my throat.

Someone coughs by my ear. Isshin Onodera glowers at

me. "Hello, Jinta. Have a seat."

Ah, my father. So warm and welcoming. Could it be any more obvious he'd rather be dining in hell than with me? Or maybe dining with me is his own personal hell.

I motion Raiden to sit beside me. "Everyone, this is Raiden Noboru. My boyfriend."

Mom looks surprised. Dad wrinkles his nose. Katsuki glances up from his phone and does a double take, then rakes his eyes down Raiden's body. Fighting back an actual growl, I wrap my arm around Raiden and kiss the back of his knuckles. *He's mine, damn it!*

Raiden bows. "Nice to meet you."

"Y-you as well," Mom says, bowing politely, though she looks shell-shocked.

Dad and Katsuki mumble greetings.

Raiden and I sit, and the waitress stops by to take our order. Raiden squeezes my knee beneath the table. "Not too bad so far."

I elbow him. "Don't jinx it."

While the chef slices and dices at lightning speed, my mother turns to me and gives an artificial twitch of her mouth. It's like how someone would smile at a stranger. Am I really that? A stranger to all of them? "You look well."

"I'm doing great." I'm not going to let the awkwardness get to me. I came here to show how well I'm doing. My parents thought I'd fail, that their spoiled son wouldn't last a second away from home. I'm going to prove them wrong. "I'm working on a photo book."

"Oh?" My mom nods with interest. "How is that going?"

"Pretty good." I sip my water to avoid talking.

Raiden smiles. "He's very talented. Your son's going to be a famous photographer someday."

"Well, that's wonderful!" Mom says. "Isn't it, dear?"

Katsuki makes a noncommittal noise around a sip of sake.

Dad has been scrolling on his phone the whole time. "Hm? Oh. What was that?"

Mom sighs. "Really? Can't you give the phone a rest? We're having a family dinner."

Katsuki and I exchange looks. It's already starting. Now, I'm really at home. Family dinners were always a war zone. Mom would get on Dad about paying attention, Dad would act like he was doing us all a favor by gracing us with his presence, and Katsuki and I would feel hurt because our own dad couldn't be bothered to listen to us talk about our day. Well, maybe he'd listen to Katsuki. More often than not, he was on my ass about not joining the baseball team like Katsuki.

Dad crosses his arms, glaring over his spectacles at me. "Yes. It's wonderful that you neglected your duty to your family to run off and take photos."

That surprises even me. "Dad—"

"You threw away all our hard work because you're a coward with no sense of loyalty to the people who raised you. And what do you have to show for it?"

My furious retort gets stuck in my throat. How dare he speak to me like this, and in front of my boyfriend. I want the floor to swallow me up as shame heats my skin. Raiden squeezes my knee painfully hard.

My dad just shakes his head. "At least one of my sons isn't a disappointment."

And Raiden says, "Shut your mouth."

My father's mouth goes slack. Katsuki chokes on his sake. My mom gasps.

Cold fury grips Raiden's face as he stares my father down. "I don't ever want to hear you speak that way to him again."

"Raiden," I begin, alarmed as my father's face turns a furious purple. "It's okay."

Raiden stands up, tossing his napkin onto the bar. "You know, if you'd just supported *Hiro* in what he wanted to do with his life, maybe he wouldn't have flown across the damn country to get away from you. You ever think about that? Your son is amazing. And it's your fault that you're too damn blind to see that."

My eyes sting with tears.

"How dare you?" My father is shaking with fury, a vein throbbing in his temple.

"No, how dare you!" Raiden's shout fills the restaurant.

Heads turn and people glare, but Raiden seems oblivious to all of it. "Let me make something clear. Hiro is mine, and I'm going to spend every day showing him how much he means to me. He's going to know every day that he's treasured. Because that's what he deserves."

I blink away the tears clouding my eyes. My mother hangs her head, and Father looks like he's about to breathe fire. Katsuki eyes Raiden with cool appreciation.

"Jinta," Mom begins.

"I'm leaving," I say, and I hop off the bar stool. I take my boyfriend's hand and squeeze. "Let's go."

Without looking back, we walk from the restaurant together and toward the car.

Once I'm outside, I suck in a breath and try to calm my throbbing heart. As I walk, my mind races and bogs down my steps. My rage at my family still has such a grip on me. What am I doing this investigation for? Is it for me? Even if I complete my investigation, I can't imagine it will make a difference. My family will never be proud of me. I'll never be good enough.

"You okay?" Raiden asks once we reach the car.

I don't know how to answer. I'm pretty sure I just ruined any second chance with my family. But does that really matter? I have Raiden. Someone who supports me and sees the best in me. What do I need them for?

Sudden emotions squeeze my heart. I'm so grateful for him. Framing his face in my hands, I tug him down into a kiss, not caring who turns up their noses at our public display of intimacy. "Thank you," I whisper against his lips.

A content hum escapes him as he nuzzles his forehead to mine. "Told you I'd always take care of you, didn't I? Now, how about I grab us some food from that convenience store over there? We can eat at home."

That sounds amazing. I return to the car while Raiden heads into the store across the street. My neck prickles. Someone is watching me. I look back toward the izakaya and scowl when I notice Katsuki in the doorway, watching me through the car window. When he approaches the vehicle, I feign sudden interest in my phone. He raps loudly on the glass, making me grimace.

I roll down the window. "What?" I ask, voice ice-cold.

Katsuki drags on a cigarette. "Nice car. Your rich thug of a boyfriend buy it for you?"

My fingers curl. "No, actually. But I bet Dina makes you buy all sorts of things for her. You know she only said yes to that big diamond ring, right?"

A muscle tics in Katsuki's jaw. "Fuck you."

"I'm sorry if you're jealous, Katsuki. Really. It must suck being engaged to someone who only looks at you and sees a big money sign."

Katsuki leans into the open window and blows smoke in. Jaw tight, I stare him down, fury heating my blood. "Enjoy him until he realizes what a disappointment you really are."

My fingers curl. "He won't—"

Katsuki snorts, a smirk tugging at his mouth. "You don't deserve a guy like that. He's hot. Rich. Way more interesting than you." Dragging on his smoke, he walks backward away from the vehicle, then crosses the street and goes into the convenience store.

My knuckles are white from how hard I've balled up my fists. The breath saws in and out in fast huffs from my nose. Katsuki is wrong. Raiden cares about me. He said so himself.

But so did Takahiro.

No. Don't do this.

Despair claws at me as I struggle to hold on to my confidence. My family threw me aside. The man I thought I'd loved cheated on me to be with my brother, the man who'd always dwarfed me in his shadow.

Love is conditional. That's what I've been taught. Love lasts until it doesn't, and you're left with a hole in your heart that never heals.

If I can't trust Raiden's feelings, then how can what we have ever hope to last?

CHAPTER 22

I haven't realized I've been staring at a carton of instant ramen for a minute until an old lady next to me says, "Excuse me."

I shuffle out of her way and give my head a shake, but I can't seem to clear it. Namikawa has been controlling me. Making me abduct people. Why? For what purpose? I wonder if the people I abducted were folks who couldn't pay their fees on time.

The son of a bitch could get me in major trouble if I'd been caught. It's bad enough Takada's pissed at me, pissed enough to threaten the pack with war. But what if I'd been arrested? Guess Namikawa wouldn't have cared if I'd spent life behind bars so long as I did what he wanted. Bastard.

Fury makes me gnash my teeth. I grab a pork cutlet bowl for Hiro and some sesame noodles for myself. Chucking both items in the basket with a low growl, I stomp over to the register and wait in line. The automatic doors whoosh open.

"Hey," someone says to me.

The sight of Katsuki makes me scowl though I'll be honest, guys like Katsuki are usually my go-to for a quick, meaningless fuck. When I look at him, though, it just does nothing for me.

How could I want anyone else when I have my sweet Hiro?

Guess my days as Tokyo's most ineligible bachelor are over.

I hand the cashier some bills. "What do you want?" I ask Katsuki, not even looking at him as I accept my change.

"To talk."

"About?"

Katsuki's mouth quirks in a smile. "Whatever the hell you see in my brother that's got you so loyal to him."

My blood's running hot, so I'm itching for a chance to let out some of that rage. Especially on an asshole like Hiro's brother. I walk out of the store, but rather than return to the car, I take a detour down an alley. Katsuki follows, eyes boring holes into my ass. Propping myself against the wall, I fold my arms and stare him down.

Dark eyes look me up and down like I'm a piece of meat.

Katsuki licks his bottom lip. "You know what my brother's doing, don't you?"

I arch a brow. "What exactly?"

Katsuki smirks. "Using you. My family cut him off after he left home. Makes sense he'd latch onto a Sugar Daddy type. What's got me stumped is what on earth do you see in him? Come on, the sex can't be that great, right?"

My fingers twitch at my sides. "Sure are curious about your brother's sex life, aren't you? Why? That pretty woman of yours not putting out?" I smirk. "Or maybe it's you who won't put out."

Katsuki's nostrils flare, the only sign that I've pissed him off. His eyes comb up and down my body. "Gotta hand it to him. He's got good taste."

I huff and fiddle with my cuff sleeve. "Stay away from him. Am I clear?" I tug up my sleeve to flash my tattoos. "I'm very protective of him, and I don't like it when assholes like you hurt him."

Katsuki blinks a couple times like he's trying to process something. Then, he grins and begins to laugh. "No way! You're a yakuza!"

I shake out my fist, wanting to punch him when he laughs harder.

"Oh, this makes so much sense!"

There's a tic in my brow.

"He's not into you for the money, or even your dick. He's investigating you!"

What the hell's he talking about?

Beaming ear to ear, Katsuki claps his hands. "Wow! Bravo. My little bro grew some balls!"

"What are you on? Hiro is a photographer. We hired him to take some photos for one of our magazines." My patience is wearing dangerously thin.

"*Jinta* is a reporter. He works for the Jiji Shimbun, and if I had to guess, he's investigating you for some story he's doing."

What? I'm too confused to even muster up a retort. That's not true. Hiro wouldn't lie to me.

Humor fading, Katsuki approaches me. He grips my jaw, and I'm too baffled to shake him off. "You're so sexy when you're confused." His breath reeks of sake as he leans in and mashes his lips against mine. Disgust makes my stomach churn. Memories of Takada's spidery fingers and rough kisses has me freezing up. When he shoves his tongue into my mouth, my heart lurches in panic.

No. I'm not a helpless kid anymore. I'm not. I—

"Katsuki!" A furious voice echoes through the alley. Next thing I know, Hiro is there, wrestling his brother to the ground. "Don't you fucking touch him!" Hiro bellows, voice thick with rage I've never heard before. He slams his fist across Katsuki's nose. Hiro hits his brother again. And again. His fist gets bloodier and bloodier. Katsuki's eyes roll back, and blood slides down his chin from his nose.

"Hiro, enough!" I seize Hiro's fist before he can land another punch.

Hiro's wrist trembles so hard that he's practically vibrating. Ragged gasps tear from his lips. Those sweet chocolate-brown eyes are unrecognizable, black with fury and wet with tears.

Slowly, I help him stand, but his knees are wobbling so hard I grip his shoulders so he doesn't fall. Hiro's lips wobble when he chokes on a gasp, and tears course down his face. Katsuki groans, wiping his nose.

"I..." Hiro whimpers.

"Let's go," I say into his ear.

I turn Hiro around and have to walk him back toward the car like he's a puppet. People stare at us, but a quick glare from me has them averting their eyes. Once Hiro is seated in the car, I climb into the driver's seat. Hiro's shaky breaths are loud in the silence between us.

I should say something, comfort him, offer reassurance. But I can't. My mind is stuck on what Katsuki said. The surety with which he said it.

Hiro's a reporter? Is that really true?

"Hiro, he kissed me. Not the other way around."

But he holds up a hand and turns away to face the window. "Let's go home." His voice is thick but resolute.

My heart sinks into my stomach like a stone. "Okay," I say, voice heavy with defeat.

I start the engine and drive us home in silence.

We don't speak. Not when we get out of the car. Not as Hiro lets me into his apartment. Not when Hiro dresses for bed. He hasn't told me to go, but I don't feel welcome, either. I can't leave him like this.

"Want me to stay?" I ask.

Hiro takes a moment to reply, like he can barely hear me. "If you want."

Hiro is pretty indirect, but never to me.

"Listen..." Fuck. What do I even say? "If you hadn't punched him, I would have. You know how I feel about you." Seeing his brother kiss me must have brought back awful memories for him. There's probably not a lot I can say to make him feel better. He needs space to work through the trauma his brother's actions triggered in him.

Hiro suddenly laughs, but the sound comes out more like a sob. "My father is right. I am a coward. I turned my back on my family, made them hate me, and for what? I've accomplished nothing!"

"Hiro—"

Wiping his eyes, Hiro suddenly stomps to the step-style dresser by the window and starts pulling open the drawers, tossing clothes onto the floor. What is he doing?

"Your father is an asshole, and so is your brother! I don't

give a damn what you've accomplished. I like you, Hiro."

Hiro sucks in a gasp, slender shoulders rising and falling. "You shouldn't."

"Too damn bad," I growl, but my insides are starting to cramp. Something's wrong. "Give me one good reason why—"

"I'm a reporter!" He whirls around and yells the words at me.

I fold my arms. "I know."

He blinks and takes a step back. "What? How?"

"Your brother said something about that. But so what? Unless you were investigating me, there's no problem."

Hiro says nothing, but he doesn't need to. The agony in his eyes says enough.

Ice falls into my stomach. "Were you?" I ask, voice barely louder than a whisper.

Lips wobbling, Hiro reaches into a drawer and pulls out a shoebox. He tosses it on the ground at my feet.

Fingers oddly shaky, I lift the lid of the box. Inside the box is a photo album. I knew he was making a photo book, so that was expected. I take a seat on the floor with the box and start flipping through the book. There's nothing in here I didn't anticipate; it's just pictures of the bathhouse, scenic shots of Tokyo, even pictures of the garden I took him to.

I flip a page, and my stomach sours in an instant.

There are pictures of the Namikawa-kai shifting to

wolves. Our bare bodies sprout hair as we drop to all fours, our faces and bodies twist and reform. Our most vulnerable moment has been captured, our biggest secret laid bare. Why would Hiro take pictures of us like this? For what purpose? If he wanted pictures, he could have just asked me. With these pictures, he could expose us to the world.

But Hiro wouldn't do that. He wouldn't.

"Read my journal," Hiro whispers. He's not looking at me, hands braced on the dresser.

I snap the book shut. There's a journal in the box, too, and my heart races faster. I open the journal, trying to ignore the tremor in my hands. At first, I don't understand what I'm reading. There are pages dedicated to the disappearances piling up all over Tokyo. Whole sections penned about the Namikawa-kai and whatever connection Hiro can string together that ties them to the disappearances. With each page I turn, everything falls into place.

A story. Hiro has been writing a story, and he's dangerously close to connecting Namikawa to the disappearances.

I reach in and lift the press I.D. with his name and face on it. Jinta Onodera.

Then, I see a photo of myself, a clipping from one of our magazines, a photograph of the Lotus, and a picture of a woman who sparks a familiarity within me.

"What's your name?"

She leans in and whispers in my ear. "Himiko."

Himiko. One of the women Namikawa forced me to abduct.

A pit opens up in my stomach.

Hiro wasn't just investigating the Namikawa-kai.

He was investigating me. Investigating my involvement in the disappearances.

All this time, he was going to implicate me in the abductions and ruin my life.

I toss the photos back in the box, struggling to breathe as horror constricts my lungs. No. No, this can't be true. Hiro wouldn't have lied to me. He wouldn't have used me. Hiro cares about me. He said it himself, and he saved my life when he could have just let me die. I didn't imagine that. It was real.

But it's happened to me before. Time and time again. I've let myself be hurt all of my life, by my parents, by Takada. Pain, abandonment, betrayal—it's all I've ever known. I've latched onto men who've shown me the barest hint of affection, and it's backfired every single time.

Have I done it again?

Did I open my heart to someone for the first time in my life, only for him to use me?

"Why?" I croak.

Hiro lifts a hand and wipes his eyes, back still facing me. "I t-thought if I connected you to the disappearances, it would be the big break I was looking for. A front-page story."

"You know I didn't do it."

He gives a stiff nod. "I do now. I wanted to please my family. Even after everything. But nothing I do will ever be enough. I'm done trying. I'll always be a failure to them. My investigation is over. It's done." A soft sob escapes him. "We're done."

His words punch me in the chest. Pain like nothing I've felt before lashes my heart.

Hiro finally turns to face me, face wet and eyes anguished. "You deserve to know the truth. I'm everything my family said, and worse. I care about you, Raiden, but I... we can't. I'll never be what you need or who you deserve."

"You are what I need!" I shout, my voice bouncing off the walls. "Don't do this. Don't let your brother ruin what we have."

With shaking fingers, he yanks off the necklace I gave him.

"Don't." The word comes out cracked and broken. "Hiro, don't do this."

"This was going to happen anyway," he chokes out. "Sooner or later, you'll decide I'm not good enough, and you'll leave." He storms over, grabs my hand, and shoves the necklace into it. "Might as well j-just get it over with now."

He might as well have just handed me the heart I entrusted to him, shattered to pieces.

When I was eight, I stopped believing in love and destiny.

My mother thought my father was her mate. My father swore my mother was his destiny. Then, he severed their bond and left, never to return. I watched as my mother's heart broke, and she changed before my eyes into someone unrecognizable.

I thought I knew how a heart could break the day she put my father's coin in my hand and shoved me at Namikawa. But now I know I didn't know anything at all. Nothing's ever hurt quite like this.

My wolf howls, *Mate. Mine. Why?*

"No," I say, and the wolf pushes through. Fur sprouts. Fangs sharpen. "You're mine, and I'm not letting you go." I take one step toward him, then another.

Hiro backs up, hitting the dresser.

Hiro. Our Hiro. Keep us. Love us. Please.

I wrap a clawed hand around his throat and lean down, brushing my fangs over his shoulder. "Tell me to leave, Sunshine. Tell me you don't want me and, maybe, I'll believe you."

Hiro's voice quakes when he whispers, "Raiden..."

"Fuck the investigation. Fuck Namikawa. Fuck all of it. I don't care. You and me, Hiro, that's all that matters. Don't do this to me. We're mates. You're my fucking mate, Hiro. Don't push me away."

Hiro's eyes close as I lean in, his breath hot on my

mouth.

Don't push me away.

Please.

Please.

"Stop!" Hiro's palms slam into my chest and send me stumbling back. The shock that rips through me dulls my fangs and claws. My wolf snarls within, but we can't defy our mate.

Blinking back tears, Hiro chokes, "Get out. Now."

And the heart I'd thought turned to stone long ago shatters in my chest.

Love always ends in heartbreak. I should have learned my lesson.

All I want is to scream. To howl my agony to the moon. But I can't even speak. Can't even look at him as I turn my back and run from the apartment. It started raining while we were inside, fat heavy drops that cascade down on me in seconds. Yanking open the door to my car, I leap inside and slam it shut so hard, it's a wonder the glass doesn't shatter.

"Fuck!" I pound on the wheel. My eyes sting. My throat aches.

What do I do? How can I make this pain go away? I can't *breathe*. I'm so fucking angry. Everything hurts. What can I do? How do I make it *stop*?

There's a beast howling in my soul. My wolf is furious, and he's howling for our mate. No matter how much I scream that Hiro isn't mine, was never mine, I can't shut him up.

If I could claw back every little piece of myself I gave to him, then I would.

I allow myself one single tear over Jinta Onodera. The first tear I've shed since my mother left. But that's it. That's all.

I will never let another person hurt me like this again.

Chapter 23

Jinta

When I open my eyes, dread pins me to the futon.

What have I done?

I pushed away the only man I've ever loved, and for what?

I know he didn't cheat on me. Raiden would never do that. Yet when I saw Katsuki kiss him, it was like I was watching him steal Takahiro away from me all over again. My confrontation with Takada where he said I could never be what Raiden needed, then that disastrous dinner with my family really fucked with my head.

It was like all my self-doubts and inadequacies boiled over until I couldn't take it anymore. I self-destructed, and now... oh, god. Raiden will never forgive me. Regret claws at my heart, and I hide my face in my pillow. I wish I could take it all back. I hate that I hurt him. I let my own insecurities destroy the best thing that's ever happened to me.

How can I make this right?

My phone buzzes on the floor.

Could it be...

Rolling over so fast I almost fall out of bed, I snatch up my phone. My hope crumbles.

Ren: *Hey. I got stood up for a lunch date. Want to hang?*

Is it lunchtime? I check the time and gasp. I slept through to the afternoon. Today is going to be a disaster. Maybe lunch with Ren will cheer me up.

Me: *Sure. I'd love to be your sloppy seconds! <3*

I'm joking. I really would like to see her right now.

I throw on some clothes and brush my teeth, then borrow a bike and ride to our meetup spot, which is only fifteen minutes away.

The café is not only a café but a laundromat as well, so you can have a coffee and a cute teddy bear-shaped cake while you wait for your undies to dry, I guess. The café is packed with people chatting with friends, scrolling their phones, or tapping through their e-readers.

Ren waves at me from a table. "Isn't this place cute?" she asks.

I grunt. "Did you order?"

"Not yet." We leave our bags on our chairs and get in line. Ren gets a latte, a bear cake for us to share, and I order a matcha with soy milk. Ren pays for us, and we take our lunch to the table.

"Sorry about your date," I say.

Shrugging, Ren sticks a fork into the bear cake and rips off a chunk of its head, revealing yellow cake beneath the chocolate icing. "I guess it will be a while before I find my mate. You're lucky." Smiling, she kicks me beneath the table.

Tears sting my eyes. "Yeah. Lucky..."

Ren frowns. "Are you okay?" She points her icing-covered fork at me.

Blowing out a breath, I say, "There's something I have to tell you."

And for an hour, Ren listens while I tell her everything about my investigation, what I've learned so far, how Takahiro cheated, and what happened with Raiden last night. My eyes sting with guilt and shame. I bow my head low. "I'm so sorry I lied to you, to everyone. You, Raiden, and Hideyoshi have treated me more like family than my own ever did. I'm giving up the investigation. I promise."

Ren is quiet for a long moment. I can't see her face, only her hands, tightly clasped on the table. "I see," she says softly. "So everything was fake."

I sit upright, shaking my head. "No. Not everything. I care about you. I didn't expect to, but it just happened."

"And Raiden?"

A lump rises in my throat. "I love him."

Ren sighs exasperatedly. "Then why are you here telling me this?"

"Because what are the chances he'll want anything to do with me? I hurt him. Terribly. After everything he's been through, he deserves better than that... better than me."

Ren chews her cake thoughtfully. She's already eaten half of it. "Sounds like an excuse to me."

My jaw tightens. "It isn't."

"Hiro—Jinta, you're making excuses. Do you want to be with him or not?"

"Of course I do. But—"

Ren throws up her arms. "Then what's the problem? Oh. Takahiro."

My face heats at just the mention of my ex's name.

With a sigh, Ren pats my hand. "Jinta. Can't you see? You're afraid that sooner or later, you'll be hurt, so you're pushing him away."

"No, I pushed him away because he deserves someone who isn't a failure who disappointed his family."

Ren arches a brow. "Someone like Katsuki?"

Her question hits me square in the chest. They'd looked good together. Like they fit. Katsuki is everything I'm not.

My parents made that clear. "I don't know. Maybe?" Sighing, I shake my head and stare into the green depths of my matcha. Maybe she's right. I am scared. Terrified, in fact. If Raiden decided that there was someone better out there for him, it would break me apart.

"Maybe you don't see it like I do. I get it. I've known Raiden since we were kids," Ren says, a fond smile breaking across her face. "I've seen Raiden at his best, and I've seen him at his absolute lowest. I've seen him hope and dream. He wanted to open a restaurant and take care of his mother. I've seen him cry because his parents left him when he was just a kid, and he never even knew why. I've seen him struggle, trapped in a life he never wanted. I've despaired over him because, for so long, I thought I was going to watch the person I care about the most die in this life, alone, afraid to trust. And then... then there was you, Jinta. And I have never seen him look at anyone the way he looks at you."

Blinking fast, I try to look away, but Ren grabs my hand and holds tight. "What if I can't be what he needs? He's yakuza. I know he wants a normal life, but what if he doesn't want it with me?"

Ren scoffs. "Can't you see it? He loves you."

My breath catches. "Really?"

Rolling her eyes, she says, "Yes! You can't see it, but he's scared, too, because he's never loved anyone like he loves you. If Raiden, of all people, has given you his heart, he will never do anything to hurt you."

I believe her. Even though a part of me is still scared, I know Raiden would never intentionally hurt me. I love him, and I need to make things right between us. If anyone deserves to know he's loved, it's Raiden.

I finally manage to smile as I scramble out of my chair. "Thanks, Ren. I'll talk to him."

Ren punches the air, almost spilling her coffee all over the table in her excitement. "Yes! Go get your man!"

The bell jingles as I rush out the door and onto the street. I swing one leg over my bike and start to peddle. I'm sure Raiden will be pissed at me, but I'll grovel on my hands and knees to make things right. I let my brother ruin my last relationship and allowed my parents to talk down to me for years. I'm not letting them come between me and the man I love.

My legs start to burn as I peddle faster and faster. The parks and gardens of Chiyoda Ward blur around me as I ride, and before I know it, I'm biking along the Sumida River in Asakusa.

I'm almost there, and I have no idea what I'll say or do. I just need Raiden to know that I'm sorry, that I was so stupid and scared, and that I love him.

I'll tell him I want to be with him, come yakuza or werewolves or kitsune. I'll tell him I'm done trying to earn my family's approval. I'll tell him from now on, he's all that matters.

I arrive outside Raiden's building and wheel my bike inside. The doorman recognizes me and smiles. "Here to see Noboru?"

"Yes," I say panting, legs burning from all that peddling. "Is he here?"

A shake of the head. "I haven't seen him since this morning."

I'll just have to wait until he comes back. Maybe he's out on a job for Namikawa.

I take a seat in a plush velvet armchair and catch my breath. Should I text him and ask where he is? The indecision makes me hesitate as I pull out my phone, reading the last messages we exchanged before I fucked everything up.

Slowly, I type, erase, and rewrite my message.

Me: *I'm so sorry about last night. Can we talk?*

I send the message and try to distract myself by watching a video.

Ten minutes go by, and he doesn't answer.

Not that I expected him to be jumping for joy to hear from me, but I'm disappointed anyway. Raiden's probably just busy.

My phone buzzes in my hands, and I almost drop it.

Ren: *Hey. Can you get in touch with Raiden?*

My stomach twists nervously.

Me: *No. Can you?*

Ren: *Do you think something's happened?*

The last couple of times we couldn't reach him, he was being tortured by Namikawa and out abducting people. Shit...

I jump when someone calls me, but it isn't Ren. It's Hideyoshi. I wonder if he's on the same train of thought as we are. Swiping, I answer, "Hideyoshi. Have you seen Raiden?"

"That is why I called you. Something has happened."

Fuck. I knew it. Heart in my throat, I spring up. "What?"

"There's no time to explain! I need to focus. I'm driving to you now."

"Wait! I'm at Raiden's place. Come and get me."

"Will do."

Fear is sour in my throat. "Is he... is he okay?"

Hideyoshi's voice shakes when he says, "Just wait for me. I'll be there soon."

My heart feels like it will explode as I hang up.

Oh, god. What's happened now? Is it Takada? Did he hurt Raiden to get back at him for what Raiden did while under Namikawa's influence? Did hunters shoot him again? Or did he run into trouble while collecting debts? And what am I needed for? I can't help. All I can do is guess, fear twisting my stomach into knots.

After what feels like forever, my phone vibrates.

Hideyoshi: *I am outside.*

My feet pound the ground as I run outside, cricking my neck as I look every which way. Someone waves out the window of a big black car across the way. Hideyoshi motions me over. "Quickly! There's no time!"

Please be safe, Raiden!

Looking both ways, I jog across the street. At my approach, the automatic doors slide open. I grab the handle and hoist myself in. "Hideyoshi, what's going—" I freeze at the sight of Raiden, sitting in the back seat. The doors close. Hideyoshi slams on the gas.

What's going on? Why is he here?

Raiden's face is stony, cold eyes staring right through me. They're... empty.

I look over at Hideyoshi. "Hang on. What's—"

Raiden lunges for me, snaring my arm in his grip and tugging me onto the back seat. The razor tips of his claws dig into my throat, dangerously close to breaking the skin. If I struggle, his claws will puncture my throat.

Hideyoshi meets my wide, horrified gaze in the rearview mirror. "I'm sorry," he says, voice shaking, and I'm not sure who he's talking to. Me or Raiden.

Tears prick my eyes when I try to meet Raiden's gaze. He stares straight ahead, eyes glossy, still as a statue. "Raiden," I whisper, and his claws twitch against my neck, making me swallow my pleas. I have no choice but to surrender and accept my fate.

CHAPTER 24

Jinta

The sun disappears beyond the horizon as Hideyoshi drives us out of the city, a lit cigarette between his yellowed teeth. I have no idea where he's taking us, but I know in my heart that wherever we're going, the missing people will be there.

Raiden's claws dig into my skin. My back aches from lack of movement, but if I move, Raiden's claws will cut me. Every time I swallow, his hand bobs on my throat. Raiden is completely still, eyes staring miles ahead.

I have no idea if he's aware of what he's doing. He's trapped. A prisoner in his own body. The despair threatens to consume me. God. He's been used enough.

"You have to help him," I say, voice rusty from an hour

and a half of silence.

Hideyoshi's head twitches in my direction, but he keeps his eyes on the road. "Everything I do is for him. Even this." His face twists in disgust, knuckles whitening on the wheel.

"What do you mean?"

"Raiden told me everything about your investigation."

I wince. "And this is... what? Revenge for that?"

Surprise widens Hideyoshi's eyes. "No. Am I angry that you were spying on my grandson? Yes. But this is not revenge."

"Then what is it?" I grit out, my patience wearing thin.

"It was always Namikawa's plan to use you in the ritual. I assume you know what I'm talking about."

My breath hitches as he confirms my worst fear. "The kitsune ritual. Namikawa is the kitsune, isn't he?" All that I need now is a motive.

Something like respect lights up Hideyoshi's eyes. "Ah. So you have done your research. You likely know all our secrets."

Raiden's claws prick my neck. "I know your clan has been murdering people since the 1900s. Sacrificing them in this sick ritual. Why? What the hell do you get out of it?"

With a suck on his cigarette, Hideyoshi blows smoke out the window. The stink is starting to make my stomach queasy. "During the Meiji Restoration Era, hunters decimated our numbers, culling us to near extinction. Namikawa believed the only way our kind could survive was if he bound an ancient and powerful kitsune to serve our pack in the fight to come."

I'm pretty sure I misheard. "Namikawa's ancestor?"

Hideyoshi shakes his head. "No."

My brain stumbles over this revelation. "How can Namikawa be that old?"

"The kitsune has granted him great longevity. A boon, or perhaps a curse, the kitsune bestows upon its host. However, the longer a kitsune possesses its host, the weaker the host becomes. Namikawa knew the demon would demand a price, but he didn't know how truly heinous the demon's request would be. The kitsune demanded that we sacrifice one half of a couple, or half of a fated pair. Only then would she serve us."

That's oddly specific. Why would a kitsune enjoy tearing loving couples apart? "But that was a hundred years ago."

Hideyoshi nods sullenly. "Yes. The kitsune curse lasts from generation to generation. So long as whoever hosts the demon sates her lust for power, she will remain in our service."

"And if you don't?"

"Then the demon will rampage out of our control. The sacrifice is vile, but it is nothing compared to the bloodshed the kitsune will unleash if we do not appease her."

Disgust fills Hideyoshi's voice. Clearly, he hates the idea, so why is he going along with it?

"And you. What's your role in all of this?"

In the mirror, Hideyoshi glances at Raiden, brows puckering as if he's in pain. "For years, Namikawa has punished my grandson for the actions of his father. All I want is for him to be free. I told you there is nothing I would not do for him. I meant it. It pains me, but I would see hundreds dead before I allow Namikawa to harm him any longer."

"But Raiden would never want that!" I say, imploring him to see reason. "If he finds out you're helping Namikawa murder people on his behalf, it will destroy him! He'll never forgive you."

A shuddery sigh escapes Hideyoshi, smoke leaking from his mouth in a long stream. "That is a price I will have to live with. Losing you... it will hurt him. Greatly. But what Namikawa has planned for him will hurt far, far worse."

Heart in my throat, I ask, "What?"

"Namikawa has been the kitsune's host for a hundred years. It is a burden he tires of as the curse eats away at his body. He planned to pass the curse onto Raiden's father, but the curse rejected him. We do not know how or why Raiden's father was able to evade the kitsune's curse, only that he did. As you know, he ran away. I begged Namikawa not to, but he was determined to pass the kitsune curse onto Raiden as revenge for his father's betrayal. Until you showed up. Namikawa does not fear much, but he fears your bond. He thinks that it may be enough to... override the control he has over Raiden."

My interest piques at that. Could it be true? The red thread connecting me to Raiden glows, still tethering us together despite our fight. If our mate bond is the key to freeing Raiden from Namikawa's influence, then that could be our way out of this.

Hideyoshi meets my gaze in the mirror. "As you can imagine, that is a risk Namikawa can't afford. If he can't control Raiden and the kitsune, then Raiden will become a threat. The Takada-kai have threatened us with war. Hunters are creeping into our territory. The kitsune is an edge we cannot afford to lose. So I have offered to accept the curse in Raiden's place. Namikawa knows I will do whatever he asks so long as he has Raiden under his control."

I swallow hard, stomach swooping. "So... he wouldn't be expecting you to betray him."

Hideyoshi's eyes meet mine in the mirror. "No. I don't expect he would. I have been nothing but loyal to him throughout the years. But even my loyalty has its limits. I will become the kitsune's host, and I will destroy the Namikawa-kai. Only then will Raiden be free."

"So... so you'll help us."

But Hideyoshi shakes his head. "I will help my grandson. I am sorry, Hiro. Truly. But the ritual must be completed. The kitsune must have her bounty of souls. Your soul included. Or else none of this will be possible."

Panic tightens my chest. "You seriously think Raiden will ever forgive you for killing so many people?"

Hideyoshi closes his eyes tight, but not before I glimpse the remorse that dampens his eyes. When he opens them, they burn with resolution. "All that matters is the Namikawa-kai will be gone, and Raiden will be free. If he hates me for the rest of his life, then so be it."

Despair wraps around my heart with an iron grip. This is it, then. I'm going to die. There's no way out of this situation and yet, I want to live with a desperation that surprises me.

I can't die. Not yet. But it's not because I haven't penned a big story for the newspaper or because I still have so much to prove to my family.

It's because of the man beside me, eyes vacant, claws around my neck. This man, who has given me the love and acceptance I've searched for my whole life. I've got to find a way to get us both out of this mess. If I want to have a future with him, I'm going to have to fight for it. Because we both deserve it. We deserve to have the love we were denied.

Reaching out, I touch Raiden's leg and squeeze. The claws around my neck twitch, but Raiden's expression doesn't change. He's still in there somewhere. He must be. And I'm going to save him.

Even if it's the last thing I do.

The sun disappears, and the moon rises over the rolling mountains. Hideyoshi drives us off the main road and into the woods. Trees flank us on all sides, the depths of the forest shrouded in darkness.

At last, Hideyoshi stops the car and unlocks the doors. He opens Raiden's side door, and Raiden tugs on me, making me wince as his claws scrape my skin.

I'm forced to step out after him. The headlights offer a small cone of light ahead but can't hope to penetrate the darkness of the woods. Hideyoshi brushes past me and leads the way. I realize they must be able to see in the dark as they navigate the dark woods with ease, skirting around the trees I would have walked into.

The ground slopes, and I almost trip when Raiden slowly leads me up a series of stone stairs. There must be a shrine ahead. Fear makes sour bile rise in my throat. We're almost there.

Small cones of light flicker into view as we pass lanterns swinging from tori gates. The lanterns illuminate a crowd that has gathered, all facing something out of view.

Hideyoshi parts the crowd, and Raiden and I follow in his footsteps. Horror freezes me in my tracks. Dozens of men and women are on their knees before a shrine. Their hands are bound, hair disheveled, and clothes torn and dirty.

These are all the missing people. I've found them—and I'm going to watch them all be murdered.

"Set him down here," Hideyoshi instructs.

Raiden shoves down, forcing my knees to bend. I collapse onto the ground, panting as fear possesses me.

"Please," I rasp, "Hideyoshi, don't do this."

But Hideyoshi turns his back and walks around the terrified captives without a glance. He goes and stands before the shrine.

Raiden trails behind his grandfather, eyes staring straight ahead.

There's movement behind me. I crane my neck to look over my shoulder. Namikawa makes his way through the crowd, but he has to be escorted by two guards on either side, gripping his arms to keep him upright.

The curse really has taken its toll. The most powerful man in Japan looks like he'll keel over and die at any moment. Hideyoshi offers Namikawa his arm, which the elderly boss accepts, swaying as he holds himself tall to face the gathering.

"Tonight," Namikawa says, "I bid you all farewell. It has been my greatest honor to lead this family for as long as I have. I only wish we weren't parting during such a time of strife for our kind. Hunters are on our doorstep. The

Takada-kai desire to take our city for themselves. But fear not. I have faith that under Hideyoshi's leadership, the Namikawa-kai will thrive even after I am gone from this world. Serve him as you have served me, my children."

"Boss, what's happening?" a yakuza asks, face pale. "Who are all these people?"

"Why have you brought us here?" a captive shouts.

They have no idea what their boss is or what he's about to do.

Namikawa grips the railing and hoists himself up the short steps to the shrine. On the altar is a wooden box and a large stone, cracked in half. The Sessho-seki, the stone said to contain Tamano-no-Mae's spirit. Namikawa picks up the box and returns to Hideyoshi. Hideyoshi opens the lid and withdraws a short sword. Namikawa looks him in the eyes and says, "Begin the ritual."

The people around me begin to whisper, frightened whimpers rising in the air. I can practically taste the fear, sour in the air like urine. Quakes rack my body. What can I do? If I don't do something, I'll be killed.

"W-why are we here? Please let us go!" a man shouts.

"Please! Don't kill us!" a woman screams.

Stone-faced, Hideyoshi marches forward and seizes a man by the arm, wrenching him to his feet. The man screams and struggles, but even though Hideyoshi is old, he's still a supernatural creature. Hideyoshi forces the man over the altar.

Namikawa lifts his arms to the skies. "Oh, great and powerful Tamano-no-Mae. Accept our sacrifice in your name. Grant us your strength! Under your guidance, we shall rain chaos upon our enemies!"

Hideyoshi slits the man's throat. The crowd, both yakuza and captives alike, cry out in shock, fear, and disgust. A hideous gurgle rattles in the air, and blood runs down the altar. Hideyoshi kicks the body down the steps. The captives scream as the corpse rolls to a stop in the dirt, throat split from ear to ear, eyes vacant. My gorge rises, and I pant for breath, shaking violently.

The prisoners scream and struggle as they're dragged up the steps. Hideyoshi cuts their throats again and again with the mindless monotony of a butcher at work. The corpses roll down the steps, piling one on top of the other. The stairs run red, streaked with the blood of the slain. The wind howls. Veins of lightning fork across the sky. Thunder booms.

Namikawa laughs and laughs, face twisting into something hideous and inhuman as the fox slowly reveals herself, thriving in the chaos committed in her name.

All I can do is close my eyes, panting raggedly as bloody gurgles claw at my ears. Then, a clawed hand grabs the back of my neck and hauls me to my feet. Hideyoshi's face is cold and impassive as he stares down at me. He looks at Raiden, still under Namikawa's control, and closes his eyes tight. "Forgive me."

Tugging hard, he drags me toward the altar. Blood makes the steps slick beneath my feet. Crimson drops pitter-patter off the edges of the altar like rain. There's so much blood in the air, I can taste it when the wind blows.

I don't want to die. I can't. Hideyoshi holds firm as I struggle, then slams me against the altar. Holding my neck in place, he grips the short sword, the blade coated in blood.

Namikawa laughs. "We are so close now!" His voice is odd. There's someone else speaking beneath his worn voice. A woman's, deep and melodic. "Hurry, wolf. I grow weary of this frail body." Lightning flashes, revealing the tall shadow of a woman with a fox's head and nine lashing tails where Namikawa stands.

It's Tamano-no-Mae, speaking through Namikawa.

My hand shakes on the altar's wet surface.

Raiden? Can you hear me?

Tears sting my eyes.

I'm so sorry that I pushed you away. I was stupid and scared. I let my family come between us. Please, forgive me. I should have trusted your feelings. Thank you for choosing me. If I could do things over again, I would choose you over everything else every day for the rest of my life.

I love you.

Goodbye.

Tears run down my face. Hideyoshi slides the blade beneath my throat. The metal is cold and wet. I close my eyes tight.

Something around my finger begins to vibrate, then pulls taut against my skin. My eyes fly open as the red thread of fate glows crimson.

A roar splits the air. The earth shakes as something huge barrels toward us. Hideyoshi drops the dagger and stumbles out of the way. Namikawa whirls around, claws long and sharp. An enormous, clawed hand covered in black fur rips Namikawa off his feet and sends him flying down the steps.

A growl rumbles like thunder, quivering the earth. Dread freezes me in place. Then, two huge, clawed hands lift me off my feet and clutch me against a powerful chest covered with black fur.

Terror grips me as the face of an enormous wolf stares down at me, a snout full of fangs inches from my face. His body is human enough, minus the claws and all the black fur covering every inch of his skin.

It's his face that unsettles me; he looks like a wolf-man straight out of a horror movie. His body bulges with muscle and his hands are large enough to crush my head between them. Wrapped around one of his long fingers is the little red thread.

"R-Raiden?" I whisper, unable to believe what I'm seeing.

The wolf parts his huge jaws and growls in a deep low voice, "Hey, Sunshine."

CHAPTER 25

Raiden

Where am I?

Everywhere I turn, I'm surrounded by darkness.

I remember running from Hiro—Jinta's apartment, my heart a shattered mess in my chest. Driving around in my car. Trying to forget. Called Hideyoshi, told him everything. Then Namikawa summoned me to his office. I went and... and then nothing. My memory is completely blank. Screams come from far away. People beg for mercy. A copper tang hits my nose, the scent overpowering.

Shit. Is Namikawa controlling me right now?

Fear wraps around my insides. What the hell is he making me do?

Raiden? Can you hear me?

My heart skips a beat. That's Jinta's voice. The sweet aroma of cherry blossoms washes away the stench of blood and death. He speaks to me and every word makes the red thread around my finger thrum and ripple. He tells me he's sorry, that he wishes he hadn't pushed me away, that he chooses me the way I chose him.

And then he says, *I love you,* and all the breath lodges in my chest as my heart races out of control.

When I was eight, I'd learned that those three little words my father once whispered to my mother had no meaning. I never wanted to love or be loved, so I'd built walls around myself.

Yet here he is, this man who smells like cherry blossoms in spring, telling me he chooses me. That he *loves* me. Words I never knew I needed to hear that defy everything I thought I knew about myself.

Goodbye.

All my joy withers and dies.

Goodbye?

No. No, you don't get to say goodbye to me, damn it, Jinta!

You don't get to give my heart somebody to beat for, only to leave me behind.

You can't.

I won't let you!

My wolf roars within my soul. The darkness around me shatters like glass. My body changes as the wolf's fury surges through me. Fur ripples over bulging muscles as I rise up on my back legs. The thread around my clawed finger vibrates, glowing so bright it hurts to look at. The last of the darkness disappears, and I stand in the middle of the woods. A pile of bodies lie at the foot of a shrine. Rivers of blood soak into the grass.

The wind carries Jinta's scent to me. There he is, bent over an altar. My own grandfather holds a knife to his throat. Namikawa is laughing. There's no time to think. I've got to save my mate.

Charging forward, I swing out a clawed hand and bat Namikawa off his feet. My boss smashes his way down the stone steps and crumples against the pile of corpses clogging the stairs. My grandfather has dropped the knife and backed away, face pale and hands raised in supplication.

Reaching out, I seize my mate and haul him in close. His hair tickles my snout, and I breathe in a lungful of his scent. Thank god. A shuddery gasp escapes Jinta when he looks up at me, chocolate-brown eyes going wide. "R-Raiden?"

I smile at the sound of his voice, though it probably just looks like I'm baring my fangs. "Hey, Sunshine," I growl, voice deep and inhuman.

"Wh-what happened to you?" he asks.

I'm not sure myself. I've heard stories of wolves transforming into gigantic bipedal wolf-men monstrosities to protect their mates, but I never thought it would happen to me. Not until he came along. "Not going to hurt you," I huff, carefully setting him down. "Get behind the altar. Don't come out!"

On the steps below, Namikawa rises. Shadows pool in his haggard face, which has taken on a foxlike appearance. But it's his shadow that reveals the truth. It isn't Namikawa's shadow, but of a woman in a kimono. She has a fox's head and nine tails lashing back and forth.

Namikawa is a kitsune? Hell, this is bad.

The gathered Namikawa-kai cheer in anticipation of watching me fight Namikawa.

Namikawa bares his fangs. He's standing taller than he has in weeks. The kitsune must be granting him a boost of strength. "This new form you've gained is impressive, Noboru. Unfortunately for you, it means nothing. You will always be my attack dog. Step aside. Our lady Tamano-no-Mae requires her last sacrifice. Do not make me ask."

My jaws click hungrily as I snap my teeth together. "No," I snarl. "Touch a single hair on his head, and yours will roll, Namikawa!"

A sneer hooks Namikawa's lips. "Insolent brat. Noboru, would you kindly step aside?"

His request tugs at my mind. The fury of my wolf threatens to falter. My claws begin to shrink, my fangs become dull. *No, no, no! I've got to fight. I can't lose Jinta.*

"Raiden, don't listen to him!" Jinta shouts, rising from

behind the shrine. "Fight him!"

"You will never be free!" Namikawa roars, body shifting rapidly to his kitsune form. "I own you, body and soul!"

"Maybe," I say, voice strained as I wrestle to hold on to my resolve to protect my mate. "But only one man owns my heart!"

The thread connecting me to Jinta burns like the sun. I focus on our bond as my scars burn. My wolf tries to roll over and submit, but I won't let him. Not this time. I charge, shaking the earth as I pelt toward Namikawa.

Fear widens Namikawa's eyes as he realizes I'm not in his control. Not anymore.

I swing at him with claws like utility hooks. The crowd erupts into noise, shouting over each other. Namikawa moves so fast, he blurs, leaping over me with grace no man his age should possess. Claws like daggers fasten into my back and rip downwards, carving open my flesh. Blood soaks the fur on my back. Roaring, I whirl around and rip my claws across his ribs.

Namikawa grabs my fist in his hands and with inhuman strength, spins me around and hurls me into a tree. My back snaps as I crash into the trunk with such force, I uproot the tree. My broken spine leaves me paralyzed. The bones begin to heal, but it's slow going as Namikawa advances on me, blood dripping from his claws.

His head snaps side to side as his face forms a snout. His body ripples and shakes, clothes shredding. "I should have left you to rot in that wretched house you called a home!" He snarls, and charges toward me, claws extended.

"Raiden!" Jinta shouts, terror in his voice.

Suddenly, Namikawa stumbles, grunting as a sword pierces through the center of his chest. The crowd gasps.

Hideyoshi kicks Namikawa hard in the back. The sword rips free. Breathing hard, Hideyoshi says, "You have hurt my grandson enough!"

My spine snaps back into place, and I gasp in relief as the pain fades.

Namikawa laughs, coughing up blood. "You old fool. You will regret this!" Fury makes his voice rise. Fur erupts over his body which shifts in seconds. A fox with bright red fur and nine tails howls. At the kitsune's command, several flaming blue orbs materialize up from the ground. Fox-fire. Hell, this is bad. Not even werewolves can heal from foxfire. The crowd scatters into the trees before they're burned by the foxfire as the orbs shoot toward their targets and erupt. I leap behind a tree as the orb of foxfire explodes, scorching the bark and lighting the tree ablaze in seconds.

Hideyoshi rushes to my side. "Stay back. Let me face him!"

"You've done enough!" I snarl, furious as I remember the way he'd pinned down Jinta and held that bloody sword to his neck. "What, you think dying will make up for what you've done?"

"This isn't about redemption!" He grabs my large arm, eyes imploring me to listen. "You have so much left to live for. Live, Raiden. For yourself. For your mate. Get out of this life." In seconds, he's shifted to his gray wolf, snout tinged with silver. With a furious bark, he charges at the kitsune.

The kitsune snaps its jaws, but Hideyoshi skirts around it. Hideyoshi fastens his fangs into the skin of its throat. Then, the kitsune dissolves into mist. It was an illusion. Another kitsune yelps as it leaps from atop the shrine and flies toward Hideyoshi. Another charges his flank. Hideyoshi snaps and slashes, dissolving the illusion. A snarl comes from above me. The kitsune leaps from a tree and crashes onto my shoulders, fangs snaring the back of my neck.

I struggle and thrash but just as I grab a fistful of fur, the kitsune leaps off my back, turns invisible, and disappears. Straining my ears, I listen for the slightest sound that might betray the kitsune's presence. Hideyoshi growls beside me, head swiveling this way and that. The ground burns hot. Barking a warning, Hideyoshi slams his body into me, bowling me off my feet. I tumble over but before I can stand, a flash of blue flame blinds me.

Hideyoshi's agonized howls split the night. His howls turn to screams as he shifts back, his body wreathed in blue foxfire that consumes his flesh. Blood spurts from the charred, melting remains of his skin as he stumbles and collapses. His body has been so severely burned it's unrecognizable.

A roar of fury and agony tears from me. What my grandfather did was unforgiveable. I can't reconcile his actions with the man who taught me to cook, the man who raised me. But he was still my grandfather, and I know he won't be walking away from such an injury. I run toward him and the kitsune materializes in front of me.

More illusions surround me in seconds. They leap upon me, fangs like needles shredding my flesh. I swipe and slash but when I dissolve one, another appears. I can't hurt them, but they can hurt me. There's no time to heal as their fangs tear into me one after another. They swarm me, bringing me to the ground. With a howl, the kitsune conjures more foxfire orbs. I hurl a kitsune illusion into one of the orbs, dodging an orb as it soars at me. An illusion tears its fangs into my ankle and I go crashing down.

Blue foxfire hurtles toward me, obscuring my vision.

"No!" Jinta's voice echoes through the woods. And then, he's there, standing over me, arms spread wide.

Horror has me reaching out my claws toward him. I've got to get him away, now, before—Foxfire consumes my mate's torso, devouring his clothes, scorching his flesh. His screams tear into me as he frantically tries to extinguish himself, but the foxfire goes on burning him alive. His beautiful fair skin is raw and red when he collapses, writhing in the grass. The scent of cherry blossoms is consumed by the stench of burning flesh, blood, and charred fabric. With a shuddery gasp, Jinta's head falls back and his body goes completely still.

I can't move. My mind can't comprehend what just happened.

The kitsune's body shudders, jerking erratically.

That was it.

The final sacrifice.

The transition is complete.

"No! I was free! I was finally free!" The kitsune wails in a woman's furious voice.

Black mist oozes from the kitsune as it shifts back. Namikawa totters forward, haggard and far too thin. A ghastly groan escapes him before he falls. The scars he carved into my skin so long ago heal, disappearing completely. Namikawa is dead. I'm free from his control forever.

The black mist swirls through the air and covers Hideyoshi's burned and blackened body, but the blood won't stop flowing. There are some wounds not even a werewolf can come back from. He'll be dead in minutes. The kitsune will no longer be confined to a host. She'll be set free to do whatever she wishes, causing chaos wherever she goes.

And I can't bring myself to fucking care because my mate *isn't fucking moving*. The shock leaves me unable to sustain this new shape, and I revert to my human form.

"Jinta." My voice is hardly more than a whimper. I claw myself to my feet and run, crashing to my knees in the grass beside his limp, bloody body. With a shaking hand, I roll him over. The breath gets stuck around a sob when I see how badly burned he is. When his bloodstained lips twitch and eyelids flutter over dull chocolate-brown eyes, I gasp my relief.

He's alive, but only just.

"R-Rai..." He tries to say my name and coughs weakly, a bubble of blood bursting at the corner of his mouth.

"Shh. Don't speak." Carefully, I lift him into my arms, grimacing when he gasps in pain. In seconds, his blood soaks my clothes. I told myself I'd only cry once for him. It wasn't a vow I could keep, because I can't stand seeing him in so much pain. "I'm here, Sunshine. I'm here." I kiss his forehead, brushing his soft hair away from his sweaty skin.

"Sorry. For everything..." Eyelids fluttering, he struggles at first, but manages to hold my gaze.

I press my quaking lips into a tight line but can't hold back my anguish. "I'm not."

I will never regret Jinta Onodera.

"You saved me, Sunshine," I whisper into his hair. "The moment we met, you saved me."

He doesn't say anything. The red thread around my finger unravels strand by strand, and his heart begins to slow.

No. No, no, no. Panting, I yank off my necklace and press the five-yen coin into his warm hand. "Take it back. Please. I want you to have it. Only you." His fingers won't close around the coin. Those sweet brown eyes close, and Jinta's head flops to the side as he loses consciousness. A strangled noise escapes me. "Jinta," I croak. My face is wet. I can't get a full breath. My heart is in pieces in my chest. "Don't do this to me, Sunshine. You can't!"

"Raiden..." Hideyoshi's voice is barely a whisper. "Bring him here. Now. Hurry."

Sniffing, I lift Jinta's limp body and carry him to my grandfather.

"I don't have much time," Hideyoshi says, coughing wetly. His eyes roll back, but he forces them open again. "I am beyond even the kitsune's healing abilities. But Jinta isn't."

My breath catches. "You can save him?"

"The kitsune can. But you know what that means, don't you? He will live, but he will become the kitsune's host, susceptible to her corruption. If you cannot find a way to lift the curse, then she will consume him as she consumed Namikawa."

I hesitate, but only for a second. "He has to live. Please."

I don't care what comes next. Jinta and I will face it together.

Hideyoshi nods weakly and holds out his hand.

I lift Jinta's limp, cold one, kiss his fingers, then place his hand in my grandfather's.

Black smoke crawls from Hideyoshi's eyes and mouth. The blackness crawls up his arm and wraps around Jinta, creeping up his skin.

The smoke crawls down his mouth, seeps beneath his eyelids, trickles into his ears. His skin ripples, veins running black. Fear grips me until slowly, color returns to his deathly pale skin and the hideous burns begin to heal.

The severed strands of the red thread of fate reach for each other and reconnect, glowing warm against my skin. Jinta's heartbeat kicks, stutters, and restarts, pumping rhythmically in my ears.

A relieved sob escapes me as I lean down, capturing his lips with mine.

He's alive. That's all that matters.

Slowly, the Namikawa-kai emerge from the woods, surveying the devastation with wide eyes. Ren fights her way through the crowd and freezes, one hand going to her mouth.

"Namikawa is dead," one of the men says, face pale and eyes wide. "The boss was... a kitsune? I can't believe it."

I nod. "Yeah. Namikawa's gone, and so is Hideyoshi." I don't know how to feel. Before tonight, I would have been devastated. Instead, I feel... not nothing. It's a mix of different things. Anger for his deception. Disgust at the lives he stole from this world. Sadness, but I'm not allowed to be sad. Not after what he did in my name.

Clearing my throat I say, "Not sure how much you lot understood, but Namikawa wanted to pass the kitsune curse onto Hideyoshi, and he passed it onto my mate. As long as the kitsune has a host, we can control it. For a time, anyway."

There are confused whispers. "Who will lead us?" someone asks.

The answer is obvious. Hideyoshi was meant to succeed Namikawa, and he's gone. As his grandson, as a yakuza renowned throughout Tokyo, the duty is mine. If no one opposes it.

"I will," I say, putting one knee beneath me and rising, cradling Jinta in my arms. "Our bond has made me strong. Stronger than anyone here. You all saw what I became. The Namikawa-kai can't afford to be weak, not now. Not with hunters invading our territory, not when the Takada-kai has promised war. On my honor, I will lead us to victory. Do you stand with me?"

It isn't what I want, not at all, but it's what has to happen. Takada will never give me a moment of peace until he's dead, and I can't face him and his pack alone. Not if I want a future with Jinta. The Namikawa-kai must remain a force to be reckoned with.

Silence answers me. My breath hitches, heart racing as I wait for them to turn their backs.

Ren moves first, shoving her way to the front of the crowd. She folds at the waist, bowing—acknowledging me as alpha. The crowd ripples as one after another, all bow before me. My heart thunders in my chest. Jinta stirs in my arms, as if even he feels a change in the wind.

The Wolf of Asakusa is no more.

I am Alpha of the Namikawa-kai.

CHAPTER 26

Jinta

Being dead sucks.

Zero out of ten. Would never recommend.

Wait. *Am* I dead? Can the dead think?

I feel like shit. Although, not as much as I should, considering I got burned alive. I probably look like Deadpool. I ease open my eyes, wincing at the bright white walls. The view outside the windows is familiar. I'm in Raiden's penthouse, in one of the guest bedrooms.

Bracing myself, I look down, expecting to see myself wrapped in bandages like a mummy. But there's... nothing. My skin is completely unblemished. How could my burns have healed so quickly? What the hell? Only supernatural creatures have that kind of power.

Before I can spiral, the bedroom door flies open. Raiden fills the doorway, and the sight of him steals the air from my lungs and kick-starts my heart. A scent like nothing I've ever smelled before hits me, and it's like all my senses wake up. The scent rolling off him is... indescribable but all I know the minute I catch his scent is that from now until the day I leave this earth, he's all I will ever want, all I'll need.

This man is going to be mine—forever.

Eyes bright with vulnerability he's never shown me, Raiden crosses the room in seconds, takes my face in his hands, and kisses me. "Sunshine," he whispers, voice shaking. He kisses me until my lips are tingling, and I'm breathless.

"If I'm your sun, then you're my moon." I kiss his cheeks, his chin, the tip of his nose. No matter how dark the night gets, as long as I have him and the light he's brought into my life, I know I'll be okay. "I love you, Raiden."

The breath shivers in his chest. "No one's ever said that to me before." He whispers the words into my neck, hiding his face from me. He gathers me close, and I melt into the warmth of his arms and bask in his scent.

"I... I want to say it back, but..." Raiden's voice falters. "It's difficult."

"Do you not believe me?" I ask.

He shakes his head. "I do. It's just hard."

I rub my hands up and down his back. "That's okay." After the trauma of his parents' separation, then his horrible experience with Takada, I can't blame him for being hesitant. "I'll just have to say it enough for the both of us—if you're okay with hearing it."

He presses a smile into my skin. "I like hearing it from you."

Bringing my mouth to the hinge of his jaw, I kiss him. "I love you."

Raiden shivers against me, squeezing me tight.

"You smell amazing," I say, breathing in his scent.

He tenses in my arms. "About that. There's something you should know." Raiden untangles himself from my arms and faces me. "When you were hurt, the ritual was completed. The kitsune was passed on to Hideyoshi, but he was too badly injured to contain her. You were dying. I thought..." His words catch, and he blinks fast. "I thought I was going to lose you. Hideyoshi offered the kitsune to you so your wounds could heal."

My heart thumps faster at his words. "I'm... I'm a kitsune now?"

Averting his eyes, Raiden nods. I don't know how to react. Obviously I'm grateful to be alive, but can I handle a kitsune? I don't feel too different. My senses are sharper, but that's about it. "What happened to Hideyoshi?"

Raiden's expression is difficult to read. "He's dead. So are all the other victims, unfortunately, and Namikawa."

What a mess. "So what does this mean for the organization? Who will lead?"

"You're looking at him."

My eyes widen. "You're the new boss? But... but Namikawa's gone. You're free."

Raiden shakes his head. "I can't be. Not with the Takada-kai still gunning for us. And maybe the hunters, though I'm not so sure about them. As soon as I'm sure my pack will be alright without me, I'll pass on leadership to someone else. We can leave. Go wherever you want. Just wait for me."

Leaning in, I kiss him. "Fine. If I have to. You're usually worth the wait."

When my stomach growls, Raiden jumps up. "I made you some food. Not my usual culinary masterpiece, so don't get too excited. I'll be right back, oh, and the visiting nurse is here!"

The door closes behind him, and I slump against the pillows. The nurse comes in to check my vitals, remove the IV, and run a few tests. She has no reaction to how quickly my injuries healed, so she must be in on the pack's secrets. Once she leaves, Raiden returns with some egg and rice in a bowl. He feeds it to me, even though I mumble that I can feed myself. I like it when he takes care of me.

"What will we do about the kitsune?" I swallow a bite of scrambled egg. "The only person who was able to reject the kitsune curse was your father."

"Really? Who knows if he's even alive?"

"Could you find out?"

He grimaces as he holds up a piece of egg, which I eat. "I could, yeah. Hate to ask anything of that bastard, but I'll do it for you." A smile softens his face. "I'll do anything for you, you know?"

I grin. "Will you help me take a bath?"

His eyes light up. "Gladly."

Steam rises from the tub when Raiden removes the lid keeping the water hot. The water looks perfect. I dip my toe in and moan as hot water heats my skin. Raiden gets in first and sits, water lapping at his tattoos. He combs his eyes up and down my body and offers me his hand. "Come on in."

I climb into the tub. It's huge, big enough for both of us to stretch out and for me to sprawl between his muscular thighs. I lean my head back against his chest, closing my eyes when he runs damp fingers through my hair and tickles my scalp.

I crane my neck back and his lips find mine, warm and damp. His cock twitches against my body as I turn to face him. Our kiss deepens, tongues tangling, teeth nipping at swollen lips. I'm hard in seconds. His scent goes straight to my cock, making my fangs lengthen. I wonder when I'll shift for the first time, and if that's something I should worry about.

When I kiss his neck, the overwhelming urge to bite down alarms me. I draw back, covering my mouth.

"What is it?" Raiden asks, panting.

"I want to bite you," I blurt out, cheeks heating. "And I don't mean in a sexy way. I mean, I may eat you."

"Most mates bite the other to mark them as theirs, so everyone knows they're taken. If they're fated mates, then the marks won't ever fade. Now that you're a kitsune, you can feel the same pull as I do." Smiling, he crooks his neck. "Want to mark me?"

More than anything. "Maybe," I say, the rasp in my voice betraying how badly I want my teeth in him. I love the idea of everyone knowing this powerful man is mine. "Is that what you want?"

Raiden's full lips sink into a frown.

"What?" I ask.

"What if I screw things up? Screw *us* up?" Raiden asks, his low voice full of uncertainty.

"You can't." I frame his face in my hands. "I promise you, you can't."

His throat bobs when he swallows, dark eyes blinking fast as he looks away. "What if, a few years from now, you decide I can't be what you need? There's a chance I'll never be free of this life, or that I won't be able to adjust to a normal life. If you... if you left me, I..." Blinking fast, he looks away. "I couldn't come back from that."

The agony in his voice makes my heart ache. I can tell we've got a long way to go before he'll be ready to meet more milestones in our relationship. But it's fine. I'll wait as long as it takes because this man is worth waiting for. Leaning in, I kiss his forehead. "I won't. I promise you, I won't ever leave you. But if you're not ready, we don't have to mark each other. We can take things slow. Being with you, that's enough."

Raiden exhales slowly. "I want... There's a lot of—" Scowling, he clamps his lips shut. I wait, stroking my thumb up and down his jaw. "I'm gonna screw this up."

"Screw what up?" I challenge him, holding his gaze. "Come on. Talk to me."

Raiden's jaw tightens. "This. All of this. I don't want to, but I will."

"Well, maybe I won't let you." I stick out my chin with as much defiance as I can. "Tell me what you want, and I'll help you."

"I want to take things slow," Raiden says, surprising me because that's what I want, too. "Want to savor this."

We have before, after he'd almost died from a hunter's bullet. I still shiver remembering how sweet and tender he was, how he worshipped me.

"Me, too. You can do that. You're good at it."

Raiden doesn't reply, restless fingers squeezing my ass.

I'm about to speak when he suddenly says, "If I can't tell you how I feel, then I want to show you. But I'm... it's not what I'm used to."

"I know," I assure him.

Raiden wets his lips. "But I want to try."

I nod eagerly, cock already stirring as my imagination runs wild. "You can do whatever you want."

Raiden's eyes darken, arousal spicing his scent. "Sit up," he commands.

"Oookay..." I'm not sure what he's planning, but I'm here for it. I lift myself and sit on the rim of the tub. My cock bobs inches from his face. "Did you want to go to the bed, or—*oh*." I groan as he leans in and wraps his mouth around me. He takes me in slow, big hands massaging my thighs. I don't know what's hotter, the hot water or his mouth, wrapped so perfectly around me that my eyes roll back and my mouth goes slack.

He bobs up and down, taking his time. It's almost reverent the way he worships my body. It's utter bliss. Sinking my fingers in his hair, I stroke his scalp when he flicks his tongue over my crown and traces the vein that runs the length of me. "That... that's good, baby. Really good."

The groan that rumbles up from his chest vibrates from the tip of my cock to my balls. Tightening his lips, he swallows me down and keeps me there for several heart-stopping seconds, like he enjoys this just as much as I do. When he pulls off, sucking me hard, I can't hold back my cry.

Pressing his lips to my hip, then to my lower belly, Raiden murmurs, "Back in the water. Turn around."

Panting, I sink back into the tub and lean on the rim. When Raiden tugs on my hips, I push my ass back. Big hands squeeze my cheeks appreciatively, then a wet finger circles my hole and sinks inside. I gasp as he fills me, swirling his finger around and lighting up my nerve endings. I'm so hungry for him that I ache.

Grasping my cock, Raiden squeezes the head, then peppers kisses over my shoulders. The glide of his hot mouth, the crook of his finger inside me, has a hoarse, desperate sound escaping me. "*Yes*. Fuck. Give me more, just like that. Please." My words come out in a breathless rush, hips flexing to push those talented fingers deeper into my body. Another finger slides inside me, stretching me wider, and all the while, Raiden lavishes the head of my cock with flicks of his thumb.

I could finish just like this, soon. Whimpers escape me, growing in urgency as Raiden takes me higher, closer. Then his fingers are gone, and he lets go of my cock. "What—" I begin, words slurred.

As I turn around, Raiden's mouth finds mine, as in apology. "As nice as the bath is, I'd rather have you in my bed."

Then his hands are beneath my ass, and he's lifting me. I wrap my arms and legs around him, nuzzling my face into his neck. He carries me into the bedroom and holds on to me with one arm to grab his discarded robe, which he throws over the bed to protect the sheets.

Down we go, my back pressed into the feathery mattress, Raiden coming down on top of me. We kiss and kiss until my lips are sore and tingling, rocking our bodies against each other in search of friction. Everything is hot, and wet, and slippery, and so damn perfect.

I need him, think I'll combust if he doesn't take me now. "Baby," I pant, "I'm ready. So ready."

Finally, Raiden yanks his mouth from mine long enough to sit up. "Me, too. Gonna fucking bust if I don't—*fuck*. Want you, too."

Water runs in little rivers along the hills and valleys of his muscles, his hair slick and shiny, eyes black with lust. He's utterly breathtaking, and he's mine. He reaches over and grabs a bottle of lube from the nightstand.

Slick fingers slip inside me, making me whimper when he swirls them around, getting me ready for him. Pulling out, he grasps himself and strokes until he's glistening. I lift my legs for him, panting with agitation as he scoots closer. When he pushes inside, the glide is so easy, so smooth, my eyes roll back.

Raiden lets out a huge sigh, eyes closing in shared bliss as he sinks inside. "Fuck, Sunshine. You feel so damn good." He takes his time, filling me with every inch until finally, he's seated completely inside me.

I'll never get sick of the way he stretches me, how full he

makes me feel, but it's the way he looks when our bodies are one that always takes my breath away. Every wall he's ever built comes down before my eyes, and I can see everything that I mean to him.

It doesn't matter if he never says those three words to me. Words mean so little when he captures my mouth with his and kisses me like he'll never get the chance to again, when we move together, and he gasps his pleasure against my lips, when his hands grab mine and hold on for life as he takes me, slow and deep, over and over again. Every kiss, gentle touch, every glide of his hips is a message in Morse code, and I've memorized it down to my bones.

"Love you," I whisper into the crook of his neck. "I love you," I whisper against the space between his brows. "I love you," I whisper against the tip of his nose. "Love you. So much." I gasp against his neck as my toes curl and I tighten around him. We ascend together, higher and higher until I'm crying out my release. He moves with me through it, chasing his own climax.

"Jinta," he gasps between our lips, breath hot on my skin as he spills inside me. I wrap him in my arms as he collapses atop me, our bodies heaving, wet with sweat and our bath, limbs tangled and slack.

I cradle his head to my chest, peppering kisses over his shoulder. That was... perfect. If that's as close as he can get to telling me how he really feels, then I'll never need to hear him say it. It's not necessary, not when he's done such a good job tonight at showing me.

Raiden slips his arms beneath me and squeezes before he rolls off me so he's not crushing me but stays close enough that our bodies can touch. I roll onto my side and seek out his hand. Our fingers brush and twist together, and Raiden holds them to his chest. His heart gallops against my hand, racing as fast as mine is. I notice then that he's wearing the five-yen coin he gifted to me. The one I shoved back at him. My throat tightens at the painful memory.

"Raiden?" I'm almost afraid to ask. If he says no after all of this...

He hums questioningly.

"Could I—If you want..." Damn it, Jinta. Just say it. "Can I have your necklace back?"

Raiden's eyes widen, and his breathing pauses.

"You don't have to," I add, heart sinking. "Maybe I haven't earned it back, I don't know. I'm going to keep making it up to you. So, whenever you're ready, just let me know. I'd really like it back."

"Why?" Raiden asks, his voice devoid of judgment or suspicion.

Why, indeed? I wet my lips. "Because, I guess when you gave it to me, it sort of felt like you were... I don't know? Giving me a part of yourself. Your heart. Or something. So until you give it back, things won't be mended between us." Good god, I'm babbling. This is awful.

"It really meant that much to you?" Raiden sounds

surprised. I know the necklace means a lot to him, even if his relationship with it is complicated.

I laugh. "Yes. Of course. It's the nicest thing anyone's ever given me."

Raiden's face softens. He reaches back and pulls the necklace off. My heart skips up into my throat as he holds it out to me. "You can have it back. Should have just said so earlier. I'd have given it back to you sooner."

Tears sting my eyes. "A-are you sure?"

Raiden nods solemnly. "Yeah. 'Course I am."

My hand shakes as I take it from him and slip the necklace over my head. My lips tremble, and I blink stubbornly to keep my tears at bay.

"Jinta—"

I throw my arms around him and clutch him to my body. A low, warm chuckle escapes him, and he wraps his arms around me, stroking my back as I shake and gasp.

I kiss him again and again, saying, "Never taking it off. Ever. Hear me? I promise I'll take good care of it. I promise."

Because it's not just a necklace. It's the heart of him, Raiden's heart, and I'm going to cherish it, always.

My full bladder wakes me in the middle of the night. Carefully, I untangle myself from the blankets. Raiden snores softly but doesn't wake. In the bathroom, I flick on the light and go about my business, sighing in relief. I flush the toilet and wash my hands. My reflection stares back at me in the mirror, hair tousled, lips a little swollen.

My smiling face in the mirror suddenly darkens. The lights flicker, electricity humming. My reflection ripples like water, and in seconds, a beautiful woman in a red kimono stands where I once did. Her skin is pale as a ghost, eyes black as the void. When she bares her teeth, they're razor points in her red mouth.

It's the kitsune. Tamano-no-Mae.

"My. Aren't you adorable?" She bares razor teeth in a feral leer, her harsh fangs contradicting her beauty. "It's so nice to finally have a body at my command that is both young and supple."

I stumble back until I hit the wall, heart in my throat. The mirror ripples as the kitsune steps through the glass. Her bare feet slap gently over the floor as she reaches out a pale hand to touch my cheek. Her touch is cold as ice. "We're going to have so much fun together. Aren't we, dear?"

The lights flicker, plunging me into darkness. When the lights come back on, Tamano-no-Mae is gone, for now. But I'm afraid that her plans for me, for all of Japan, have just begun.

Chapter 27

Kensuke Namikawa's remains are cremated and laid to rest in a family grave. Hundreds of yakuza from all over the city fill the streets in their black cars as we ride to the temple where his funeral will be held. I wear a black kimono. Wearing minimal makeup, Ren wears a black kimono as well and carries a black handbag.

Once we arrive at the temple, I climb the steps and wait outside the doors to greet those who enter. Every person to approach offers me their condolences with a bow, writes their name in a book once inside the temple, and places an envelope of condolence money on the table nearby.

Closing the doors behind me, I join my pack inside. On an altar covered in flowers, a portrait of Namikawa smiles at the gathered crowd. You'd think he was just a normal businessman from that picture. Incense burners fill the room with sweet smoke.

The service begins once we're all seated, and a Buddhist priest recites sutras in a deep low voice. Namikawa never took a wife or had children. The only family here is the one he created. Namikawa was a lot of things, mostly bad, but he gave people a place to belong, he gave them purpose. I'll give him that.

Tense whispers fill the room and when I smell him, a growl rises in my throat. I turn in time to catch the eye of Takada as he enters the temple with Hirano. He sits in the back and observes, eyes crawling over my skin like a spider.

The funeral concludes after we've burned pinches of incense, filling the temple with the scent of smoke. A light meal is served at Namikawa's home after the funeral. Everyone from the service attends the dinner. I don't eat and stay outside, burning through a cigarette.

I've had my share of wakes and funerals for the week. Hideyoshi's was... complicated. Not the service itself. That was simple and intimate. I invited a few of his friends from the pack to my apartment and set up an altar for him that will remain a permanent fixture in my home. It's my feelings for him that have changed. He was my hero growing up. The father I never had who understood me and supported me when no one else did.

But he murdered people in my name and would have

killed my mate if I hadn't stopped him. I wish someone would tell me how I'm supposed to feel.

"Hey, 'boss.'"

I grind my teeth at the mockery in Takada's voice. He sidles up beside me, cigarette smoking between his teeth. Many of Takada's men had been sacrificed in the ritual. I'd had the bodies returned to him so he could oversee their burial. I wouldn't tell him how they died. Nobody needs to know about the kitsune. Especially not him. I'm not naïve enough to think that makes us even, but how nice would that be?

"Shame about Namikawa. Man was a legend in this city. Now, he's just ash." Takada snorts, smoke puffing from his nose. "Those are big shoes to fill."

I grunt around a drag of smoke.

Takada grabs my arm and yanks me around to face him. "You better be up to that task, Noboru." His lip curls around a fang. "Because the minute I sense weakness, I'll be over your territory like maggots to meat. Got it?"

Tension tightens my jaw. I tug my cigarette out of my mouth and blow smoke in his sneering face. "Give it your best shot. Tokyo will never be yours."

I will never be his.

Takada huffs, a nasty smile twisting his face. "You should have joined up with me when I offered, Noboru. I would have gone easy on you." Leaning in, he hisses in my ear. "I always get what's owed to me." With a low chuckle, he mashes his smoke beneath his shoe and walks away down the temple's steps.

Ren comes to stand beside me, body tense, glaring holes in Takada's back. "We won't let him touch you," she vows, then cracks a smile. "Boss."

I sigh. "Hey. None of that from you." I wish I could believe her about Takada, but the broken boy in me wonders if I'll ever be safe from him.

My friend squeezes my arm. "Come on. Let's make things official."

As the hour arrives to celebrate my ascension to head of the Namikawa-kai, my pack piles into the temple for the ceremony. Other yakuza bosses from around the city have come to pay their respects. Fortunately, Takada stayed home.

I'm dressed in a traditional kimono, but I still feel like a kid playing dress up. I can't afford to appear weak. There's too much at stake. Takada will strike while we're vulnerable during this transition of power. We'll need to be ready.

Then there are the hunters, but to be honest, I'm not as concerned about them. Nobody's seen them since I got shot. Maybe they've crawled back into their holes. I know they were probably itching to kill Namikawa, but they missed their chances. That must be demoralizing.

"Hey, boss." Ren bumps her shoulder against mine. "You're brooding."

Scowling, I massage between my brows. "I know."

"Try and relax, okay? Have some sake. Fawn over how cute Jinta looks in his suit."

A smile makes my mouth twitch. He does look cute. I could barely keep my hands off him in the car on the way here.

"Where is he?"

Ren points to the east wing of the temple. "I saw him talking to some guy over there."

"Who?"

She shrugs. "Don't know. I didn't recognize him, but we rarely gather like this, so I can't know everybody."

My stomach is a mess with nerves. Not sure what I have to worry about. We've been making preparations for weeks. All the hard stuff is almost over. All I need to do is drink from a cup and that'll be that. Maybe seeing Jinta will calm my nerves.

I follow the scent of cherry blossoms that winds over the crowd until I glimpse him. I can't see the face of whoever he is talking to. He's tall and broad-shouldered, black hair slicked back. I can't tell what he smells like, there's too many different odors in the air. But it's the unsettled expression on Jinta's face that has me quickening my stride.

Before I can reach them, I'm cut off as a crowd of

Namikawa-kai men walk past. In the seconds it takes for them to walk away, the man has disappeared from Jinta's side. As soon as I'm within reach of him, I ask, "Who was that?"

Jinta frowns. "No idea. He didn't introduce himself."

I grip his wrist tight. "What did he want?"

He shrugs. "Nothing. Just to meet me. He said he had to see me for himself."

What the hell? Maybe because Jinta is my mate? I guess word has spread fast among the pack.

"You look good," Jinta says, giving me a heated, appreciative look from head to toe.

"It's the kimono."

"Nope. It's the man in it." He glides an appreciative hand over my chest.

My mate looks ravishing in the suit I bought him. Pulling him close, I press my lips to his ear. "Soon as we're home, this suit comes off. Except for the tie. I'll use that to bind your wrists so all you can do is lie there and let me have my way with you."

Jinta shivers, sinking his teeth into his plump lower lip. "I like the sound of that..."

"You'll like what I do to you even more. That's a promise." I drop a quick kiss to his lips.

"Who are they?" Jinta asks, motioning toward a crowd of older men who are gathered together and talking.

"The Namikawa-kai bosses of the different wards, and

the higher-ups in the organization. Presidents, managing directors."

"So, the equivalent of a boss's boss."

"Something like that."

A voice calls out, "Starting now, we will begin the Namikawa-kai Ascension Ceremony!"

My heart gallops.

Jinta smooths down my kimono. "Go get them, baby."

Feeling much better, I follow my people into the next room for the ceremony. My people kneel beneath banners that cover the walls. The ceremony begins once I've knelt before the Namikawa-kai's most respected president, Taoka Ishii.

The ceremony is highly choreographed, down to even the slightest step as one of our men places two altars before us. Two cups of sake await us, symbolizing the blood connection between the father, Ishii, and myself, the son.

As the father in our parent-child relationship, Ishii drinks first until no sake is left.

Now, it's my turn.

The eyes of my pack fall upon me, watching my every move as I raise the sake cup to my lips and drink. The last time I did this, I was a lowly underling beneath Namikawa's watchful eye. We each wrap our cups in special paper and place them within our kimonos.

Bracing my knuckles on the floor, I look my superior in the eyes and say, "Please accept my pledge," and bow low.

Ishii says, "I accept."

Now, I'm the leader of the most powerful yakuza organization in Japan.

I'm not free, not yet, but I realize it doesn't matter. I've got a reason to fight for my freedom, for my future. Everything I do, I will do for my mate, for us, so I can be a man deserving of his devotion.

A quieter reception begins in the temple where there's a feast. I carry some sake to Jinta. It's noisy in here, so I motion for him to follow me out onto the balcony. The evening is quiet and cool, and the city is lit up, lights sparkling against a violet sky. "Cheers," I say.

Jinta smiles. "Cheers."

We drink, then I lean in and kiss him. His lips are sweet from the sake. Heart lighter than it's been in days, I lace my fingers with his and lean my forehead against his. "Things are going to change. So promise me something."

"Anything." His gentle fingers weave through my hair.

"That this won't change. Us. Stay with me."

His supple mouth tilts sweetly. "Always," he promises as he kisses me.

I'm about to slip my tongue past his lips when my phone buzzes. Sighing, I pepper kisses over his jaw as I reach blindly for my phone and answer. "This is Noboru."

A voice I've never heard before says, "Hello, Noboru."

I pause, lips stilling against Jinta's soft skin. "Who is this?"

"You don't know me. In all the festivities, there wasn't time to say hello. I do apologize."

I'm being toyed with. Like I'm prey. I don't like it. Leaning back on the railing, I growl, "Tell me what you want. Now."

A low chuckle answers me, then he says, "I want you to know how close I was to driving my blade into your pretty little kitsune's stomach."

My fingers sprout claws that dig into the railing. Fear turns my blood to ice. "He's not—"

"I'm a hunter, Noboru. I know a kitsune when I see one."

I can't speak, frozen to the spot.

"You didn't even know who I was, did you?" His voice is positively gleeful. "It was so easy to just wander right into the temple. I was a bit disappointed."

There was a hunter among my pack, inches from my fucking mate.

Shoving my fear down, I infuse my voice with as much fury as I can when I snarl, "Tell me who the fuck you are."

"Oh, you've already met my associates. They put a bullet in your arm, remember? They were *supposed* to kill you. But this is much more fun. I've always preferred a challenge to my hunts. My name is Akira. We are the Swords of the Onryō. And we're going to cleanse this city of all paranormal filth."

Jinta's eyes are wide, and I realize he can hear every word.

I reach out and take his hand, squeezing it tight. The fear in his warm brown eyes shifts to the same fury lighting up my blood.

To Akira, I say, "The Wolf of Asakusa doesn't hunt alone anymore. Come for what's mine again, and I will burn your world to the ground."

I hang up, draw my mate close, and brace for the storm.

Thank you for reading!
What will happen to Jinta and Raiden next? Find out in the thrilling finale:
Curses & Kitsune (A Paranormal Yakuza Duet Book 2)
Want more Raiden and Jinta goodness?
See what happens when the pair move in together when you sign up for my newsletter at www.CJRavenna.com!

About CJ

CJ Ravenna loves to tell stories where the ordinary meets the extraordinary. Her books often feature an explosion or two, possessive and protective werewolves who adore their mates, steamy and swoony romance, and of course a happy ending. Connect with me on:

My website: cjravenna.com

My Facebook group: Ravenna's Ravens

Instagram: @cjravenna

TikTok: @cjravenna

Goodreads: goodreads.com/cjravenna

Bookbub: bookbub.com/authors/cj-ravenna

Get bonus shorts, sneak peeks of upcoming books, and more on my Patreon: https://www.patreon.com/CJRavenna

Secrets & Sake (A Paranormal Yakuza Duet Book 1)

Curses & Kitsune (A Paranormal Yakuza Duet Book 2)